Sweet Tea and Zombies

SL Figuhr and T. Golgan

ISBN: 0991149882
ISBN-13: 978-0-9911498-8-9
Library of Congress Control Number: 2015918292

In Memory of Solstice, my real life Pepper.

Thank you to Bland, for all the advice with weapons, and military matters. Any mistakes made are my own.

Edited By:
Janie Goltz

Acknowledgments
Shutter stock Image by:
Kiselev Andrey Valerevich

Prologue

Leave it to science to destroy humanity.

The vaccine was supposed to help against the new form of H3N2 virus. They thought it would protect us, but they didn't foresee the side effects. The shot was sent and given to "first responders-" schools, our friendly countries, and hospital staff, like my girlfriend, Spacey, who got it first. This antidote? It turned out to be our downfall.

By the time the rest of the population received the shot, there were people complaining about fever and muscle stiffness. We found out about seven in ten people showed the antiviral had mutated into something deadly. Those who received the virus, died of "complications" within days or weeks, but they didn't stay dead. Those who treated the infected never knew what hit them. No one knew why, but the bodies suddenly came back to "life."

Those who cheated death bit or scratched their caregivers, who never knew they became infected. Within twenty-four to seventy-two hours later, depending on the severity and location of the bite or scratch, the newly infected turned into mindless flesh eaters. They went after the scent of new blood to feed, and further spread the infection. Government officials downplayed the intensity of the new virus while the CDC and WHO scrambled to unravel what had gone wrong with the chemical and biological makeup of the H3N2 virus and manufacture an antigen. While this was going on, the virus raged unchecked across the United States and other countries who had received shipments of the H3N2 inoculations for their citizens. By the time those in charge admitted their mistake three months later, the infection couldn't be halted. Martial law was declared, panic set in, and the government went into hiding, ready to form a new order when the time was right, though we wouldn't find out until later.

The world leaders tried to impose travel restrictions, shutting down their borders. The virus had already spread, and infected billions. The following story is ours—of family, and the will to survive.

CHAPTER ONE

Hey, babe, where u @?

I glanced briefly at the text message, debating the wisdom of what I was doing. My plan seemed so logical and easy inside my head. I hate when I begin to second guess myself. Plus, I was starting to hyperventilate. I had the shakes of a Parkinson's patient. I swore, fixing my answer.

"Fucking autocorrect!" I screamed as I deleted and retyped. The end was here, and I was still concerned with proper spelling.

Caught on highway, trying to get off

I sent back, then cringed at the all-too-close screech. A pitiful mew came from behind me. I tried reaching one hand back while craning my neck to see out the side window. "It's okay, baby. It's okay," I crooned to my cats.

What 1?

Seventy-Eight, I sent back.

Not good, babe, u need to get off onto safer roads, less traveled.

I hadn't seen him since we'd kissed goodbye four days ago; before we both left for work. By the time word went out the country had a national disaster on its hands, I was unable to leave the hospital where I worked. We were considered essential personnel. My place of employment went on gray alert, their code for community disaster. We slept, ate, and worked in shifts.

Don't worry, trying 2 get 2 safe place. How far away are you from joining me, and having some sweet tea?

It took a bit for the message to go through, and just as long for his reply to return.

A while, got an errand to run first. I'll b there soon.

For some reason, his words didn't sit well. What type of 'errands' could he possibly need to do while humanity turned on each other?

Please tell me you're not trying to get more food and ammo, it's too dangerous. Wait until the chaos dies down, and we can raid together.

The send bar slowly inched across the screen while I sweated inside the hot truck.

Don't worry, we will, after my errand.

Five minutes passed before Wade's reply came through.

The sick feeling inside of me intensified as I furiously tapped:

What errand?

Nothing to worry about, it won't take too long. Stay safe, I love you, came back after another agonizingly long wait.

My nerves slowly became replaced with anger.

What errand? Why won't you tell me?

I don't want u to worry, k?

You are not helping, just tell me.

His evasiveness sparked off my anger.

I peeked over the dash once more. The road before me filled with vehicles, screams, crying, gunshots. You know, the usual post-apocalyptic end-of-the-world mayhem. My stolen ride was a truck with a U-Haul hitched to the back. I had driven it to a local bookstore and hid behind the building. I knew I shouldn't have made this stop, but my greed got the better of me. Fuck guns, ammo or food or water or any other useful shit. Nope, I wanted books. I needed books. I was so fucked.

My phone vibrated continuously. Sheesh, I should put it in my pocket since it was likely the last good feelings I would get in a while.

"What?" I snapped out.

"Look, why are you angry at me? What did I ever do?" Wade asked.

"Why is it so hard for you to just tell me where you are? The world's ending."

A huge sigh carried across the airwaves. "You're not going to let this go, are you?" he asked.

"Wade," my tone flat, warning.

"I've got to get my kids once they're safe we'll come back to you," he ran all the words together.

For one moment, a chill raced through me, and my ears buzzed. I had to remind myself to breath.

"Hello? Space? Babe? You still there?" Wade's voice sounded tinny. "Just hang in there, and I promise, I'll come back for you."

He had already lit out. That's why he didn't want to answer my question. His mind was on Joan and Anne, his kids, over six hundred miles away at college.

The highway with its traffic, gunshots, squealing tires, wavered before my eyes. The heat pressed down on me, irrelevant thoughts crossed my mind: Dumb-ass. He'd never make it. Even if he did, there was no guarantee they'd still be alive, or that he'd be able to find them if they had to move. It was only a matter of time before communications went down. Even now, getting through to others was spotty. To say I was resentful of his daughters, and what I considered a suicide mission on his part: big understatement.

"Did you at least manage to get your sword, or one of the guns I left for you?" He continued. "Did you make it out okay?"

Really, fucker? That's your biggest concern? I should have known. I rolled my eyes without thinking, anger mounting inside of me.

"Barely," tears trembled. The fear of not being able to do what needed to be done to survive rose higher. Visions of getting ambushed, tortured, held prisoner by psycho shitheads, flashed through my mind, my anxiety levels nearly overwhelmed me.

"I barely managed to leave the hospital. I didn't think it was real at first, none of us did; I mean, this stuff doesn't happen outside of fiction. Then I thought I was dead. I . . . I should have just left when it became obvious, not even attempted to go back to our place, but, I couldn't leave the kitties to starve to death. Our fucking neighbors were trying to force their way into everyone's apartment to loot!" I spewed out.

A zombie—once someone's loved one, ironically—saved me from being beaten and raped, maybe even killed. The thought still made me shake with anger and fear. I should have told him about the attack, but just having to think about it made me nauseous.

"But you're safe, right? You got out; maybe I should come get you. Then we can rescue my kids."

"No, too late; you should've thought of it sooner. Go get your kids, don't waste time turning around and coming back. I'll try to stay safe and sane. Meet me at the beach," I sniffed, needing a Kleenex.

"WTF? I can't leave them to die. My kids come first, besides, which beach? There's only four, and hello, zombie infestation."

"I knew I should never have gotten involved with a single father," was what I blurted out instead, my brain-to-mouth filter broke again.

There was a pause on the line. "I can't believe you're going to bring that up again. If you had . . ."

"Don't even give me that fucking bingo!" My voice rose, and the cats mewed. I trembled now with anger.

"Damn it, Space, I love you," he replied.

"Gee, thanks. Your kids, who're grown-ass adults, still come before the person you claim to love with all your heart. They're over three hundred miles away. " I bulldozed over his spluttering. "Be safe, good luck. You're going to need it since communications will go down soon, and I doubt you'll even make it. Besides, I got the shot too. I had to. All the hospital staff had to. I-I may still succumb to it. I found a gun; I've got bullets. If I think I'm gonna change, I'm gonna kill myself. You know I will."

There was a long silence on his end. He replied in a tone shaking with barely suppressed anger, patronizing me, "I'm gonna put your bitchiness down to fear, and try to forgive you for it."

My anger crested, irrationally, toward his daughters. I raged at him.

"If your adult kids don't know how to care for themselves by now, they can suck it like the rest of the population, and turn into fucking zombies. You think I want to listen to you blubber about how torn you are about leaving me to go after them? Clearly I'm not high on your priority list."

If he felt concern for me, he would be here, and not on a futile quest, the idiot. My stress rose as a part of me knew I acted hateful and jealous. I checked the area to make sure I hadn't been spotted. Still chaos, and getting really, really smelly. I was gonna puke soon.

I might never see him again, yet his attitude pissed me off. The realization I was losing the one person I knew I could trust, forced me to slap my inner bitch and be rational. "I gotta go. I can't concentrate on staying safe while we argue. Good luck, you'll need it for the fool's errand you're on," I said, convulsively swallowing as saliva pooled in my mouth. Oh yeah, hurl fest in three . . . two . . .

I hung up on his outraged squawking, opened the

door and puked. Damn, that was dinner, too. I shut the door quickly, getting as comfortable as I could, laying back the driver's seat. My vision wavered, as hot tears poured down my face, scalding me. I peered back at the cats, who gazed blearily at me. I'd had to drug them with Benadryl so they would remain calm, and not screech during our ordeal. Any noise would bring zombies to us. Any change made them anxious. A soft mew came, as I reached my fingers through the wire door and stroked the fur I could reach.

"Kitty babies," I whispered, my throat burning from tears as my sinus clogged.

There was still too much activity around me. I would be noticed if I moved, so to keep my mind off my worries, I texted my sister, who lived in D.C.

Hey, sis, I hope you're safe as I am. I don't know when, or if, we'll ever see each other again, but remember I love you and miss you.

My phone buzzed incessantly, the number my partners. I didn't have any patience left to soothe Wade's wounded feelings or listen about how wrong I was about everything. I'd be amazed if he lived past a single day. I sent his calls to voicemail, and glanced out the windshield, noting the current frenzy was slowly dissipating.

I tried to call my parents, who still lived back in Pittsburgh, but their answering machine picked up.

"Hey, Mom, Dad, it's me, Spacey. I hope you're safe. I got out of the hospital alive, and I'm free from infection. I haven't talked to Helen, but I managed to get a text through. I'll try calling again later. I love you both, and I miss you."

A fresh spurt of tears coursed down. My dad was in the first stages of dementia. My mom was most likely frantic with worry over what would happen to them, and to my sister and me. Mom had a pay-as-you-go phone, so

I tried calling it. I was swiping at the tears, using an entire packet of tissues to keep my nose clear. Neither of my parents picked that phone up, so I left them another message. It wasn't like my mom to ignore her phone during a crisis, especially one that affected everybody. A sinking feeling overcame me, and I repeatedly swallowed as bile tried to force its way out my mouth. After my calls, I turned my phone off, not wanting to waste what precious battery life it had left. I checked on the cats one last time, then scanned the area. I was clear so far. It was now or never.

The trek into the bookstore was nerve-wracking. I don't know how many times I nearly passed out from fright. I could barely keep my panic away. I breathed much easier once inside the (hopefully) empty store. I listened for voices or moans. None greeted me. I grabbed several totes, then cautiously made my way farther inside. Okay, who was I kidding? I was power-walking, barely checking. I was zombie bait; I couldn't compartmentalize, or keep the fear and panic shoved down inside to do what needed to be done.

"Be Alice. Be Alice. Be Alice," I chanted softly. "Oh, who the fuck am I kidding? I'm so zombie chow."

I dared to turn on the flashlight, quickly scanning shelves. There was no time to stop and read the backs. I grabbed what looked useful. *Remember, dumb-ass: you have limited space.* I needed books on plants, natural home remedies, survival, and living off the grid. I set my stash by the back door and dashed to the small cafe. It had been raided, but there were still items of use. A lot of what food remained in the cases or cooler was perishable. Well, this was my last chance to eat dessert or any other type of pre-made, yummy, so-not-healthy-for-you-before-it-was-rotted food. Oh, and drinks. Couldn't forget the hydration even if it was heavy on the juice/soda side. I had used every tote and basket in the store without realizing it. I waded through my small sea of booty to the metal back door.

I paused by the back door, hyperventilating in fear and panic again. I lost precious time trying to find my spine and an imaginary pair of balls. In my anxiety-ridden state, I wasn't thinking about personal safety; I was thinking of loading up and getting out. Thus, when I opened the back door, I saw I was within arm's reach of several zombies. I momentarily froze, which almost cost me my life. I swung one of the bags toward the nearest deadhead, forcing him backward. It allowed me enough time to draw my weapon. In my panic-induced state, I merely grazed the side of the zombie's head. It pissed me off and helped me refocus. I managed to finish them off, but I was out of ammo. I hurriedly grabbed the bags, re-stuffed them with what had fallen out, and bolted for the truck. After loading the gun again, I went back for the rest of my booty. It took a while, as I had to stop and kill more zombies attracted by the initial gunshots.

"Oh shit, oh shit." I gripped the steering wheel, crying. I had loaded everything up and added to my zombie kill count. Also added to "dumb-ass nearly bites the dust" too from my greed. *No time for a nervous breakdown, bitch! Get your pansy ass in gear! Fuck you!*

Great, my inner bitch reared her ugly head and wasn't helping me at all. The mewing from the back was beginning to become more insistent. I did not need to listen to howling the whole way. I was already bat shit crazy. That would just tip me over the edge. It was almost midnight; I had gone beyond sleep into a deceptive second wind. I ignored the sensible part of my brain that said I should find a good hiding spot, nap, and then move out. No, I had to listen to the crazy side. The side that said, *I can do this*, just like all the other sheep before me who thought that and then wondered why they were in the hand basket, and where had it all gone wrong.

#

I woke up screaming, kitties crying in fear, the scent of excrement, and dead things all around. The truck was rocking, flesh slapping wetly on the outside, trying to break the window to get breakfast. I could only hope the cats didn't get underneath my feet. It was a mistake to have let them out of their carriers while I slept, even if it was so they could use the litter box, eat some food, and drink water.

"Oh shit, damn, fuck.!" I fumbled with the keys, trying to get the engine to start. I held it too long, hearing the starter grind before I mentally slapped myself and got the motor going.

"You have a litter box!" I howled at the cats as my left foot squished in poop.

My driver's window cracked; I floored the gas, forgetting about the U-Haul attached to the back. The tires spun, chirping on the asphalt, while the engine screamed, then with a lurch, the tires grabbed traction, and I shoved the horde away and under the wheels.

"The engine! The body! The undercarriage!" I screamed out loud to myself as a reminder not to wreck my ride. "Shut up!" This last bit to the crazed howls of the cats.

I felt the truck weave, wanting to tip as the U-Haul bounced over bodies. I slowed down, pumped brakes, twirled the wheel, and fuck if I know how I managed to get the vehicle back under control. The horde was still within reach, plodding after me as I sat sucking in air, pretty sure I had just wet myself. Gah, the feel of wet, stinky shorts was only marginally worse than the horde. I pressed on the gas.

"Remember, stupid, slow and steady. Look! Keep your eyes open! Everyone is the enemy." *The humans are worse than the zombies. They just want to eat you.* The living, as I had found out to my detriment, wanna do bad things. They are the real force to be feared.

My breathing started to slow down; my hands still shook, my left foot beat a nervous tattoo on the floor, the howl of my cats my music.

"I'll replenish your food and water in a minute. Just shut up," I yelled to them.

Yup, my nerves had gone beyond frayed and shot. My cats didn't deserve this; they had no clue. The orange tabby crawled into my lap, shoving his head with enough force at my face I had to slam on the brakes or drive off the road. I spit fur out of my mouth and lost skin off my thighs, getting his back claws out of my legs. The horde was still behind me, albeit more of a speck. I wasted precious moments getting my attention whore of a cat situated, and the scratches smeared with antibiotic ointment and covered before continuing to drive.

His front paws dug into my shoulder, kneading while he constantly rubbed his face over the side of mine and on my chin, his purrs vibrating my chest. I hoped nothing came at me from the left; I wouldn't see it until it was too late. I passed several wrecks that had almost blocked the entire road. It was called a highway, but it was a two-lane blacktop with trees forming effective barriers to each side. I didn't get much farther before another wreck loomed in the distance. I stopped and just observed.

"Please don't let this be a trap. There's no way I can get this turned around in time." Panic time: we were becoming really good friends.

My eyes darted everywhere at once, not seeing. *Stop it!* I firmly commanded myself. Carelessness *is how idiots die. Quit being an annoying movie loser! Scan the sides of the road, look at the wreck, look for things that seem out of place.*

I must have sat there for five minutes, dithering, scanning. Well, if this was an ambush, they either had an incredible amount of patience or were sneaking up the sides of the truck in a way that couldn't be noticed. I cautiously drove forward and stopped halfway to the mess. I spent another few minutes scanning, waiting. Nothing. No shots, no masked raiders. The only sound cicadas and flies, with an occasional bird.

Do something, genius. Shit or get off the pot. I couldn't go forward unless I cleared the road.

"Eh, fuck it. That's less work than trying to turn this shit around."

My decision made; I shut the engine off and contorted myself inside the truck. I filled the food and water dishes for the cats, bitching at the pee/poop stains. I climbed down out of the cab. My bladder immediately lets me know it was unhappy. Really? I could've sworn I soaked the seat. I needed to change my shorts. Here's hoping the smell helped disguise my scent.

I cautiously scanned the roadside as I walked forward, my feet already sweating inside my boots. The stench overpowered the Vicks clogging my nose. *Don't puke, don't puke. Oh shit. I'm gonna puke. Oh, that's so much better.* I was vainly trying to blow puke and Vicks out of my nose. I hacked, spitting, gagging and blowing. *Ew.* Now I was messy. I rubbed my hands off on the grass as best I could before making my way forward. Dead people trapped in the cars beat on the windows. They didn't have fine motor skills or the memory of how to open doors. Their teeth snapped, moaning. As long as the windows stayed intact, the sounds they made wouldn't travel too far. I had to work fast, though. It was a sizable wreck. At a guesstimate, people trying to flee had hit people with the same idea as me. Move to a less populated area with land for growing food and hunting.

Bits of bodies littered the road, people eaten too much to rise again. There were only two corpses that worried me; I knifed them through the eye, hitting brain to be on the safe side. The zombies trapped in the cars made their prisons rock with their desire for my flesh. Adrenaline coursed through my body, brain synapses firing as I saw two of the cars wouldn't move under their power. I winced. I would have to bash them out of the way, which meant noise. Even with moving non-mobile patients on and off the gantry at work, I still didn't have the upper body strength to push vehicles out of the way. I only weighed 125. *Damn you, fuck-up fairy.*

I found a minivan that still had keys in the ignition and gas, with only minor damage. I hoped it would start, and cheered a little as it did. By the time I got done bashing vehicles out of the way, the minivan had died.

Let's just say I was in such a bad mood when I finished, I worked my aggressions out on the reanimated victims, and then had a post-victory loot. My stomach growled as I climbed back into the cab and started the truck up after cleaning myself off with sanitizer wipes. I re-brushed and pulled my shoulder-length, brown-shot-with-gray hair back into a ponytail. I noshed on a granola bar as I carefully drove by my handiwork. How long could my good luck last? I mean, the place had people . . . inhabitants. Not all of them went to the safe centers when the government told us to.

"Hello, paranoia, my friiiiiennnnd. It's nice to see you agaiiiiinnnnn," I sang off-key under my breath. "I know they're out t' get me. I know my luck's gonna run ooouuutt. Fuck it all. Tear it down. Not gonna die on my knees. Shoot me where I stand. Oohhh oohhh oohh!" I was belting out my made-up song, bopping my head to the imaginary beat as I rolled along.

THUMP. I screamed and slammed on the brakes.

My wide, terror-filled eyes met those of a zombie. Inattention will get you killed fast. I gassed the truck, slowly picking up speed, going as fast as I dared. I risked a glance in the side mirror: the rotten shit was running after me.

Oh, that's so not right. *Why do they have to run?* I whimpered. I saw the only bridge onto the island ahead, rising and dipping down in such a way I wasn't sure what lay beyond. I kept driving, passing more wrecks, cats back to howling protests as I scanned frantically. I drove further into Wadmalaw Island, cursing the amount of churches here in Bible Belt Land.

"And each one is no doubt full of the faithful and the suddenly-found-Jesus-because-the-world's-ending so here's hoping the first zombie Himself can save us all while we do some last-minute repenting. Only, surprise! You can't pray away this epidemic, and I bet everyone left inside is now a flesh-eater. Fucking morons!"

My rant kept my mind off how long it seemed to be taking to reach my end destination. Finally, the turn off I was looking for.

"Fuck me!" I screamed in frustration, slamming on the brakes. My luck had run out. The entrance and road up to my destination was jammed with vehicles and zoms, people who hadn't fled fast enough. There was no way I was getting in. I had fallen into a trap all right, a natural made one. I looked in the side mirror: runner zombie going for the gold. *Fucker.* I hate the newly turned. The other zoms hadn't noticed me just yet; I had seconds before I would be screwed. I wiggled out the back window, nearly losing my shorts in the process. I shut the window so the cats wouldn't escape, or at least so the orange tabby wouldn't. I could hear his frantic meowing as I crawled over the boxes and bags. I hastily cleared a spot to stand, and steadied myself in the bed. I still jumped as runner zombie attacked the truck, growling, moaning, reaching for me.

My sword was part of a five-year anniversary present my partner, and I gave each other. We are both geeks and gamers. I had even gone so far as to take fencing lessons. Wade was a gun nut and managed to drag me to the shooting range, so I knew how to handle firearms, and could hit a stationary target in the center mass. Head shots farther than 50 yards away, however, still took me half a mag to accomplish.

My sword is a custom make to my build; hopefully its twin was with him. I had to get that thing to shut up; too late. I could hear the moans from the horde as I shoved the blade through the eye and brain. My sweat-slippery hands nearly lost the sword at the sudden re-dead weight.

"Hah! No gold for you," I said while cringing at the largish horde coming my way. Craptastic, more runners.

"Please don't let them have learned climbing." The truck rocked from the force of the zombies. I was so dead. No. More than dead. I was lunch.

I let the sword clatter to the truck bed and grabbed the gun at my side while dropping to my knees. Forget about being quiet; I needed to thin the herd. The only good thing about this much up close and personal touchy-feely meant even I could make every shot a head shot. The world narrowed to the vicious rocking of the truck, flying gore, keeping balance. To this day, I'm still not sure how I managed to survive without being bitten or dragged out of the bed. I lay exhausted over my spoils from the bookstore after the last zombie dropped. I hadn't the energy to move all those vehicles. At that moment, I felt every one of my forty-odd years. I couldn't stay where I was, there was no telling what or who would be coming to investigate the noise.

I hauled my ass up, and carefully leaned against the metal of the cab roof. Now that I didn't have to worry about fighting, I could survey the jam better. It looked like with a little maneuvering I could get the worst of the offending vehicles out of the way to give me just enough room to squeeze past. The other problem would be if there weren't any gas left in the tanks.

The sun rose a little higher; I had to get the cats out of the oven the truck would fast become. I hauled my sweat- and gore-soaked body into the truck cab just long enough to comfort the kitties, reload, and drink some water. The high cab for my door allowed me to barely clear the bodies. I adjusted the strip of cloth tied across my face. It didn't help much in blocking the stench, especially as I had to step on those same bodies.

Carefully I approached the morass. So far so good. I shook from nerves and fading adrenaline as I jostled vehicles around. I didn't care where I put them . . . Well, mostly. I just wanted in. By the time I'd made enough room, the inside of the cab had reached dangerously high temperatures. I blasted the air conditioner while trying to remember just how long the kitties had been in the rising heat interior. The slightly open windows were clearly not enough to help in the still air.

They lay panting on the floor.

"I'm sorry," I sobbed as I fired the truck up. "Just hang on."

The stench of cat excrement joined the aroma of my piss, puke, and gore covered self. "Ah, Eau du Apocalypse, now in Zombie and Dirty Survivor scent. J'Adore."

In my haste to get off the road, I slewed left so I could minister to my cats. The U-Haul rocked and jounced, and took out a fence post.

Ouch. That's gonna leave a mark. The rutted drive forced me to slow down. Okay, not really, it was the U-Haul. I was never so glad to be alive when I could finally rest in temporary safety.

# # #

I woke bleary-eyed, confused as all get-out. Then it came crashing over me. The world ended, fleeing for a haven, trying not to die—or worse, become some sicko's idea of fun. How long would I be able to stay here? There was no security, zombies and living free to wander around. The house was quiet . . . too quiet. My heart started thumping anxiously, breathing becoming shallow. *Get a grip!* At this rate, I would either pass out or give myself a heart attack from stress alone. I slipped out of bed, dragging the sword with me. Yeah, I slept with it. So what? I crawled over to a window, pressing back to the wall, inching up enough to peer out. I stayed that way, observing the yard I could see, before moving to see it all.

The noise that must have awakened me came again: gunfire or fireworks. *Oh shit, please let it be friendly people and not the other kind.* I scrambled away from the window, into clothes and boots. I darted from room to room, trying to keep out of the line of sight from windows, taking care to peer out and scan. The yard was nearly empty; two horses trotted in endless, frantic loops. I wasn't sure why they hadn't succumbed to wandering zombies. The sound of battle echoed. It must be people on the road, as there was no activity other than the horses in the field.

A nose nearly made me pee myself a second time since this all started. "Damn it, kitty."

I petted Buttons, scratching his head as he purred and lavished my hand with love. The sound of thunder kept up as I made rounds inside the house. The fields still held two nervous horses. I tried the TV. Only a few major networks still broadcast. I kept the sound as low as I could while still being able to hear it. Maps flashed up; the infection had spread to other countries. The anchor came back to the U.S.

There was a lot of red, for once not Republican-related. The woman was telling people to make their way to refugee centers because it was no longer safe to occupy private residences or public buildings. The centers were spots, highlighted on the map.

"Yeah, right lady. 'Cause that always works, and nobody who's infected ever gets in." I kept getting more cynical and anti-government as I aged.

The more I read and researched on the hot topics of the day, the history behind how they came to be, the more I realized how much those with power lied, cheated, and stole. It seemed those in charge were more concerned with pushing their personal agendas, and not what was good for the country.

I shut the talking head off and tried the internet. Still there, but slow enough to remind me of the days of dial-up. The airwaves were full of deejays trying not to sound panicked as they broadcast the list of local safe shelters for survivors. Curfews were in effect, martial law in order, anyone caught out at night would be shot on sight, blah blah blah. At least I learned what all the thunder was. Fighter jets, helicopters being deployed. The local military bases had mobilized, trying to hold off the horde, getting people to safety. The army was airdropping units in to help.

"Thanks, you draw all the zoms to you, keep them occupied while I reinforce my end-of-world spot."

I shouldn't stay here much longer. The house was an individual's attached to the plantation. It sat near the main road, and even though this part of the town was an island with limited access, it would fill with fleeing refugees. I wanted to hunker down before it happened. The refrigerator hummed, letting me know the power still worked. I made a meal out of what I could find in it before loading up with weapons and apples, to deal with the horses.

The poor animals twitched, sweat lathering their bodies from fear. Instinctively, they knew something wasn't right. I didn't want them to bolt and get hurt trying to jump or break through the pasture fencing. I was hoping they would let me approach them and use them. I worked quickly, opening the pasture gate next to them, leaving the gates touching so they could make their way into the new space.

I tossed red apples from the fridge into the field, trying to make a line to help. My aim sucked at first, not getting better until I was done. When I was out of apples, I headed toward the water trough I had seen from the windows. It was made simply, not hard to empty and refill. I think the animals knew I was trying to help, even though they didn't know me. With that chore done, I moved on. I would muck out stalls later if I had a chance.

The sun had started its downward trek. I moved a few more vehicles to re-block the entrance, hoping I wouldn't need to leave in a hurry any time soon. Technically, this was the country, and the South. People loved them some guns down here. I needed to try remaining calm, and think rationally.

My pulse fluttered, fear at the ready. The road was strangely empty, even for a country highway, the thunder of far-off gunfire and air support letting me know what was going on near the city. It wouldn't be long before raiders—or worse, other survivors—got the idea into their heads like I did that this place would be empty. I jammed the vehicles as close as possible to make it look worth more effort getting in than moving on to find another spot. If I survived another day unmolested, I would try draining the vehicles' tanks. The thought alone made me shudder, anticipating the foul taste of gasoline already.

My nerves were wrecked, shot. I just wanted to collapse with my cats, but I couldn't. Reality is pain. I needed to clean, and patch up cuts, scrapes, and minor wounds, along with fortifications to build. Damn my partner, I needed him. I was so pissed he was ignoring common sense to trek about infested countryside after a family who had a ninety percent chance of already being infected or dead. I would use my anger as fuel for what needed doing, even as tears poured down my face from stress and fear of having no technology to rely on, only myself.

CHAPTER TWO

"Bitch!" was the last thing I said to a dial tone.

If she thought, she was getting the last word in. She wasn't picking up. "The only idiot is you," I ranted into her voicemail. "Real mature there, ignoring me. Ya know what? Not only will I survive, but I'll be better at it than you."

My obsession with zombie movies could only help me get to my kids, save them, and get back home.

I should be kicking my ass for trying to go after my kids at college during a zombie outbreak. Lord help me, I love them and need to know if they're alive, dead or worse. My hard-headed partner would never understand a parent's love for his kids. I'm still worried despite our fight. I know her hateful words are just her stupid self-defense mechanism she uses when she's scared and won't admit it. I would have felt better if we both went together. I waited patiently for the hospital lockdown to end, for her to be able to come home, but it never happened. Once the government made the plague official, all first responders and medical personnel such as Spacey where on 24/7 duty.

Three days ago, the media had stopped telling everyone to stay indoors, and only to call 911 if it was life-threatening. Now, they were telling us to head toward designated safe zones and only bring the essentials such as food, water, and medication. It was the point at which I realized I'd have to leave my partner, gear up, and rescue my children. I've been trying to get a hold of my kids in this chaos—what is it about the end of the world that makes people call everybody just to say, "I love you"?

Meanwhile, I'm trying to find my kids. *Fucking people.*

"Fucking traffic, MOVE!" I yell to nobody. Gotta love road rage. "Somebody better be dead."

Fuck, did I just say that? "Dead" means a whole different thing now the rules have changed. I didn't need to add getting eaten to the list of ways to die. I shouldn't have left Spacey, especially since she got the shot that started all this.

"Please don't let her turn," I pray to the gods, "and let me live so I can make her eat her 'I told you so.'" I tried my kids again.

"Hello? Dad?" Anne picks up, thank Odin.

"Honey, I'm coming for you both," I yell quickly, not sure how long the connection will last.

"Dad—"

"Listen. Do not go to a safe center. You get out of the dorms and grab as much food and water as you can. Head to the nearest gas station, and fill as many gas cans as you're able. Be on guard. Don't let anyone near you, and don't trust anyone."

Static drowns me out for a minute. I think my heart stops, and then I hear Anne calling my name, and I blurt out the first place I can think of on short notice for her and her sister to join up with me. It's close to the North Carolina border, and I barely make out her tearful acknowledgment before static drowns us out again. I hope it's another fluke, but no, I can't get back through.My anxiety ratchets up to near-unbearable levels.

I may have to ditch the car and find a better mode of transportation. Maybe a bike, SUV . . . Anything with off-road capabilities will be better than my car. I was hemmed in on three sides, with a cable barrier to my left that prevented anyone from crossing the wide grass median into the other lanes. I sat there kicking myself for not going after my kids sooner. I should've gone when all this started. Two months ago, my brother visited me during his last shore leave before being recalled by the Navy. We had both drunk too much one night, and he told me the military had stopped giving out the H3N2 shots because of strange side effects. Unfortunately, he was unable to tell me more, as only the higher-ups knew what was truly happening. My suspicious nature immediately thought the worst, because if they stopped using it, it must be something big and potentially dangerous. I saw an asshole blast past my left side, thinking to use the median as a way of getting ahead while I sat cursing myself for taking a main highway.

"Oh, hell no," I shouted, cranking the steering wheel hard left, gunning the gas. If he wants to play asshole, I can be much better at it. I've got my kids to rescue.

There wasn't enough space in front of me as I heard a sickening crunch. My bumper nudged the car in front of me, rocking it. *Fuck it*, I thought as a tear came to my eye with the sound. *I hope it doesn't come off completely.* I had almost caught up to the asshole who had blown past us all. Another irate driver decided to teach people like us a lesson. The person had enough room to move their vehicle half on the median, half still on the road.

The driver in front of me tried to swerve to go around, but the barrier was too close, and he didn't have as much room as he thought he did. Tires screeched and smoked in a failed attempt to stop before hitting the wiring or the car blocking the path. A horrendous sound of metal crunching, plastic breaking, and glass shattering reached all our ears.

Slamming on my brakes, I watched in stunned disbelief as the SUV I was following ricocheted off, causing an even more FUBAR traffic jam. The driver who'd thought to block us became forced into the cars beside and in front of him. We all watched as the SUV pin balled between the cable barrier and the other cars until finally coming to a stop.

I was so concerned with what was in front of me, I didn't see the other car behind me. The driver's reflexes mustn't have been fast enough to stop his car. I felt myself slammed forward as the seatbelt lock engaged. As the air rushed out of my lungs, my thought was: *Damn my love of my '96 Z26 I restored myself. If I live, I'm gonna kill the son-of-a-bitch behind me.*

Other drivers popped out of their vehicles, running to help the people in the initial crash. I yanked my seatbelt to loosen it. I pushed my door open forcefully, forgetting about the barrier beside me, with how pissed I was. The door bounced off the wires into my elbow causing pain to lance up my arm. "Motherfucker!"

I rolled down the driver's side window as a few motorists stood in front of the hood asking if I was okay.

"We're calling 911, and it's telling us the lines are jammed."

"Maybe you shouldn't try getting out until they arrive."

"It's gonna take 'em a while."

"I hope one of the roving police patrols comes by soon."

These came from several trying-to-be-helpful souls.

Traffic flowed by on the outbound lanes, albeit slower as people rubbernecked. I waved letting everyone know I was fine. A few motorists leaving the city pulled over onto the opposite median, wanting to know what aid they could render. I thought I heard one person say he was a volunteer firefighter. I was trying to work my way out of my car by crawling out the driver's side window, wincing in pain. It wasn't easy hauling my six-foot, three hundred fifty-pound frame out. Once out of the car, I was effectively on the other side of it, so close was the wire barrier. I reached back in, grabbed my gun and strapped it to my thigh before walking toward the person who'd rear-ended me.

As I got closer, I could see his head lolling. "You hit me, asshole. Don't even think of faking a serious injury," I yelled to him.

His head slowly raised, face gray, sweating profusely despite the mild weather, eyes bloodshot. *Oh, shit,* I thought, *he's having a heart attack.*

"Hey! Hey! I need some help over here. The guy looks like he's having a heart attack," I called out. I was still pissed off, but more worried about him.

My fellow motorists and I managed to haul him out of his car and lay him down on the ground. The volunteer firefighter was jogging over to us when the man stopped breathing.

That's not good.

"Anyone know CPR?" a person next to me called out.

The firefighter had reached us by then; he dropped down and started administering CPR. He turned enough to suck in a breath and suddenly the head of the man he was tending snapped up. We didn't understand at first. Then the screaming broke out. We all jumped as the firefighter fell backward, leaving a large portion of his cheek in the heart-attack man's mouth while trying to push the "victim" off him.

The two struggled while the idiots around me jumped in to help restrain the biting, snarling man and pull the firefighter away.

There was only a slight hesitation on my part before I reached for the Beretta strapped to my thigh, pulled the weapon out, and clicked off the safety.

"He's infected. Get away." I knew enough from hearing Spacey talk about her job to know the "victim's" reaction was not normal.

They still tried to restrain the man, receiving scratches and bites in the process. I yelled again.

"Goddamn it, move," I fired a shot into the air.

Finally. All but one person scattered at the sound of the gunshot. The unlucky soul was being savaged by his attacker. I aimed, squeezing the trigger. Bone, brain, and blood burst from the front of his head like popping a zit.

I ignored the few remaining people nearby who were now calling me a murderer. It was time to leave. I ran the few feet to my car. I didn't have time for this climbing-back-inside-the-car shit. I shot out the rear window on my beloved ride, sending the people who'd been heading toward me in a change of direction.

How I managed to get onto the trunk of my car with the wire barrier in the way I still don't remember. I was running on pure adrenaline, scared shitless. I gathered my stuff, checked the magazine on the AK-47 and 12-gauge tactical pump-action shotgun. I set everything from my backseat on top of the trunk and geared up.

First on was my Army surplus ACU tactical vest. I quickly patted the pouches to make sure the ammo hadn't fallen out during the crash. They were all accounted for. Next, I slung the tactical sling of the AK over my shoulders and strapped on the three-day MOLLE pack. Next I slid the sheathed sword on the inner side of the holster belt, and tied it off, before chambering a round in the rifle. I caught my reflection in the side mirror, I look like a reject from a Mad Max movie. Two helpers stood lingering nearby, discussing how to detain me until the police arrived. The looks I got from the rest of the motorists: priceless. People were locking their doors—like I want their stuff. *Got enough of my own, thanks anyway.* Before I could move off, a lone figure came running up the verge.

I wave and yell, "Hey, over here," and that is what

almost killed me. The smell of feces hit me, and by then it was on me.

"Fuck me," I said as I almost lost control of my bowels.

The shotgun was still in my hands, so I swung it up and the zoms jaws snapped shut on the barrel. *Gotta think—no, gotta act; thought will get you killed.* I brought a leg up, kicking the thing back with everything I had.

"Yeah, bitch, enjoy the flight. Whoa, shit," I almost lost my own footing. "Eat shotgun, you undead prick," A pull of the trigger blew half the zombie's head off.

Hey, no feeling of needing to puke. In my younger days, I'd wanted to follow my brother into the Navy, and volunteer for the SEALS- a dream that never happened. They wouldn't tell me why I had been rejected.

"Hey, fucktards in the cars, get out of them and move your ass before you become brunch," I yelled at the unhelpful pricks still in their vehicles.

A humanitarian is what I was, even at the end of the world. "Time to go." *Shit, I said that out loud, didn't I?*

A wave of death washed over me, followed by running figures breaking out from the woods.. A few broke off to pound on car windows while others chased screaming people. I'm glad I gave up smoking, because I hate running.

"Hey! There are more coming! Yinz gotta go, like NOW," *Great, now my Pittsburgh accent is showing.*

I beat a hasty retreat, hoping to find a safe place for a bit of rest and a chance to grab another ride. I slid across the back end of a car beside me, plunging into the woods farther down the interstate. The screams of trapped motorists followed in my wake. Dumb-asses. I ran until I was panting for breath, stopping to lean against a tree. The only sounds were of the forest. If it went silent, then I would know I was in trouble. I pulled my phone out, praying to Odin there was a signal.

How can this be? It uses satellite, for fuck's sake. I should still be able to pull up a map. I go so far as to step from cover, thinking the trees might be blocking the signal even though I know they've never before. *Son of a bitch!* I stopped myself from throwing the phone at a tree just in time.

It seemed my only option was staying near the road until I could access GPS. I put my device away, adjusted the straps of my pack, and start trudging inside the tree line. I didn't want to get caught outside after dark.

Hours later, I paused for a break. My whole body was soaked in sweat. A sharp pain shot through my chest, please don't let me have a heart attack. I knew I should've exercised more, and spent less time sitting, playing video games. If I died now and turned, well maybe I'd still retain enough "memory" to make my way back to Spacey; so I could bite her smug ass and zombify her.

"Come on, Wade, you can do this. Better than she could," I gulped down another Gatorade, crumpling and pitching the bottle to one side.

I swore, realizing I might need the empty whenever I next came across any water. I limped over to the discard, nearly pitching head first onto the ground from the weight of my pack and weapons. My knees slammed into the grass while pain shot up my arms as I caught myself. I grabbed the bottle before struggling to my feet.

"I will make it. Suck it, Spacey," I mumbled as I continue.

# # #

The sun's down as I finally discovered a tertiary road. Every part of me screamed in pain as I stumbled along it. I'm about to just find a nice, big tree to climb up and sleep in when my boots kick gravel. I turned my head, and saw a long driveway leading up to a house. I'd cheer if I had the energy for it.

It's time to switch tactics—could be twitchy people inside. I use the surrounding trees and shadows to get close to the house. There are no lights inside, but it's not wise to assume no one's home. I creep up the three steps of the porch to test the front door.

WTF? I mouthed silently at each creak and pop of the boards. I pause before trying the knob, which turns easily beneath my hand. This is either good or bad: dead, undead, or empty inside.

The smirk grows across my face. Finally, all the Call of Duty I've played is going to pay off. I let the rifle swing from its strap, taking out my pistol for these close quarters. Slowly I open the door . . . wow, what a wonderful smell of dead things inside. Quietly as I can, I enter—*remember, kids, lead with the gun first, no Rambo shit and check your corners.* Lord knows I bitched enough about nobody doing it while playing my games. That's how your opponent gets your ass. I check room by room. There's no sound or movement except my own. I'm almost done when I come to a closed door. I paused outside and and heard the moaning of the undead.

Shit, I'll take "I might be fucked" for 200, Alex. I switched out the pistol for the silence of the blade. God, I love my sword.

I open the door wide with one hand, taking a step back, "Oi!" I don't care how much noise I'm making now. That's the point.

The shout gets its attention. I wait until I see the zom's head in the doorway and thrust. My blade enters the head. The zombie hits the ground as I withdraw the gore covered blade. I let all my stuff clatter to the ground and groaned in relief. I can't sleep just yet, not with a corpse in the house. Mentally, I gird myself for the icky part, getting the body outside. *Ewww* touching, *ewww* naked big man. I'm gonna need a hundred showers, and a shit ton of eye bleach after this.

I should've spent more time working out. My muscles shake from fatigue. This sucks, I do a quick check for any signs or sounds of the dead before I dragged the corpse out. Random shots echo, but I can't pinpoint the location.

I get back inside the house, and locked all the doors and windows. My self-imposed chore finished, I can start looting. I find food, and yes, booze.

Hm, I didn't get a full look at the master suite. Need to rectify that. I walked back to the bedroom of death. Okay, the fat man wasn't alone. He had been feeding on another body. Whoever it had been, was too eaten to come back as a zom. I decided to leave the remains as is. I didn't have the strength to deal with them.

I turned to exit the room, and spotted a gun safe. *Please let it be open.*

"Score." It looks like the fat guy must've been going for his weapons before he succumbed to the infection.

It's slim pickings inside: hunting rifle with scope, shotgun, and. . . A .50 Desert Eagle with a laser sight. I've always wanted this hand cannon. Beside it on the shelf is five full mags, and an extra fifty rounds in a box. Also inside is one hundred rounds for the .30-06 rifle and shotgun shells.

The scent of offal from the bed is making me dry heave, I cram all the weapons and shells inside a duffle bag sitting on the safe's floor. This is the first time I've ever been in a hurry to leave a bedroom.

I dumped my find in the guest room while my muscle fatigue grew. My legs and arms are shaking so badly, I have to drag my stuff into the room. It has its own bathroom, so I don't have to deal with the blood on the floor of the master suite. I let my pack fall beside the sink, getting a look at myself in the mirror. I looked like a serial killer poster boy. No wonder people didn't want to get out of their cars. I'm glad I don't have open wounds 'cause I do not want to find out what happens if I get zombie goo in it. *Please, let the water still be on. Woot! It is.* I get cleaned up a bit and have a drink for the nerves. My last chore is to quickly service my weapons before getting some well-deserved rest.

CHAPTER THREE

Several days had passed before all communications failed. Despite all my calling, texting, and voicemails, I never got ahold of any of my family.

I had been super busy fortifying my spot, pushing myself to the limits. The taste of gasoline still lingered in my mouth. I was slim to begin with, I didn't need to lose more weight. I heard motorcycles pass by one night, and the thought of them turning off to inspect this place gave me a bad case of fear- induced diarrhea.

There's nothing better than being incapacitated by the shits in the middle of a good old zombie apocalypse. Gah. At this rate, I would need to raid just for toilet paper. I never heard the bikes again. I could only hope the riders got chomped on, but that would take more luck than I possessed. I figured the gang might have holed up either at the local distillery or the fish preserve. Two places now further down on my list of spots to be raided.

I scanned the house before me from the long driveway, looking for movement, or the thunder of bikes. The hot air shimmered, an anemic breeze couldn't make up its mind if it were going to swell or not. This was the farthest I had ventured from the safe house. I rolled the truck toward the back, parking so it was nose out, a feat in itself with the U-Haul attached. I opened the roller door, less concerned with zombies getting in than not having quick access to space. I gained the deck of the house and crept toward a door. I had only moments to gain entry, zombies wandered in a cluster near the front of the place. The truck let them know food was near. I realized now this place had been a private club. The door didn't budge, so I broke a window instead. I cringed inside at the noise of shattering glass, replacing the gun I had stolen back into the makeshift thigh holster.

Moans started, a little closer than I wanted, drawing the zoms inside toward me. Great. I killed four of them before I could climb into the room. Good thing I had found some work gloves, or I'd be crying from the pain of lacerated hands.

"This is so gross." The first of the outside zoms sounded on the deck as I heaped my kills under the broken window. "Here's hoping this helps." I ventured deeper into the clubhouse, encountering more zombies.

"Crap, lost count. Um, let's just say 120. Yeah, that sounds impressive. Go zom killer queen." I backed away from another re-dead body.

The quiet unnerved me. I had to keep reminding myself not to talk out loud. I didn't want to become zom dinner at this point. The place was a bonanza for more than booze and food. I emptied the cloth bags I had used to carry books in from my backpack. They were little worse for wear. I had packing loot down to a science. It seemed my corpse relocation service worked, as a peek out an upstairs window showed me the outside zoms back to wondering the lawn.

"Don't get greedy, you don't want to get caught with the U-Haul. Load up and get the fuck out."

Of course, my loading up meant the zoms wandering the lawn would smell me and come back for round two. I wasted precious time killing them, time which could have been better used securing my loot. I had just done one last sweep of the place, including outbuildings, adding a few more items to the truck bed as I had used up all the space in the U-Haul.

A faint roar floated on the breeze. "Good advice, too bad you never take it."

The sound was muffled, but if it was what I

thought, then it wouldn't be for long. Normally I don't like making assumptions, being as I can make an ass of myself without help, but in this case I would make an exception. The rumble of bikes meant it was time to go. The last thing I needed was to be spotted by a motley assortment of bikers. Who knew if they were of the naughty or nice variety? I sure as hell didn't want to find out. Humans scared the crap out of me, more than the zoms did. At least with zoms you know what they want. A juicy brain, a succulent thigh, prized sweetmeats in a tender skin covered belly, or perhaps some ribs coated in Blood-b-Que sauce. Humans, however, could be nice one minute, mean the next or just plain scheming until you turned your back and Wham! You woke up trying to wrench the proverbial knife out of your back or rattled the cuffs chaining you to the solid, inescapable object while you cried, screamed, begged for mercy that would never come. Humans played games: mind and body.

Most of my early life I had suffered from being too trusting, and a magnet for bullies. By the time I hit high school, then college, I had learned to trust no one, and to stand up for myself and take no shit from anyone. Zoms, they just wanted their next meal. At least when the zombies overwhelmed you with sheer numbers, you knew there was no hope of salvation. Not us, not the living. Sheer numbers gave false hope there was a rational mind, or several in the crowd of bullies. That they would protest and try to stop the others or at the least, help you escape.

I slammed the roller door of the U-haul down, using the included mechanism to lock it. I could see zombies struggling up from the pluff mud by the river. As much as I wanted to watch the battle between bikers and zoms, I liked myself too much to put me in that much peril. I left the house behind regretfully, driving farther back toward the creek and the surrounding trees. I drove across adjoining lawns, scratching the paint while I squeezed the vehicles between the trees. See, this is why I can't have nice things.

I could still hear the thunder of large guns and combat vehicles sporadically when the wind blew a certain way. I had a feeling the refugees, what was left of them, would soon come seeking a haven. I wanted to be set up before that happened. I wasn't about to share my space with those who thought they wouldn't have to work to survive.

Until then, let's see what happens first, the bikers find me, or the wandering zombies. It turned out neither did. An explosion rang out, quickly followed by several more. I used the sound to cover the truck's engine noise. I drove across yards for as long as I could, hoping I was heading away from the bikers and they wouldn't spot me. The roaring got louder, shit! I stopped behind a stand of trees, engine idling as the sound swelled, then it was passing like an angry hive of yellow jackets. I waited a few more minutes to be sure there was no rear guard coming, then eased out into the driveway, picked up speed, and swung out onto the road. My attention shifted between the silent road before and behind me. I decided not to raid anymore today. I thought I knew where the bikers were. I needed to get back working on defenses.

# # #

It took almost the rest of the day to unload my loot, bringing me dangerously close to twilight. It had been worth it, however. With judicious rationing I could survive on what I had for at least a month. That didn't mean I wouldn't seek out food if I had the chance. At some point, I would need to search for a feed store. I didn't know much about horses, but I didn't think there was enough grass for them to free graze. Besides, if we all made it to winter, there would be no grass, and they would need oats or something. The two horses needed care still. They hadn't let me touch them yet, but waited till I set out food and water or opened pasture gates to move them between fields. I had some defenses in place, but not enough to give me an advantage over a pack of bikers, or anyone else with malicious intent. By the time I finished with stable chores, the light was fast slipping. I hurried inside and had a hasty meal. Buttons climbed into my lap as I worked, Pepper curled under a chair nearby. Eventually, we all ended up asleep in bed.

# # #

A rattle and shaking woke me at the ass crack of dawn. "Fuckers. People are trying to sleep here," I grumbled.

I am not a morning person. If I could slap someone for this, I would. The noise wouldn't let up, nor the shaking. I gave up on sleep and hauled myself out of bed. By the time I stumbled outside, bits of ash had floated out of the sky like black snowflakes.

"Oh, this isn't good." I could smell smoke, and a wave of noxious fumes comprised of burning... stuff. My over-active imagination filled in what the stuff could be. Sometimes, it sucked.

The thunder of guns and military vehicles had ended. The zombies had overrun the safe centers. I figured the gathered survivors would keep them busy for oh, maybe thirty minutes. People would already be fleeing. I had to get my ass in gear. I didn't know how long it would take before I would have unwelcome guests. I'm a bit of a loner, and I really enjoy being by myself. More than three or four people naturally stresses me out. I'm more toward the extreme end of the introvert scale.

I checked my projects on the porch. They had hardened overnight but were covered in ash. It must have been coming down for a while. The trick would be not cutting myself on the embedded glass. That would have to wait. I dashed to the pasture, not an impressive feat. It was two arm lengths from the house on all four sides. For once the horses crowded the gate. They must have decided to take their chances with me as a means of getting out of the ash. They knew where their stables were. I just had to keep from getting trampled as they bolted for their home. I did a slap-dash feed and water, earning a '*Really, fucker?*' look from both.

"Yeah, yeah. Unless you want to end up as dinner just go with it for now," I called to them. I raced to a second truck I had driven out of the mess of vehicles clogging the entrance/exit to the plantation.

I didn't want to unhook the U-Haul from the vehicle I had arrived in, more out of fear I wouldn't be able to get it hitched back up. So far both trucks had served me well. I used the second truck to load up my project and take it out to the driveway leading to the side road access.

I had dug shallow ditches several days ago in preparation for this. I set the concrete and glass into the ditch, using dirt to fill in the gaps at the sides and help anchor them. I now had a line marching across the side access. The glass wouldn't be easy to see unless the sun shone on it the right way. It wasn't the best method for tire puncturing, but I didn't have enough nails to do the same thing. This would have to do. The quiet was complete, unnerving, with no animal noises or birdsong. Every time I had encountered zombies, the eerie stillness preceded them. I cautiously walked to the road, out onto it, and peered both ways. The sun was going to be bright and hot today. Oh, joy.

I squinted my eyes, lack of sleep and the early hour not sitting well with me. The staged wreck I had placed where side road meets main highway didn't appear to be disturbed. I had left just enough space on the berm to squeeze out if a person was willing to sacrifice some paint, maybe a side mirror . . . or two. I wondered how many people would be able to stop shitting themselves in fear long enough to help themselves instead of waiting for someone to come rescue them.

The second part of my project I scattered on the berm leading up to the opening. I left a distance I figured I could miss but others might not; especially if they backed up or swerved early in preparation to take advantage of the opening. I scuffed dirt over them just enough to try and hide but not bury. My surprise comprised of home-made caltrops. The internet is a beautiful and scary thing, at least when it was still working. I walked back to the driveway and the line of trees. In the event the vehicles did or didn't make it this far, I had project number three for those on foot. I decided against more caltrops, once would be enough. If they had any brains, they would look out for more, and I wasn't going to leave them lying about to be picked up and used against me.

Project three was a mono-filament line, or fishing line if you will. Strong, clear, deadly if used right. Another internet find. I spent hours wrapping it around and between the trees in lovely patterns. Making sure each section between the trunks was individual, so if one was cut, the rest wouldn't sag for no good reason. The longest stretch went across the opening to the driveway. I made a second pattern using the fence posts marking the sides of the drive. Double trouble. If nothing else, it would slow someone down the few seconds to cut through it, seconds which could be all I needed to turn the tide my way or run.

Now then, what to do about the sides not facing the road? Or the approach from the plantation fields? I didn't want to be predictable, besides, I only had so much fishing line and I might need some to actually use it for what it was meant for. Hmm . . . there were four tour buses. Maybe if I could tip them over on their sides, nose to an end, I could use them as a blockade? The only problem would be killing the zombies inside. Once those doors opened, I would have my work cut out for me. What would be the odds anyone would actually use the other road cutting through the plantation to see if any houses sat on it? Locals would know one existed, if any were still alive, and if any outsiders cared to go far enough they would find it. The only drawback to my blockades would be alerting people perhaps there was more than just the houses nearby. I would have to chance it.

The most stomach-churning of my projects was still to come. The air around me was relatively free of the heavy scent of decay unless the wind blew the wrong way. I contemplated something that would change all that. I drove back down the road that cut through the plantation and parked the truck near the visitor center. I had cleaned out any lurking zoms from inside and out, except the buses. They would hopefully stay quiet if I didn't approach their metal prisons.

That still didn't mean I could be sloppy. I hugged the tree line, moving slow and steady, sword out at the ready, but so far no new zoms had made it my way. I hoped the large pack of bikers would draw the zombies to them. At the rear of the processing plant, I found the diesel storage tanks for the farm equipment. I figured it had to be pretty full–the plague struck at the beginning of the harvesting season. What else could I find that would be helpful? Oh MY! I didn't expect the place to have its own mini-digger! That would make my job so much easier if I could only figure out how to work the damn thing. I couldn't help the little hip-shaking boogie dance I did.

It took three-quarters of a frustrating hour to figure out how to back up, turn, and go forward before I was rolling. I hummed to myself, happy for the first time in days. I spent the rest of daylight digging. My project would take a while even with this machine, considering the depth I wanted to go. I briefly wondered how my (as I now thought of him) ex-boyfriend was doing. How long would he last before his stupidity got him killed? My musings kept my mind occupied as I dug.

CHAPTER FOUR

"What is with all the pounding," I mumble, feeling muscle twinges from yesterday's crash and escape from the chaos on the highway.

Now I remember: zombies. How in the hell do they know I'm here? I hope there's not a lot, they could get in. I look out and see seven of them. Not bad, but it looks like more are on the way.

I should text Spacey, just to let her know I'm still alive, and she's wrong about me not being able to save my kids. Yes, childish, but I was still pissed off at her smug assumptions. "Well fuck me, dead battery." I mumble, as I pull out the spare battery, and put it in.

Life comes back to my phone. My sigh of relief turns to bug-eyed disbelief when no signal is found.

"No, no, no!" I shout. "What the fuck? It should've taken longer for stuff to fail. Unless . . . the damn military probably has all us civilians blocked from accessing the phone and power grids. Fuckers!" The noise and smell outside have grown.

Okay, this is bad. The dead are on their way. A few are outside the door already. To make matters worse, the garage, I just realized, is detached. Damn my luck. I find the keys near the dry-heave inducing mess of what was once a person. Please be for a lifted truck with a gun rack. I do a quick check on the banging. Oh goodie, we're up to ten with about twenty more zoms coming. If I'm gonna do something, it better be NOW. I don't mind a head-on fight, but with opponents like zombies, it will get me eaten. I squash my impulse to rush in fighting and gather my stuff. I need an opening so I don't get surrounded and overwhelmed. A crash of glass lets me know a few could be downstairs.

"Fuck me," I say under my breath.

I regret loading myself down with the MOLLE pack, my weapons, and the duffle bag filled with loot. I'll be damned if I'll leave everything behind, even if it almost does kill me. I make a last check of the cords holding the duffle to my pack. It would be a shame if they loosened mid-fight. I decide to use the shotgun. Even without a head shot it will knock zoms down long enough to get out the back to the garage. I creep downstairs, looking into the living room. I see at least two of them. *Hope they're slow and not the fast kind*, I think. A third zombie comes into view. It's now or never. I make a break for it. They turn at the noise, one sprinting. I fire a round and hit it at chest level. The slug tears through dead center, and the force of the hit sends it flying back over the couch. I keep racking and shooting, knocking them down like dominoes. Something shifts on my back; the duffle—I knew it. Turning my head enough to check how much it's moved almost leads to my doom. I'm rounding the corner into the kitchen when movement in my peripheral vision resolves into a fourth zombie. I get my forearm across its throat as it grabs me, my quick reflexes to the rescue. *Well, no shotgun now*, my brain says.

I let the weapon fall in its cross-body sling, fumbling for my holster and the pistol. The entire time, I struggle to keep the zom from biting or scratching me, while the weight on my back shifts even more. Finally, I manage to free my Beretta. The zom is lunging for another attack when I press the Beretta to the zom's temple and pull the trigger. Its body falls away. My ears ring, and I feel I'm covered in brains. The duffle is still attached, but hanging on the left side of my pack. I don't have time to fix the uneven distribution of weight. The scratching of nails on tiles alerts me to danger. The zoms I shot a moment before are crawling for me, the shotgun blasts having severed their spines. The sounds of shattering glass and wood mean more are pouring through the windows and busted front door. I've got to get out of this deathtrap. I unlock the back door, and open it enough to see my way is clear.

"Thank the gods." *Please let the garage be open.* I dash across the lawn as two runners appear around the corner of the house.

Feet, don't fail me now. My luck ends as I crash into the locked side door of the garage. "Fuck, it never ends." I'm glad I found the Desert Eagle. I shoot around the lock—"Can't a guy catch a break?" My new love jams on the third round. The growls of zoms sound scary close.

I back up a bit, then batter the door with the left side of my body. The AK and rifle swing, getting in the way. The pack and shifting duffle messes with my center of gravity. A strong tug yanks me back.

Nope, that little girl scream wasn't me, and I dare anyone to say otherwise. The rifle's stock saves me, as a zom chomps on it. I reverse my grip on the Eagle and use the butt end to bash the deader's head in. In a panic now, I raise my booted foot and kick madly at the door. *Thank Odin!* I pitch forward as the door finally gives way. *Ouch, that's gonna leave a mark.* My hands skid across concrete. My fear gives me the strength to scramble inside. I'm tangled in the stocks from my weapons, but they're the least of my worries. I flop onto my side, kicking the door closed with my feet and holding it shut. The runners hit it, sending it slamming into my feet. Pain reverberates up my legs. My hands are bleeding from where the Eagle's butt gouged my right palm, and the floor my left. The gun's no use right now. I let it lie on the floor. I lunge up from the ground, and the door nearly bursts open from the zoms outside. I let the weight of the pack and duffle tip me forward. I slam the door, holding it closed as I frantically cast around for something to keep it shut.

I see metal shelving beside me. *Light bulb*. The heaving door is getting harder to keep closed. I swing the rifle into my hands to pop a few rounds through the door. I'm trying to buy time. The shelves are full of stuff, so I just grab things and hurl them at the door until I think the shelves are light enough to tip. I reach up, grabbing the top shelf, while moving my foot to the bottom of it. It takes a bit of pulling, but the unit starts tipping as the door moves. I get out of the way as the unit crashes to the floor, the rest of the contents scattering. The door hits the shelves, driving it shut again. The quick peek I got, though, shows me a small herd.

This ought to buy me a few minutes, pausing to scope up the Eagle, to get into . . . OH MY GOD. Can this day get any worse? Wait, don't ask, yes, yes it can. I guess fate likes to fuck with stupid. A rusting, primer grey Toyota truck greets me. At least it's got a front guard. I throw my stuff in the bed, jump in, and immediately adjust the seat.

"Did a midget drive this thing?" I complain as I fish the keys out of a pants pocket and fire it up.

I hit the garage door opener. As it lifts, I see the lower half of zombies. They're already shambling inside by the time the door is half-way up. I gun the engine and peel out. A brief jolt and screech lets me know I've hit the bottom of the door.

"I hope this piece of shit holds together," I say at the thumps on the push bar as I make zombie roadkill. A head hits the hood and leaves a nice sized, bloody dent.

The truck jolts again, as I run over another zombie. "That will do wonders on the old suspension. I should see if there are any working car washes open," I mutter.

I race down the road, fumbling in another pants pocket for my phone. I put a few miles between myself and the horde before I feel it's safe enough to stop. Let's try bringing up a map so I can find my way to my girls. An agonizingly long wait ensues, then rewards me with the message: No satellite. I'm cursing the lack of GPS. The satellites can't be shut down, so why won't anything using it still work? I bet my smart-ass partner would know. I can almost hear the egg-head, lecturing tone she gets when imparting information. My temper rises. She doesn't know any more than me. Grimly, I mash down on the gas pedal as I rummage in the glove box. I find much-used state and local maps. Once more, I pull over to look at them, trying to figure out where I might be. The highway would keep me from getting lost, but back roads are safer in terms of avoiding the dead and most humans. A few hours of driving on unmarked, country roads pass before I spot a couple trucks blocking the road about a half-a-mile away. This can mean only one of two things: The trucks were abandoned, or in the words of Admiral Ackbar, "It's a trap!"

I pull over into the woods, still pissed with the lack of satellite feed. The Toyota needs gas. I hope the nearby vehicles have enough for me to re-fuel. I grab the AK and the .30-06, making my way farther in under cover of the trees. I find a good shooting position and check out the scene through the scope.

"Let's see here," I whisper, "I spy with my little eye, four armed men."

They're so sloppy. Hell, if I can see them, they're amateurs. They could have found better cover. I'm confident I can take out two of them before they figure out where I'm at. It's time to take out the trash. I'm slowly creeping from tree to tree, getting within firing range. I spot a nice little bit of cover: a fallen tree to steady my shot. I head for it only to hear a crack behind me.

My blood freezes cold as please gods, don't let that be what I think it is, pokes into my back.

"Well, now," the thick country accent makes it difficult to understand words. "Jus' whut you thinkin' you were gonna do, boy?"

Fuck! Keep calm, and hope he doesn't alert his Bubba friends. Maybe I can get out of this without being shot. The barrel of what has to be a rifle pokes harder into my back.

"Hands away from yer toys, Rambo. Lace 'em on top your head, and kneel real slow."

I start shaking in anger, not enough to notice, but he will soon. I let the guns fall to either side, so he has to kick them away. Slowly I kneel, watching from the corner of my eye as his boot kicks the AK first.

Now or never. I twist, falling sideways as I kick out. Boom! I think I screamed a warrior cry, not a cry of pain. Fire lances across my upper back, the one spot not covered by my Kevlar vest. Bubba lands on his ass. . I kick out, as my hands scramble for a rifle. Finally, Lady Luck.

I manage to knock his hands away from his rifle. Ass munch's mouth is moving, but I can't hear over the ringing in my ears. My fumbling comes up with a rock as he launches himself at me. His ham- sized hands are squeezing my throat as I bash the crap out of him. Suddenly, blood sprays out of a new hole in his forehead. I close my eyes as blood and brain coat me. So much for not being noticed. The effort of rolling his fat ass off me causes a scream of pain to rip from my mouth. Three men run at me with rifles at the ready. The fourth is steadying for another shot.

Abort! Abort! Where's my guns? I hear the zip of a bullet as I scramble up. I'm not in the mood to test their aim. I take off running, zig-zagging, hearing cracks, and wood chips are pelting me. I fall face first against the side of my truck.

Those assholes cost me my guns. The fuck this

isn't happening. Hell no. I rip the door open, jump in, and start the truck. I peel out while grabbing the Glock laying on the seat. Tears of rage, not pain, course down my face. If I can get 'em alone, I can kill 'em, and get me some new guns. Let's see how you like this, mother fuckers. My tin can shudders as shots punch the body. I'm hunched over the wheel, jerking back and forth on the road. Damn apocalypse. A cop would be welcome. I glance in the rearview and see trucks with Bubbas inside chasing me. They keep firing, hoping to get a lucky shot off and kill me. Yeah, keep wishing. The low-gas idiot light blinks on. I pound the steering wheel and swear. I almost miss the dirt road to my left. What the hell, things can't get any worse. Finally, a break, if you call a collection of broke-ass mobile homes a break.

The truck sputters and dies fifty feet from the nearest tornado magnet. I can barely hear the whoops and laughter over the sound of engines. I throw the truck in park and bail out. A grunt of pain escapes my lips as I hastily grab my stuff and take off running. I'm darting between the structures, frantically looking for anything to help. A door hangs open, and I bolt inside, not caring what might be waiting for me.

The stench of rot burns my nose hairs. I just need a moment to access the rifle in the duffle bag. I let my stuff crash to the garbage strewn carpet. I'm kneeling, pawing the bag open when voices sound out.

"Hey, boy! I said, Hey, boy. You ain't gonna hide from us here. Come on boys, we got's ourselves a nice little hunt."

"I hate mobile homes. I hate good ole boys," I grumble as I load the hunting rifle.

"Hey, Jimbo! Get Lem and the dogs over here!"

"And I now officially hate dogs," I add under my breath.

Once I've got the rifle and extra mags situated, I

re-attach the duffle bag with the cords to my pack. Then I slip it onto my back, wincing as it brushes against the bullet track. I use the rifle's barrel to nudge aside one-half of a pair of limp, ragged curtains. From the direction of the front of the mobile park, I hear the throb of engines. Maybe the back has a better view. The kitchen window shows more mobile homes, a small tanker truck, mounds of dirt, and woods.

Shit! I can't believe I'm even contemplating leaving the house I'm in. I have no other choice. Just thinking about it makes me gag. Balls. I bail out of the home, doing my best to stick to the shadows cast by the homes.

A shout reaches my ears, along with the sound of a small fusillade. I don't know what the Bubbas are using, but flying debris hits my back. I'm running and dodging like one of my favorite Steeler's players.

There's a pause as the men stop to reload. Thank you for ringing the dinner bell, idiots. Please, Odin, send zombies. Over the whoops of the men, I hear hysterical barking. It sounds much closer than I like. I risk a look back and see a medium-sized pack of slathering dogs with lots of sharp teeth. I bring the rifle up as I renew my efforts to make it to the tanker and the small ladder attached to the back when the sensation of falling overtakes me.

Sploooosssshhhhh!

Putrid fluid fills my mouth, nose, and eyes. I vomit as I re-surface, nose hairs singed from the stench. Desperately I claw at my face with one hand, trying to clear the gunk as I continue hurling. If I can just get my stomach to come up, I don't need it. I'll never be able to eat again.

Shadows race across me. Another splash sends a wave of liquid shit over my head, followed by yelping. I smash against the side of the sunken containment unit as a hound flounders nearby. Don't get me wrong, I love dogs, but this mutt means to kill me no matter what. It's swimming and lunging at me. Its jaws snap shut over the barrel of the rifle I've somehow managed to keep ahold of.

"Sorry, puppy," I whisper as I use the rifle to shove him under, drowning him in fecal matter.

What kind of luck keeps the men and pack from hearing our struggles, but doesn't help me avoid landing in the pit?

"Hey, Lem. What's wrong with them dogs a yours?"

I can hear snuffling, whining, and soft woofs from the pack as they search to pick up my scent. I hold my breath, for more than one reason. I try not to think about what all this waste is doing to my wound. I let the weight of my pack drag me back down until my head is the only part above the sludge. The gold medal winner for floating in shit goes to Wade.

"He can't a disappeared. Probably trying some dumb city slicker trick to throw 'em off the scent. Don't you worry. My boys'll find 'em."

"Spread out! I want alla ya fuckers lookin' fer 'em."

"Ya think he's hidin' in one a these trailers?"

"Not fer long! YeeeeeeHaaaaawwwwww!"

The rapid discharge of a rifle follows and is soon joined by the others. I'm forced to take in another foul breath, trying to suppress my gag reflex.

"Hey, Jimbo, let's just burn the fucker out. There ain't nothing a use in these tin cans anyway," suggests one of the Bubbas. "He ain't worth wasting bullets on,. Iffin' he is in one a them, he'll come out right quick or burn up."

"Ya know, that ain't half bad, Clem. All righty, we're gonna burn it down. Every one a them. Gonna have ourselves a weenie roast!"

More sounds of glee as I force another breath of

air into my lungs. I think I'm growing light-headed from the fumes. Must escape soon. I eyeball the rim, looking for anything to grab onto, and haul my ass out of the cesspit I'm currently in. Fuck the noise.

It's not long before I smell smoke and hear the crackle of flames. Please be a boom soon from gas igniting. I can't hear the dogs anymore. They must have been recalled to their owners. I flounder, the weight of the pack hindering my best efforts. I shuck it off and toss it up and over the rim, followed by the rifle.

I haul myself out of the septic system, and into a roiling mass of smoke, hot air, and flames. Eyes streaming, I flop on the ground, wriggle back into the pack, and grab the rifle. Fuck dogs, Bubbas, and potential zombies, I gotta get outta here before the truck catches fire or explodes. Despite my aching body, the throb of my wound, I crawl in the direction of the tanker.

Now, if only the door is unlocked. Sweet Freya's tits, it is. I toss the rifle onto the seat. My wound screams for mercy as I drag the pack off and throw it inside the cab. I heave myself up and inside, slamming the door shut. In my haste, I bash my knees on the steering column, sending the key ring sticking from the ignition jingling.

Here's hoping the Bubbas didn't drain the tank. I crank the starter. The big engine roars to life. I offer up quick thanks to Odin, as I check the gas gauge: half a tank. Fuck these motherfuckers! I mash the pedals, shifting into gear. The whine of tires spinning reaches my ears before I feel them grabbing purchase on the grass. I turn too quickly and feel one side lift. Whoa! I've gotta remember this thing has a whole different center of gravity than the Toyota. I don't wanna tip my new ride over.

I burst outta the flames and smoke, catching the men off guard. I plow between two of the Bubbas' lifted trucks. The tanker shudders and lurches. Steel shrieks as I force my way through their blockade. I wish I could've seen their faces. I'm cackling, which turns into a hacking cough before I clear my lungs and throat.

"Eat shit and die, assholes!" I howl as I force the truck into greater speed, rolling the windows down.

The tires chirp as I hit the blacktop. I'm increasing my speed to put distance between us. It's time to find a safe place where I can literally wash the shit off me and tend to my wounds. Odin knows what possible infections might be festering.

CHAPTER FIVE

I estimated two weeks had gone by since I fled the city. My peaceful ideal was about to be shattered, though I didn't know it at the time. I woke as usual, took care of the cat (Pepper didn't look too good), and then the horses. I was slowly making friends with them, but they knew they were in charge. I had finished my tiger traps, re-locating the zombies in the bus to the pits. A pain in the ass project which still makes me want to hurl. The buses I had driven closer to the dirt access road running throughout the plantation, and also served the house I occupied. That was a lesson in frustration, not to drive the buses as they had automatic transmissions, but on trying to tip the damn things. I eventually gave up, instead letting the air out of the tires to prevent crawlers from getting underneath.

The poor horses still didn't like me for the ruckus, and the smell of the captured zoms. I had to admit it wasn't my best idea either, especially with the temperatures rising. The still air brought to me the sounds of bikes, occasional gunshots, and screams. I had raided nearby houses lining the highway for more supplies and added to my food and liquid stores, and my kill count. I also used what vehicles I found to arrange more 'wrecks' around the roads surrounding the plantation.

My backpack now had a bottle of mouthwash in it. I had more than enough gas for the trucks, and a sports bike I had found. I kept the use of the bike to a minimum. It was a crotch rocket. It's noisy, enough to make people want to find out about it, or signal to lurking zoms that lunch was nearby. A few of the houses had boats attached to their docks. I piloted them up the waterway to the two nearest docks by my house, and buried caches of supplies nearby. Those would be my escape plans D and E. I loved the water and knew how to boat and sail.

My family had always had boats while I grew up, and I had helped my Dad enough times with repairs to be able to do basic to medium maintenance. Just thinking of my family and boating on the river every summer while growing up caused me to break down and sob uncontrollably. By the time I finished tinkering with the boats, I was emotionally wrung out.

Knowledge is power. What my dad taught me, along with what I raided from the bookstore, ensured I was able to take out a needed part of the engines so no one else could steal them. The bookstore also had maps— good to take as back up. I don't always trust technology. It has a way of failing right when you need it the most. I might not be particularly brave or a great warrior, but I could make plans out the ass. If I could avoid a fight to live another day, I'm turning tail and running. Call me a coward, but I bet I'll be the one laughing last while less prepared people's asses either turn into a zombie or become a happy meal.

On this day, I was worried about the diesel tank. It was a big temptation to those who might think of it, and had back-up generators to power. The ground around it was concrete, which made it not so easy to defend—meh. I used small, yet sturdy branches, to make a grid. The ends were sharpened and hardened with fire. I found some rope to rig up a lever system. I set my traps just outside the perimeter of the concrete. The fishing line came in handy once more as a trip wire to set the whole thing off. Once triggered, the stakes would spring up from their shallow ditch, hopefully impaling trespassers. My last ditch, scare 'em effort, was to scatter little novelty pop-its around the tank itself. I used last year's leaves and some dirt to spread far around the area and conceal my trap. The only flaw in the plan was if it rained, the poppers would be ruined. Oh, well. I wasn't going for perfection, just pre-warning, and a measure of safety.

If I had enough cans, I would've drained the tank into them and buried them, like I did with my other stores.

My morning chores done. Lunch eaten. It was time to start on my afternoon project. I was scratching my head trying to think how to protect myself from wandering zombies coming through the surrounding woods. I had some empty food cans, but not enough to make any real noise. I put the project aside, turning instead to the horses. They were filthy. I used sugar cubes to bribe one to come close. He let me snap a lead on the halter and wrap it around a fence post. I started trying to curry. I had a big book of horse care open on an upturned bucket as I worked. The horse didn't try biting or kicking me. Instead, he amused himself by constantly knocking the book and bucket over. I figured I was doing something correct. During this project, I heard revving engines, gunfire, and screams. The noise sounded way too close. I finished with the horse and let him free. I hustled to the house, grabbed extra ammo, raided guns, and my sword. I jumped in the truck and was soon bouncing along the fields before I could get back on the access road. The spot I came out at would do little to hide me.

I grabbed my scavenged binoculars off the front seat, to get a closer view. The bikers seemed to be in a battle with the remnants of military personnel, zombies, and civilians. Crap. My haven was about to be invaded. I drove the truck closer, then used the access road to avoid my blockage, stopping at what I considered a safe distance. I had no turnaround with a fence to the right of me and a big-ass ditch to the left. I would have to reverse to get out of there, and I can't do that in a straight line at speed. Hell, I can't do it slowly, either.

I grabbed the rifle and propped it on the lowered window ledge of the opened door. A poor shield, if the bullets from the defenders were of high enough caliber. I lined up my shots through the scope, taking my time to make them head shots. A waste of effort. I still needed more than one shot. There was a shit load of zombies. Where had they all come from? I took shots until it became too dangerous to do so without hitting non-zombies.

Some of the smelly fuckers turned my way. They tumbled into the ditch, then clawed their way out and toward me. I switched to the handgun. It took me more than one shot to explode heads as I didn't have a scope to help me, just the sights. My ears constantly rang by the time the last zombie fell. I nearly started going *mawp mawp* just to discover how deaf I currently was. I had switched to my sword by then, as I was out of ammo. I still didn't feel confident I could drop the spent mag and reload with a full in time to not be lunch. I was wiping off the blade and re-sheathing it when one of the military men turned my way.

"You. By the truck. Hands in the air. On your knees," Or at least that's what I thought he said. It was hard to tell through the ringing in my ears.

Seriously? The look I gave spoke volumes to the man keeping me in his gun sights. I pointed with a free hand to my ears and screamed, "You're fucking welcome for the help."

Okay,. so my mouth was going to get me killed.

"Down on the ground. This is your last warning," he shouted at me, making accompanying hand gestures to get his meaning across. His squad mates drew down on the bikers, who were also not complying.

Oh, so not good. I really didn't want to be caught in cross-fire. Now that I was done metaphorically shitting myself in fear and nerves, my usual skeptic self came to the fore.

I kept my hands up, heart racing as I cautiously started to kneel. I was near the back tire, the driver's door shut. Just as I had finished kneeling, shots rang out. I found myself staring up at the under carriage of the truck.

"Wow, that's gross and dirty," came out of my mouth as I worked my way out the other side, standing in the space between truck and fence. "Great, I need a new pair of pants, again."

I used the distraction to open the passenger-side door and crawl inside. It's kinda hard to keep hunched over with a sword on one's back. Gunshots rang out, more than was warranted for a pack of bikers. I risked a quick glance over the dash. While we were all getting to know each other, another pack of zombies had burst out. This group seemed even larger than the last.

"Oh, hell no!" The truck rumbled to life, sword digging into my back and seat, hampering me actually. I ripped it off over my head, letting it fall onto the center console. "Reverse. Reverse. Where the hell is reverse?"

The rear tires spun, then bit into the dirt as the large vehicle fishtailed backward. I slammed the brakes in time to keep myself from going bed first into the ditch.

"Think, Stupid," I screamed at myself as I got the truck straightened.

Zombies fell in the ditch trying to get at me. The zombie runners are even more terrifying to watch as they pull themselves out and to my side.

I powered up the still lowered window with one hand while trying to guide the truck backward down the access road to the fence opening. Unfortunately, my lack of coordination meant my speed matched that of a snail's. The runners slammed into the driver's side, pounding, clawing on the glass, trying to get at me. Fuck this! I slammed the gas down while yanking on the wheel. The fencing held a moment, then gave with a splintering crash.

I still winced .

"Great, I hope that didn't fuck the tailgate up too much," I mumbled, then screamed, "Get the fuck away from me."

Yeah, like that would just shoo the stinkers away. I was gaining quite the following as I spun the truck, nearly tipping over in my haste. The only thing to keep me upright was bodies of zoms as the vehicle smacked into them, sending some spinning away. Others got caught by the tires and dragged underneath. I stomped on the gas to plow over a few more. I needed to flick on the wipers to clear gore off so I could see.

I raced around the field in a big U, heading back to the military as runners and slower zoms followed in some demented game of Tag, You're It. I could clearly see the entrance again as I barreled along the inside access road, making no attempt to avoid zombies. I brought the truck to a skidding halt, a wave of running survivors and zombies in a big nasty group just behind the vehicles I had left blocking the entrance.

Most of the zombies following me broke around the truck to get at the easier prey as I hurried to reload the guns. That done, I backed up a few feet before throwing the truck in park, letting it idle. I twisted, kneeled on the console, opened the back window, and fired at the zombies surrounding the truck. They were so close even I could make head shots. Once the mag was empty, I slammed my ass back in the driver's seat and reversed.

The big vehicle shuddered, grinding more zombies under the tires. "Oh, my poor much-abused truck. Last just a little bit longer. Fuck."

I almost couldn't see the entrance, but I could still hear the gunfire and a few screams. I grabbed the handgun, switched mags, before lowering the window a bit. I finished off the smelly biters still trying to shatter my glass.

"Assholes," I huffed, slamming the truck into drive and closer to the front before I stopped at an angle.

The pack was busy feeding with no sign of how many bikers might have escaped. The military Humvee driver apparently decided to not risk the ditch. He turned the vehicle so it was facing inwards, the gunner on top keeping a very nasty looking weapon trained my way. His teammates threaded their way around the cars. There was shouting, Did a caltrop or two go through the boots? I didn't think they'd be thanking me for that anytime soon. Behind the lead vehicle a troop transport idled. More soldiers lay on top with rifles, guarding the rear, followed by another Humvee with a scary-ass gun.

The stench had me retching out the window. I wanted to help, but didn't want to accidentally shoot any soldiers. Given my poor marksmanship at this range, shooting them would be just my luck.

"Fuck." I hurried to switch mags on the handgun. The soldiers and I finished off the pack. The Humvee advanced forward. An inverted piece of metal welded to the front nearly touched the first line of cars.

"Crap on toast, what a nasty looking gun." I hoped no one could read lips well enough to know what I was saying. The cab cleared the mess enough for me to step out. I had a WTF? look on my face as the Humvee used the metal plow to shove vehicles out of the way, and clear a path while the barrel of the big gun held steady on me.

"Ma'am, are you the only survivor?" the team leader called to me.

"Those were my defenses you're fucking up. I was perfectly safe, now what the fuck am I gonna use to keep assholes out?" Nice, piss off the brave men and women serving our country.

"Ma'am, are you the only survivor?" the leader asked again, bite in his tone.

I just stared at him a moment, anger clear on my face before I looked at the transport vehicle idling on the road. Scared, dirty faces of what looked like regular people stared at us.

"I sure as shit hope you don't plan on dropping a bunch of useless survivors off and expect I'll happily take care of them. There's housing down the road, and enough land for them to find their own farms."

"Ma'am," he began, before stopping and speaking softly into his mike as I continued to glare.

The passenger-side door opened as another man in uniform stepped out. I couldn't help the tightening of my stance, the way a hand drifted to the butt of the gun strapped around my waist. Even though I knew any one of the soldiers could kill me before I drew the piece.

"Ma'am, I am Colonel Travis Downing of the United States Army. If we can all just calm down a little . . ." he continued talking, but my buzz of temper made it a wash of noise.

I started to shake a bit in anger, the adrenaline zipping back into my bloodstream. The glare 'o death should have clued him into my state. We stared at each other in silence. Some of the troops cautiously walked forward in a crouch, rifles at the ready as they called out warnings to avoid the caltrops scattered over the ground.

I managed, barely, to keep from spewing a vile torrent of verbal abuse. My left arm lifted, forefinger pointing toward the left of the road. "Housing and land to farm are down that road. I do not want, nor need, company. Get out so I can fix my defenses you just fucked up."

The Colonel bawled out an order for his men to halt their forward movement. It must have finally penetrated his brain I either didn't hear a word he said, or didn't care. I was still standing pointing down the road, right-hand fingers clenched around the gun, knuckles white.

He held his hands up in a placating gesture and tried again. "Ma'am, it's not safe to be alone. Those zombies should be proof. Besides, some of your neighbors are not nice people. If you come with us, we can offer food and protection."

I really needed to get the brain to mouth malfunction fixed one of these days. "A: I was safe until you fucked up my defenses. B: Those are the most zombies I've seen since the start of all this, no thanks to the small crowd behind you. C: My neighbors didn't know I was here until now. Fuck you very much. D: I'm not joining the mobile food truck. Thank you so much for your service to this country. Now, kindly fuck off, and help those who need and want it."

The last bit was a tad more sarcastic than I had intended.

The zombies and me, aggravating bitches to the end. My poor partner was going to get his ass chewed off, if and when he finally made it back. That should increase my popularity with his kids. Damn it. Of course, this assumed the military didn't clap me in chains first, or shoot me.

A huge sigh of irritation from Colonel Whatever-The-Fuck-His-Name-Was seemed the only outward indication of his deep displeasure. "Ma'am. I'm sorry about the defenses, but you must see it would be better if you came with us. Do you know of any other survivors on this island? Have you come across any?"

"Other than those bikers? Nope."

"Ma'am, perhaps the rest of your family would like to come with us."

I just barely kept from letting him know I was alone. "Seeing as how they're even meaner and bitchier than I am, fuck no."

His jaw tightened a moment, then he gave a signal

to his troops. They began to retreat back toward the transport carrier, still scanning the area for threats. "Ma'am, we're gonna go now. If you change your mind, we have a base set up ten miles down the road." He paused, then said, "Any chance you can back your truck up so we can turn around?"

"Are you kidding me? Just back up the way you came. It's not like my defenses can get any worse now."

He looked like he wanted to reply, but kept his mouth shut and climbed back into the Humvee. The vehicle slowly backed up, the gunner keeping his eye and weapon trained on me as they retreated. I swear the Colonel had to have told the driver to move the vehicles he missed the first time. I now had a large, straight gap inviting anyone to come on in. The transport vehicle had backed up also. The troops on foot jumped into it, and they rumbled past to complete their mission.

"Now I've got to figure out a way to fix all this. Fucking government, always making messes and expecting someone else to clean up."

CHAPTER SIX

I had just stepped out of the shower and was toweling off when gunfire erupted.

"Great, there goes the neighborhood," I clomped down the stairs and out the back door after scrambling into clothes. Except for the shots, scratch that, except for the explosions, all was relatively calm.

I chewed my bottom lip. It didn't sound like something I wanted to be involved in. On the other hand, it sounded like I was going to have unwanted visitors again.

"Crap on toast." There was no way my hasty fixes to the defenses would hold. "Kitties, stay safe. I'll be back. Hopefully," I added as I loaded up.

The much-battered truck sat blocking the stairs where I had left it. I tossed some stuff into the bed before I climbed in and fired it up. The headlights illuminated the windswept dark as the trees swayed. I bounced across the fields and checked the perimeter. No moans greeted me over the noise of wind coming in my three-quarters open window. No biters came out of the dark. I stopped a moment behind the mangled vehicles, headlights illuminating the entrance. Just the sounds of gunfire and an explosion or two, gee, from the direction of Camp Food. Imagine that. So, retaliation of bikers, or zombies found them. I turned around, driving to the onsite visitor/gift store. I spent several minutes maneuvering the truck into place, then idling several moments more while I tried to look and listen. It seemed safe. Still, *seemed safe*, the key words as I shut the truck off.

The keys I left in the ignition, doors locked, and

crawled out the back window. I shut it enough to not latch close. The body of the truck bed blocked one-half of the entrance doors. I tossed stuff to the ground, loaded myself up with guns, then climbed down. I opened the other door, waiting to see if biters would pop out at me. When none did, I brought in my stuff and secured the doors. It wouldn't help if zombies came. They could just break the large display windows. I had boarded them over with scavenged wood, leaving only the very tops un-boarded. Let's face it: Unless giants searched the area, they weren't getting that high up. I let my eyes try to adjust to the near-darkness, then gave up.

I switched on the flashlight I had brought and got to work moving the display platforms together, not an easy feat due to the weight. The fragile china, pottery, and stoneware I piled before the double entrance doors, and underneath the front windows. I placed my sleeping bag, emergency pack, and guns on top of the display platforms. I crawled into the bag, cradling my sword, lying there listening to the racket. Eventually, I drifted off to sleep.

# # #

I'm not sure what woke me, the sudden quiet, or the rattling of the door. It felt like a huge bruise crossed my back, about where the sword had been when I rolled under the truck yesterday.

"Ouch. I'm definitely getting too old for this shit."

I slithered out of the bag, re-armed myself with weapons and pack, before moving in a crouch to the door. I peeked out the small hole I had left, to be met with a dead eye. I jumped up, scraping my arm against the push bar, heart pounding in terror. "Motherfuckers," slipped out before I could help it.

The rattling increased. "Great. Just a great start to my morning," I groused. "How many of the fuckers are there? No, don't want to know."

I sprinted toward the back of the store, and up the

stairs to a raised level.

This part had large windows giving an overview of the processing floor, and machinery below. Darkened TVs overhead no longer explained to tourists each piece of equipment and what it did. No zombies had breached the large roller doors that once allowed trucks to bring in the harvest, from what I could see. A door painted the same color as the wall near the end of the walkway led into the plant. It was unlocked, mainly because I left it that way. I cleared the door, pausing with the rifle at the ready, but nothing moved. I quickly ran down the stairs, open, metal tread stairs mind you. Just perfect for letting arms and hands through to snag pant legs. No, not freaked out by that thought at all. My heart pounded furiously, not entirely from all the running.

The back entrance door to the plant remained clear and free of zombies when I cautiously peeked out. I moved swiftly, rifle at the ready, building on my right side. A ladder leaned against the wall to the shop. I hate heights, but in this case I was prepared to make an exception. Never have I climbed so fast, fear and zombies a great motivator.

The horde from the front of the visitor's center crowded around the ladder, reaching up while I sat my butt down on the slightly tilted roof. Two lines of rope lay nearby, attached to metal handles screwed into the metal roof. Already the sun had started to warm the material, It was going to suck even more very shortly, when the metal became burning hot. I needed a way to retrieve the ladder if ever I knocked it over in haste or fear, or hasty fear. I began shooting the zombies now clustering around, not caring who or what heard the shots. I needed to thin the herd enough so I could get in the truck.

"Where are you fuckers coming from? And why won't you stay there?" I screamed as I lined shots up.

When I burned through two rounds of mags for

the handguns, and a dozen shot gun shells, I reloaded
everything a third time. By the time I finished, I had
judged it safe enough to climb back down. I sprinted for
the truck, clambering into the bed. I yanked the sword and
rifle over my head, shoving it through the back window. I
climbed inside after them, got seated, and fired the truck
up. I could've just headed back to the house, but no, I
needed to see how the front was holding. I passed the
visitor toilets with a sigh of regret. The bumpy road doing
nothing for my bladder, which protested at its abuse. At
this rate, I could see another soiled pair of pants in my
future. I cut across a field, seeing movement near the
entrance and stopped near a stand of trees.

"Again with the unwanted, uninvited guests." I
went through the motions, dropping zoms. When nothing
twitched, ran, or shambled in from the road, I brought the
truck up.

I turned it off. No point wasting gas. I left the
door open as I got out to inspect the bodies. Some were of
older zoms, probably from the first outbreak, some
slightly more recent. Then some so fresh they had to have
been bit and turned last night or the day before. I removed
what items of use I could, then drove to retrieve my
sleeping bag and take care of personal needs. No doubt
there would be more guests before the day was over,
which meant getting my ass in gear.

I really hate mornings.

# # #

The sun blazed down from high overhead. By the
very short shadow I cast I judged it to be noon. I had just
taken a break for water and food. My eyes burned from
the work, the lack of sleep, and the stench of death. I had
sprinkled a new batch of caltrops around and on the
vehicles at the entrance. A few other trucks and cars still
sat in the parking lot, and on the road leading out of it,
from where their owners had abandoned them. Many of

them t still had keys in the ignitions. I had to pour enough gas in the tanks to start them up and move them. I used them to fill in the gap the Humvee had made.

I got some more mono-filament line and wrapped it around trees, welcome sign, anything I could. The ditch I sprinkled with caltrops, and more to either side of the fence. One of my previous scouting expeditions turned up a hunter's stash of snares and traps. It took half a day of trial and error, but I eventually figured out how to set them. I sprinkled them throughout the dense trees surrounding the plantation. I used the truck and rope to drag bodies off to the forest side in a haphazard pile. I had to go back picking up parts left behind, adding to the gore factor. I was a sweaty, smelly mess by the time I ate my lunch.

Before I could finish eating, screams rang out, voices shouting in terror near the entrance.

"Oh, joy. Here we go." I geared up, crossing the pasture on foot. I carefully made my way to where I thought the commotion sounded.

At this rate, every zombie within hearing distance would soon be homing in. The screams amplified, followed by gunshots. I started running. Some dumb bunny had opened the restroom doors. There was a reason I had closed and blocked them. For the second time that morning, I became confronted by a pack of zombies. The good news for me was they already had food to chase. The bad news was they were the survivors who came with Colonel Fuckwit and his squad.

Some people tried the doors to the gift shop, only to find them locked. They turned to flee, not caring which way as long as it got them away from the horde shambling after them. I started killing zombies, the men in camo joining me. A few civilians who possessed guns or other weapons helped out. We shot and killed until the zombies got out of range, chasing after people. The survivors looked at me with a mixture of hate and fear as my irritation boiled over, and I spewed.

"What part of staying the hell away do you people not understand?"

"Colonel, I've got a hostile."

"No shit, dick head. First you smash my defenses. Then you sneak in here and let some fool give a homing beacon to every zombie around. Not to mention the Darwin award winners."

He must have received a reply through a headset because he turned around and walked to the parking lot. His buddy addressed me.

"Ma'am. I regret to inform you we will be confiscating this land . . ."

"You and what army?" passed my brain-to-mouth filter. I really need to get that fixed.

That gave him pause. He frowned at me. "Ma'am, you do realize who you are speaking with, right?"

"The remnants of a defeated force burdened with common sense devoid dead weights?" I received glares from people as I continued, "I take it your superior forces were overrun by the enemy and you barely escaped. So you come here wrecking my peaceful ideal. Who the fuck keeps making that noise?" I started forward.

The remaining military man just shook his head from side to side, motioning me to come along. We rounded the restrooms to find Colonel Fuckwit kneeling beside a screaming young man, trying to pry a steel trap off his leg. Scared, worried eyes met mine. A woman in full battle regalia, unless it was a very small, puny man, stood guard with a rifle at the ready. An older gentleman was helping the colonel.

"Sir," my escort raised his voice to be heard over the noise, "I have the hostile civilian who wishes to express dissatisfaction with our arrival."

"Gunner, I don't give two fucks. I've got a

wounded civvie."

"That's one fuck more than I give right now. Can't you stuff a rag in his mouth before he draws more zoms here? In fact, it will be my pleasure to help with that particular bit."

"Ma'am, what is wrong with you?" the gunner asked.

"You want the short or the long list?"

An exasperated sounding sigh was my answer. The young man had passed out as the two men finally got his leg free. The trap had snapped his lower leg, both jagged bones sticking out of the skin. They gleamed a wet red. I couldn't help the shit-eating grin plastered on my face at the sight of the wound.

"Cool, it's like I'm back in Imaging school. No way he'll ever walk again; at least, not without a limp." *Was that out loud? I think it was. Oops.*

The colonel turned, standing to face me. "Ma'am, how many more of these traps are there?"

I shrugged. "Enough. Unfortunately, it doesn't seem to have done much to discourage idiots from bothering me. If you'll excuse me, I have to re-set this."

He moved to block my path. We had a serious stare down going when the female coughed.

"Sir, where should we put the wounded civvie?"

I beat him to the punch. "If he's zombie bit, a bullet in the brain pan, and drag his corpse into the woods. He can be useful in death at least. Probably a change of pace for him for once."

"Ma'am," the colonel barked, "my men only take orders from me."

"Super duper, then you can order them the fuck off my land along with the left-overs you dragged along."

He threw his hands up. "I could have you arrested!"

"Yeah, yeah, yeah. We know there is no law and

order anymore. Fine, I'll make you a deal. The lack wits stay out of the fields and woods. They can rest up in the visitor shop before moving on. I'll even include a few non-crushed vehicles. Can't promise there's much gas left in them. I haven't got more. There's a school back the way you came, which should do for a defense. Or, any one of the homes lining the road. The restrooms still have water, and will work as long as no one clogs the toilets up."

"You're a real humanitarian. This is the last of humanity. Don't you care?"

"At one time, I would've. I have no more compassion left to give. Besides, considering how stupid the majority of humans are? Not really." I gave a one shoulder shrug.

The disaster had sucked out any kindness I once had. My years of being an Imaging Tech had left me on the jaded side. I had experienced the best, and the worst, in humanity. I had seen too many injured people whose lack of common sense was one of the main contributors to their problems. Some were sick because of bad lifestyle choices. Then there were people looking to scam the system so they didn't have to work. The few bad ones toward the end lingered more in my mind. They made it hard to remember those patients who made caring for them a pleasure and honor.

He looked at me, trying to bore holes into my brain. I've had better try and succeed, come to think of it. "Gunner, how many civvies remain?"

"Seven who didn't run away."

"Any bit?"

"Sir, yes sir. I'm sure of it. Those zoms came out fast and hungry. They got an entire family."

"Hold up. If they're bit, they are not staying here. Either you put them down, or I will. I won't have my safety further compromised."

The two men looked at me. The female seemed to

hold back a snort. The old man shifted his feet.

"We need to do something for this young man." He gave me a stern look. "He's in danger of bleeding out."

"That would probably be kinder to him, and less painful. He's never going to walk normally without surgery, and not become zombie food."

"It's on your head. You did this to him." The coot shook his finger my way.

"Sorry, gramps, it's not my fault. The blame lays on him for not paying attention to his surroundings." I turned back to the colonel, effectively dismissing the man, ignoring the rest of his tirade. "How long do you think you'll be irritating me before moving on? I know the governments full of dumb-asses more concerned with saving their own worthless hides, but surely even they have a major safe center somewhere?"

"The injured first, or I clap you in restraints."

"Kinky, but you're not my type." He glared. "Fine," I gave an airy wave instead of the finger and led the way back to the visitor center. "Wait here. I have to open it another way."

I took off with the gunner dogging my steps, and re-traced my way through the processing plant to open the front doors. The military men carried the bleeder in, setting him down on the floor. A middle-aged, black haired woman knelt beside him, trying to administer aid. The other survivors huddled in a clump near the front. Colonel Fuckwit snapped out orders for his men to try to find the stragglers.

"Watch your step. The whole place is booby-trapped," was my only advice.

"Ma'am, unless you tell us where and what they are, you're hampering our efforts."

"Now you know how I feel."

71

CHAPTER SEVEN

"*Nice smell, dumb-ass, I see you found the shit hole the hard way,*" *Spacey dispassionately looked me over.*

"*Bitch, I've been out here busting my ass, trying to save my kids.*"

"*Oh, the dead ones? The part of the horde daughter's? 'Cause ya know, zombies and all. How's that charging off half-cocked thing working out for you?*"

"*Fuck you.*"

She gave her amused yet contemptuous smile, "*You're all going to die.*"

"*We're getting out of here.*"

I sat straight up, jerking out the dream. Damn my love of disaster movies. Even in my dreams, those I loved and cared about quoted them.

What had woken me? I listened hard, coming to the realization it was storming. I had run across the rotting, half-standing barn a day ago. My wounds felt on fire, despite my attempts to clean and bandage them.

Every item I possessed reeked of dried shit sludge. The MRE's were still usable, thankfully. A large mud puddle formed on the floor near the front doors of the barn. I squelched a groan, forcing myself up.

Why a space here?

"No zombies, no zombies," I mumbled, lathering up with soap, forcing myself to reach up and scrub the bullet track across my back.

Heat rises from my flesh. Something slimy, not soap, oozes down. I stop, breathing hard, willing myself to not pass out from the pain. I grab up the rifle, carefully padding to the door, and listen. The only sounds are rain and the booming of thunder.

It's now or never. Despite my upper back screaming in pain, I remove part of my barricade from the small, inset door. Rain pelts me as I peek out. I squint to keep soap out of my eyes. I step outside when no moans of the damned or eternally hungry sound out. The water quickly drenches me, and I rub the soap off with one hand. I scrub again at the back wound until the pus stops oozing and blood comes out instead. I'm so light-head I can barely stand, and my body is wracked with shivers. *At least I'm finally clean.* I step inside and re-barricade the door.

In between thunder and lightning, I fill all my water bottles, including what I scavenged along the way before my wounds forced me to temporarily stop my trek. I forced myself to walk the inside of the barn as I air dried, fighting dizziness the whole time. When I'm finally dry, shivers rack my body so hard my teeth chatter. I plop down on a wedge of blanket stolen from an abandoned house. I managed to find some clean clothes, even though they're a bit on the small side. The only footwear I found to fit me turned out to be knee-high waders. I opened the med-kit, dolefully surveying my supplies.

"There has to be some rinky-dink throwback pharmacy around here. I'll even take an old folk's home,"

All my supplies I had carefully packed into zip lock bags didn't survive the septic tank dunking. A small, plastic first-aid kit was all I could salvage. Whoever once lived in the dump of a house near the barn didn't seem to feel the need to keep a stocked medicine cabinet like the rest of humanity. Or it had already been raided by the time I stumbled across it. My only other reward besides the clothes and blankets were two travel-size bottles of aspirin and ibuprofen. They rolled out of the woman of the house's purse when I tossed it aside. I nearly missed them.

Two pills per bottle were all that remained. I gulped all four down with half a bottle of water and prayed I wouldn't vomit or have the Hersey squirts.

My bones ached, my head swam, I couldn't keep warm. I rolled up in the blanket, falling into an uneasy sleep.

# # #

I finally discovered some small, backwoods town on my second day of travel after the Bubba Incident, as I called it. The place looked like a war zone—half-eaten bodies with holes in the head, and re-dead corpses littered the ground. Brains, blood, and guts splayed everywhere. I could feel the bile rise in the back of my throat from the stench. I idled, the diesel truck rumbling more than I cared for as I waited. I sat blinking sweat out of my eyes, willing myself not to pass out. I've gotta do this smart, lure out any assholes, or deadheads. After a dry-heave inducing wait with nothing human or zom moving, I pulled farther into town.

"Damn, not even a one stop-light place." I parked in the middle of the carnage, shut off the truck, and stepped out.

I had to leave the tactical vest back in the barn because I couldn't get the stains and smell out. I jerry-rigged a cross-body ammo carrier out of several belts and duct tape. A rope replaced the ruined straps of the 9mm and the rifle. Pockets cut from a pair of too small jeans, more rope, and duct tape form a makeshift holster for the .50AE. My dream gun better not jam on me again, as it seems to do on every third shot. I taped three mags each for the handguns, on the belt strap, and shove shells for the rifle in one of my pockets. I move slow and steady, from cover to cover.

The unrelenting quiet seemed spooky. "Don't like this. Nothing moving, living or dead. Feels like I'm being watched," I mumbled.

It all seemed way too easy. I slowly opened a diner's front door as I thought: *Taking out the dead is easier to do in tight spaces with the 9 mil.* I caught the door with the toe of my boot and eased it closed at the last minute as a tinkle sounded from a bell attached to the top of the doorframe. Three walking stiffs inside turned my way, and I quickly put them down. Wodin, please let there be edibles. Flies buzzed as I passed a counter with plates of rotting food. I held my breath to halt my gag reflex. I spotted a swinging door to one side. It probably led to the kitchen. I paused long enough to listen for movement. Faint shuffling filters through: zombies. It's probably gonna be dark back there. I fished a flashlight out of my back pocket, flicked it on, and held it in a cross grip like cops do. Easing the door open as quietly as I can, I see four shamblers slowly turning my way. For some reason, I can't stop my hands from shaking, and it takes me the whole mag to bring the targets down.

-And we all fall down. My mind works in weird ways. I finish clearing the stock room, back office, restrooms, and end up back in the kitchen. Two industrial steel doors; freezer and refrigerator, are the last areas to be cleared. I knock on one door as a precaution. They're so thick I can't hear if anything undead is inside. I try the handle and it moves. *This is not good. It's unlocked,* I opened the door and discovered a lone female zombie dressed in a waitresses uniform. After I dispatch the zom, I realize nothing's edible inside unless you count maggots and worms, which I don't.

The store room greets me with shelves of canned and boxed food when I go back for a closer look. I'm a bit off put by the fact that it appears no one raided the place. My Spider Sense tingles.

"Gotta git out of here." Why is it when I'm mad, drunk, excited, or upset my Pittsburghese comes out (aht)?

A wave of dizziness hits me, the ever-present buzzing in my ears growing louder. I turn, trudge back to the truck. I get inside just in time to pass out. When I wake, the sun is low in the sky, and I'm still alone with the dead. My back feels on fire, my whole body is racked with pain. I gotta get meds, antibiotics at least. What are the bacteria and germs from the septic system doing to me? I also gotta get a better truck than the shit hauler I currently have. The gas mileage is horrible on it, and there's not much room for my kids when I find them.

My kids. . . eyes burn at the thought of them. Please, Odin, let them still be safe and alive. I gotta push on. They need me. I eat some nuts, drink some water, ignore the growling of my intestines as I survey the street. I have my pick of vehicles if I can get 'em started, and if they've got gas. I'm shaky and fatigued from the small movements I've been making to contemplate wasting diesel by driving around the minuscule town vs. walking.

The whole place screamed Hicksville, right down to the general store. I have a plan in place. I finished off the water and carefully stashed the empty bottle in a garbage bag that replaced my ruined pack. I didn't even have the energy to be angry at how I had to burn everything that could, or would. Waves of dizziness washed over me as I replaced my spent mags with new ones.

I don't step down from the truck so much as fall out. While I struggled to regain my feet, I heard rapid footfalls coming toward me. I looked up through the curtain of hair hanging in my face to spot a runner. Despite my shaking hands, I manage to bring the 9mm up and fire. Missed.The rotter is now on me. I hate these fucking zombies. Fuck all these motherfucking runners, shamblers, pus-ridden, ass smelling fucks. I have my hand on its head as I try and get the gun in the direction of the fucker's brain. Four shots later I'm welcomed with a spray of brain, bone, and congealed blood as I finally hit the head. Of course, the noise brings more zombies out. Twenty of them. Where the hell were they hiding?

I gained my feet as the herd moved closer. It's no use trying to move and shoot, I can't keep the gun steady enough. I'm reduced to shooting, then moving. I barely made it to the door of a local vet's office ahead of the last zombie. It goes down just as my gun clicks empty.

I breathed hard, realizing how close to death I came. Sweat dripped into my eyes, and I blinked to clear them. The bodies of the zoms I just shot have disappeared. It's like they were never there to begin with.

"Not good, this is not good at all." A chill of fright slides down my back. I've just wasted precious ammo on phantoms, it seems.

I twisted the handle to the vet office. Tripped over my own feet as I strolled in. I barely felt the thud of my body hit the floor. I must have blacked out, for I startled awake in a panic.

"No, no more passing out, damn shamblers'll get me," I groaned as I forced myself into motion.

I banged through a 'staff only' door is to one side of a nicely appointed waiting room and stopped abruptly as a wave of rot and decay assaulted my nose. I barely made it to a sink before I'm heaving up what little I ate.

"I can't go on like this. Gonna get dehydrated." I panted while I tested the faucets.

The pipes moaned and shuddered before a thin trickle of water arrived. I did my best to contort my body so I could drink while it lasts. As I finished, another wave of dizziness hit me, and I thought I heard barking.

"How did a dog survive this long?" I must free the poor animal, who had to be near starved by now.

It doesn't take long to find the door leading to the back, but opening it was a mistake. I'm smacked in the face with a stench so potent, my eyes water. I'm gasping and gagging for air. The door slams shut as I stumble away from it and almost back to the waiting area. Once I've mastered my gag reflex, I try again.

It only takes a brief glimpse around the small space to realize every animal is dead and has been for quite some while. Yet, I keep hearing barking. I cover my nose with one hand and cautiously venture inside. Flies rise in a large cloud, buzzing in anger over being disturbed. My left hand is batting furiously to keep them off my face. I force myself to check each cage and any space large enough for an animal to hide. I couldn't find any, and I wondered if I were beginning to hallucinate.

A small cloud of flies follows me into the treatment room. Most of them buzz around behind me as I search for medicine. The cabinet is locked, but I find the key for it in the vet's desk drawer, along with a fob holding more keys. One of them looks to belong to a vehicle.

"Yay," is all I can manage at the discovery.

It takes a few fumbling tries to insert the key in the lock and get the cabinet open. I've had pets before, so I know some medicines will do in a pinch for humans. The trick would be avoiding the ones that would only harm me more. My mind is too fuzzy. I grabbed it all. Tried to remember the long-ass clinical names for antibiotics. I think I've found some, so I dry swallowed a handful. Please modern meds, kick in soon. My body ached, and my head swam from all the trudging back and forth.

Dusk fell when I stumbled for the last time into the diner to lock the door behind me. A brief nap, then I'll look for the vet's vehicle.

"I'm impressed you made it as far as you have. But you're gonna die, you know. The infections spreading throughout you. And your kids? Tick Tock, Tick Tock. They're coming for you."

"I've got more than bad movie quotes," I retorted

to my girlfriend, realizing as I woke up I'd been dreaming.

When did I go blind? I flailed about in panic before I realized a thick crust of sleep glued my lids together. Several swipes later, I pried open my eyes. My whole body is throbbed in more pain than I knew existed, and my clothes were soaked in sweat. My swollen tongue mades swallowing difficult. Shit! How long had I been out? My hand hit something plastic, A rattle signified my flashlight. I groped a little to pick it up, and flicked it on. The best I could reach was a can of fruit cocktail, and I felt my stomach churn with its new addition. My body screamed for more sleep, but my mind felt frazzled with worry over the safety of my kids. I'm praying to Wodin the animal meds kick in soon. I can't stay here longer. I've got to find a better ride.

# # #

The keys I took from the vet's office went with an older model Ford 350. It's got crappy fuel mileage, but out here in BFE I'm not about to get picky. I drive it to the diner and load the bed up with food, fuel, and water. I use every container I can find. Last, I threw in several duffle bags I've scavenged. They now hold my guns and ammo, and clothes. I even managed to find a decent pair of work boots that fit me. Now to get the hell out of zombie town despite my exhaustion.

Several hours later, on another deserted back-country road, I parked the truck. "Where are you hiding? I hope you girls didn't take the main roads," I mumbled to myself while un-balling a local map.

The animal meds help Not a lot, I could tell, but enough to keep me moving. I still have to take rest breaks more than I want to, but the alternative of passing out and accidentally killing myself is too risky. It takes me another two days of getting lost on back roads, avoiding more country-boy traps, to get just outside of Eden, NC. I took half-a-day to circle the suburbs, looking for clues. I pulled out binoculars with a rangefinder.

"Let's see here . . . nothing. . . nothing. . . nothing. . . nothing, dammit." I ditched the binoculars and picked up the rifle. Through the more powerful scope, I saw better, along with a flash of sunlight on glass.

WT. . . Ping! Instinctively I ducked as something hot and wasp-like zinged past my head. Shattering glass tinkled inside and out of the truck. I dropped the rifle onto the seat, slammed the truck in gear, and peeled out. I'm so close. I can't risk whoever's out there tracking me down before I can find my girls. I guessed at directions, as I backtracked outta town and made a full circle around it. The maps I found aren't as detailed for this area. It's a good thing I've got a great internal compass. I come across the first clue my girls left: a heart enclosing our initials with an arrow pointing toward the center of town.

"Smart girls, hang in there, Daddy's coming." I smiled.

The sun lowered when I managed to make my way back toward the main street, all thanks to the hearts and arrows.

I parked in a lot with dust-covered vehicles. Glad mine blended in. I worried about my cache in the bed, wasting precious time covering it with an old tarp, and worthless garbage dumped on top.

The medicine I found was fighting whatever infection from the shit I landed in. Unfortunately, I still got exhausted quickly, and my back felt like things were crawling inside my wound. I left it mostly alone. Expect to change the dirty bandages out for clean ones. My body screamed for rest, but my heart pounded in fear for my girls. To my disgust, my body won, all but shutting itself down as I sat in the driver's seat.

"The worms crawl in, the worms crawl out, the worms play pinnacle on your snout." Spacey's warbles are out-of-tune.

"For someone who doesn't like kids, you sure know a lot of nursery songs," I taunt her.

My words wipe the smirk off her face. Her eyes darken in anger, then become two holes in a grinning skull. "Ring around the flu shots, a pocketful of bullets, brainsssss, brainsss, we all turn zombieeee." She ends her song with a mocking laugh that fades into blackness.

I'm jerked awake by the sound of my own voice. "Fuck you, bitch! I'm sick from falling in shit. Not from a damn flu shot or a zombie bite."

Damn her, and damn my brain for producing nightmares and not sweet dreams. I rubbed the sleep from my eyes, tried to force my aching, creaking body upright instead of leaning against the door. Dawn isn't far off, and no matter how I felt, I had to get my kids.

I down the last of the meds, a protein bar, and water. Two men slink past on the cracked sidewalk, making me thank Odin I took the precaution of hiding the truck. Their voices drift to me in the stillness.

"Come on, Ted, I know them girls are hiding out. Stupid whores, thinking we didn't notice 'em sneaking about town."

Assholes didn't know I'm here. Good, they could lead me to my daughters, and I'd pay them back for talking trash about my girls. I geared up and slipped out of the truck. Walking in a crouch between vehicles as I moved to the sidewalk. I kept my body hidden behind the corner of the building next to the parking lot. Only my head showed.

The men didn't walk far. One stopped by a two-story place with a large mural of barges and men from an earlier time. The second guy cut through a small park beside the mural.

A back door ambush. Oh, hell no, I thought as I hustled as quietly as possible to the back of the lot. Plenty of cars shielded my approach. I waited for the right moment. In the still air, everything sounded amplified. I had to use my knife, not the guns.

The first dudes used something to hammer on the big plate-glass window. I heard a crash as it shattered. The fucker in my sight licked his lips. An expectant, excited leer pulled his mouth up. A tremendous racket from inside filtered out, permeated the area with shouts and yells. Shit eating grin headed for the back door. I sprinted, or at least attempted one, my body still not healed enough for the abuse I gave it. He turned to meet me when I plunged the knife at an upwards angle into his side, and twisted it. He got off a shot, which moved off wild.

I saw red, all Norman Bates on his ass as the commotion inside grew louder. I heard a female scream, which snapped me back to what I needed to do.

"Hello, semi-auto rifle," I scooped up the weapon, quickly looted the body for extra mags.

The back door burst open, caught me off-guard. It's a lucky break for my daughters. They're so panic-stricken, they barreled into me, and we all crash to the ground.

"Joan, Anne," I hoarsely shouted at them.

It took a minute, which we didn't have, for them to realize it's me.

"Dad!" they cried.

"Well, ain't this just heartwarming," a rough voice said.

Sniggers and guffaws ranged out as I squinted my eyes against the rising sun to see the outline of five men. They must have followed my daughters through the building. My girls clung to me. I didn't like our chances as the men spread out around us.

"Anne," I whispered against her ear, "in the parking lot is a Ford 350 truck. The keys are in the ignition. No matter what happens, you and your sister get to it and get to Spacey on Wadmalaw Island. Remember, sweet tea," was all I had time for before the men yanked us apart.

I still had the rifle in my hands. I took the chance they wanted the girls alive more than they do dead. I emitted a sudden scream that jolted and alarmed everyone, and sprayed the men to my left with bullets.

"Run!" I screamed, "Run."

I didn't have breath for anything more, as a new pain ripped through my leg. I fell toward the ground, still squeezing the trigger.

CHAPTER EIGHT

The boy, or rather a young man, whose leg had been caught in the trap a few days ago still suffered. I learned his name was Branson, and he had fancied himself an artist before the zombies came. At least that's what I thought I heard amidst all the moaning, crying, and screaming in pain he did. The woman who tried caring for him said her name was Tanya; she was an LPN. There was not one doctor in the group. Branson was fucked, and not in a good way.

"We have to get him some help. You have to contact your commanding officers, get an airlift, or supplies or something!" Tanya argued with Colonel Fuckwit.

"Ma'am, we will, once we have secured our mission objectives."

"He's dying! He's suffering! You're supposed to help us! Isn't that more important than, than, your. . . whatever it is."

"Mission objectives," I drily reminded her as I passed by with an armload of clothes the gunner and I had scavenged. I received a glare in return.

They continued arguing, or more correctly, she berating him while he stood stone-faced, merely repeating what the talking heads had drilled into him. The pregnant mom with her two hellions had complaints of her own. I let the gunner deal with it. The old man, Ed, was trying to keep Branson distracted from his pain as I approached Tanya.

"All right. Normally, I wouldn't care, but if completing your mission means you'll get out of here faster and take them with you, I'll ask. What is it, and what help do you need?"

I received an incredulous look. "Ma'am?"

"I am serious. Is this mission just to look for survivors? Or are you trying to contain the scourge?"

The Colonel still didn't know if I was sincere or not, but decided he wasn't going to push my seemingly good mood. Oh, how little he knew.

"Our mission objective at this point is to re-gain control of our vehicles and weapons from enemy forces and escort any survivors to safe centers."

I didn't think it was the main one. Wade, Tom, and I often had conversations about some of the exercises the Navy went through for protecting the country from potential invaders. The descriptions left Wade and me feeling there was more going on than what Tom was able to talk about. In fact, we were pretty sure the government's objectives would be to only rescue those they deemed useful to re-building the nation, with themselves being first. People such as scientists, surgeons, engineers, people at the top of their field, would come next. My love and hobby of studying history brought me to the conclusion governments considered the population as a whole as expendable. They may help 'escort us to safe centers,' but sure as shit they were poorly manned, poorly funded as all FEMA projects tended to be.

"Fine. I may know of one or two places the bikers might be headquartered in. Either the distillery, or a private club."

"Ma'am? How did you come across this intelligence?"

"Gee, lemme think. A group of bikers who've decided to live up to the stereotype of being big, ruthless, and kill indiscriminately. I'm sure they love them some liqueur. Besides, I narrowly escaped from said club after they showed up."

"How many of them are there?"

"I didn't stop to count. I got the hell out of there. I heard them before I saw them. Those bikes are good for advance warning if nothing else."

"Do you think you can point out this club on a map?"

"Probably."

He radioed to a squad member, who came over and unfolded the map on one of the display tables. I studied it a moment, then pointed out the likeliest spots. The colonel and his men walked off to confer. I turned to leave when Ed came up to me.

"You should be ashamed of yourself, setting out dangerous traps, and for being so unfriendly."

I dodged around him, meaning to ignore him, but he kept after me. "When the world's in trouble like it is now, everyone needs to lend a helping hand to their neighbor."

"Holy shit, gramps! What fucking era are you still living in? Today the world is all me, me, me. An act of kindness toward the wrong people mean they see you as weak. Look around you: Trusting anybody first without them proving themselves can and will get you killed. And guess what? So far, none of you, save the military, has shown you can be trusted. So until that time comes, you're all parasites. Unless you can do something useful, such as hunt, fish, or even plow a field, then I suggest you keep your gob-hole shut. Oh, and somebody needs to learn how to control those two hellions."

"My precious children are not hellions! How dare you! Do you have kids?" The mother spat, holding her grotesquely swollen belly.

Ew. It looked like it was gonna pop and she grossed me out. She wasn't small to begin with, and looked like she had let herself go further since last sluicing. Plus, she stunk. I didn't even think she knew where her kids currently were, as they had been suspiciously missing for most of the morning.

"Yo, moo cow, your so-called 'precious' don't listen to you. They destroy everything they get their sticky, germ-covered hands on, and they have no respect for others and their personal possessions. So, unless you start controlling them better, I'm gonna take care of it, and not in a way you'll like. Got it, pet?"

I stomped off as she squawked behind me, Ed joining in to soothe her injured feelings. I found those damn kids taunting the horses. They had managed to climb over the fencing and were in the middle of the field. The boy had found some rocks from somewhere, occasionally chucking them, and hitting the animals while his sister whined because they wouldn't let her pet them. The horses moved, trying to get away from their tormentors. I was livid. They were destroying all the hard-won trust the animals had for me.

"Oi! You fucking brats. Get the hell out of there, and stay the hell away from those horses," I entered the field, meaning to chase the kids out.

"I can do what I like! You're not my mom!" The boy didn't even turn away from what he was doing to yell at me.

"I wanna ride! Make them hold still so I can pet them, or I'll tell my mommy on you!" The girl stomped her feet.

"You do that," I told her as I passed by, intent on grabbing the boy.

"I'm telling!" she yelled after me.

The boy ran away, laughing, daring me to chase him. "Ha ha ha! Try and catch me! You can't!"

I felt something hit the back of my head and turned to see the little girl standing with a smug expression on her face. Her hands were covered in horse shit from the patty she had flung at me. I really had to

resist the urge to not shoot either one of them. I ran after
the girl. She shrieked and yelled for help as she bolted.
Her screaming would draw any zombies nearby. I just
managed to catch her as several of the survivors came
sprinting up. I hauled the little shit down off the fence and
gave her a whack on the butt the way my mom did to me
when I misbehaved as a child. I didn't think it was
possible for someone to yell even louder.

"Don't you touch my child, you bitch," the mom
shrieked at me.

"A well-deserved paddling never really hurts
anybody," Ed huffed. "Especially if kids don't listen and
behave when you tell them to."

"Calm down, all this commotion will bring
attention to us. Ma'am. Let the child go. We can sort this
out calmly," the gunner said.

I dragged Ashleigh toward the gate, to get her out
of the field. The little beast tried to bite me. Without
thinking, I shoved her away. She stumbled and fell down.
Her shrieks turn to cries. The gunner, meanwhile, had
climbed the fence and retrieved the boy, handing him
across to his mother.

"You bitch. How dare you. I want her arrested.
She shouldn't be left free around decent people. Is my
precious okay? How badly did she hurt you, Ashleigh?"
she cooed over the little nine-year-old girl.

The brat sniffed, playing for attention all she
could. Ed scrutinized the house and horses.

"You will control your feral crack monkeys. They
need to learn what the word 'no' means, and that there're
consequences for not listening. You keep them out of this
field and away from those horses. I caught them taunting
and throwing stones to injure them."

"You stay away from my kids, you monster. You
lay a hand on them again and I'll. . . . "

"Mrs. Breckson, she does have a point," Ed

interrupted. "Those horses will attack if they feel threatened enough, and the damage they inflict could be fatal."

She didn't care, just kept ranting. The rest of what she said was lost in a buzz of white noise inside my head, rage and adrenaline growing. I wanted so badly to beat some sense into her, in pig or not. I didn't know I moved toward her. The next thing I knew, I was held in a body lock by the gunner as the now silent mother followed Ed away. Her kids trailed after her, eyes wide in fear.

"Ma'am. I need to know if you can hear me. Nod if you can."

I fought my rage back down as the gunner talked to me. After a very long time, it seemed to me I was able to spit out, "Yes. I hear you."

"Ma'am, the colonel will need to be informed of this incident. I'm afraid I'm going to have to confiscate your weapons, and restrain you."

"You do, and I *will*, explode in an awful way. I'm calm. Call him over if you must, but I'm not putting up with those kids a moment more."

The gunner frog-marched me back to the visitor center where the colonel and his two other men waited for us. The group of survivors, except for Branson, stood in a knot at one end of the cement porch. I was stopped at the other end as the military man came up to us.

"Ma'am. We have a volatile situation here. You can't just go pulling guns on people and threatening them, especially not a pregnant woman. Now, I'm of a mind to lock you up, unless you can give me one good reason why I shouldn't."

I shook from rage, forcing myself to speak calmly, I replied. "They were hurting the horses, and wouldn't stop when I asked them too. The boy ran off. The girl I had to discipline since her mother refuses."

"Ma'am, Mrs. Breckson says you were beating

her child, and then pulled a gun on her when she tried to save the girl."

"Of course she would. I spanked the kid's ass once and tried to get her out of the field when the child attempted to bite me. Instinct kicked in, and I shoved her away. The mother verbally attacked me when I requested she keep control of her kids and keep them away from my field and horses. She wouldn't accept responsibility for her failure to parent. I let her know it wasn't an option anymore. It was a fact."

He looked at me, weighing our stories in his mind.

"I want them gone. I don't care if she's preggos or not. Her inability to be a caring parent will get those kids injured, or worse, killed, and she'll blame me for her failures. There's enough empty housing down the road."

The colonel sighed, then made a sign to his gunner. The man released me. "Ma'am, leaving is not an option right now. I will speak with Mrs. Breckson on the need to keep a closer eye on her children. In return, you will not take it upon yourself to discipline them, or be alone with them. This is not an option for you. It is a command; otherwise, I have no choice but to treat you as a hostile prisoner."

I gritted my teeth, knowing the kids would most likely go out of their way to torment the horses, and possibly me in retaliation, knowing nothing would be done to them. "Fine. I promise, as long as you get them out of here as soon as possible." Those kids were in for a nasty surprise if they thought they could continue their ways.

"Ma'am. Mr. Gregson says you have a house back in those fields."

I almost asked, Who? Then I realized it had to be Ed, the old coot. "Unwanted guests are not an option. I've already told you where free housing can be found.

Besides, my partner and his kids live with me. There's no room," I fibbed.

"Ma'am, this is the first I've heard of them. Where are they?"

"Coming from North Carolina."

I received disbelieving stares. "Ma'am. You can't seriously expect them to survive such a trip."

"Not really, Colonel, but even if they don't, I'm a minor demon. I'm still good all by myself. Haven't you figured that out by now?" I smirked, biting down on what I really thought of Wade's chances, which hovered around minuscule and not a snowball's chance in hell.

CHAPTER NINE

Incessant crying made Anne stop the truck. That, and the realization they needed fuel. She wiped her runny nose on her sleeve as she shut the vehicle off.

I miss you so much, Dad. Why'd you have to die?

She knew he'd be furious with her for taking the main roads, but she couldn't face getting lost. Joan remained curled in a ball. Wearily, Anne slid out of the truck and to the bed. The tailgate had a line of bullet holes stitched across it.

* * *

"No! Daddy! We can't leave him! We can't!" Joan shrieked, fighting her sister's hold.

"We can't stay, Joan. Those men'll hurt us. We'll never get free if we don't go now."

"Dad!" Joan screamed, as her sister dragged her to the parking lot. "Let go of me."

Gunshots filled the air, along with hollering. Anne kept forcing her sister to run toward the lot, and their way out. She risked a quick look back. Two of the men had broken off to chase them. It was the wrong thing to do, as Joan broke free and turned to run to their father. She didn't get far before stopping, and letting out the loudest scream yet.

This is why everyone says don't look back, Anne thought.

She got a glimpse of her dad on the ground, bleeding, being hit with the rifle stocks. The two men chasing them were within touching distance. One of them lunged for Joan, who went wild.

Anne had her own problems, fighting off the

second man.

"Little bitch," he snarled, "I'll teach you not to go running off."

She wasn't sure how she managed to escape the much bigger and stronger man's grasp. She only knew blood and a chunk of flesh filled her mouth. The guy staggered back screaming, one hand clamped to the side of his head. Blood poured down.

He was fumbling around for his rifle when Anne grabbed a beer bottle off the road. She smashed it over his head, spitting in his face. While he was temporarily blinded, she kicked him in the groin. She kept kicking him after he fell down until something zipped past her. She looked up to see one of the men had stopped attacking her dad to fire at her.

She thought she saw her dad's ruined mouth move to form the word, "Run."

"You stay right there, or I'll shoot your leg out. You won't need it for what we got planned," the man yelled at her.

Suddenly, Anne felt a weight crash into her, sending her stumbling into a brick wall across the street. Her sister screamed and fought. Without a second thought, Anne launched herself at the back of the man attacking her sister.

They can't shoot us, or they'll hit their friend, was her frantic thought.

More men now left off beating their father and came toward the group. A loud slap as Joan was backhanded rang out. Her older sis staggered, lip split. The man reached behind him to dislodge Anne. She had ripped at his face and neck with her nails. Before she could gross herself out, Anne sunk her fingers into the man's eyes.

His screams of anguish were rewarding, even if the feel of popping eyeballs made her stomach lurch. She went tumbling to the ground as the man tossed forward onto his knees. Anne didn't remember springing back up, nor grabbing her sister. She only felt bullets flying past as she forced them both to run.

The two girls skidded around the corner to the parking lot. Anne saw the truck parked for a quick getaway. She redoubled her efforts. Joan was of no help to her. The younger girl yanked the driver's door open, then grabbed her sister by the neck of her T-shirt and shoved her into the seat.

"Get in," she screamed, trying to lift Joan.

The sound of a bullet hitting the truck did the trick. Anne climbed inside after Joan and fired the vehicle up. The sound of more bullets striking had her stomping on the gas. The large, powerful engine growled as they lurched forward with tires shrieking against the asphalt.

Anne peeled out of the lot. She swore she could hear her father, *"Drive it like you stole it, baby."*

# # #

Now she stared numbly at the holes. Her hands shook. *How are we gonna make it? How many more gangs will there be?*

She reached for a gas can, grunting at how heavy it was. *Don't let it slip!* Anne dragged it over to the tank, unscrewing both caps. She spilled a little of the precious stuff trying to lift and balance it. The sharp scent on top of the heat made her nose itch. Slowly, the container became lighter, until she had emptied it. Anne carefully stowed it back in its spot on the bed.

"Gee, Dad, it would've been nice if you had something smaller, too, instead of a large twenty gallon."

She carefully climbed up and grabbed some food and water before securing the tailgate again. Her hands reeked of gasoline, but she thought she had seen a bottle of hand sanitizer in the back seat. Yup, there it was. It didn't do a whole lot, but it made her feel better.

"Here," she nudged Joan. "You gotta eat and drink something."

Her sister just hunched tighter, so she tried again. This time, she received a swat. "Fine," Anne snarled, dropping half the stuff on the passenger floorboard. "I miss him, too, you know."

There was no reply. Anne sat, mechanically chewing and drinking as she surveyed the area around them. She tossed the trash out the window, then fetched the worn and creased maps out of the glovebox. It took her a while, but she finally pinpointed their location. Her finger traced the road they were on.

"It looks so easy," she murmured.

Before all this happened, their dad would almost always go visit them. On the times they did come down to see him, they usually flew. Only once did they drive down—a long, ten-hour trip. Something in the pit of her stomach made Anne think they'd be lucky just getting to the border between the Carolinas without trouble. As much as she wanted to sleep, she felt it would be wiser to keep moving.

"Hey, Joan, let's just keep on the highway for now, okay?"

She received no answer. Anne blew her bangs out of her face and started the truck. The needle hit the half-way mark. *I hope dad has a lot of gas in the back of this thing.*

As she drove, the young woman kept being distracted by all the abandoned vehicles on the opposite side. Debris and corpses lay strewn over the highway. She had to keep reminding herself not to look, or she'd break down and end up like Joan. Their speed wasn't very fast, as Anne had to frequently navigate around wrecks. After an hour of driving, she noticed signs for Greensboro.

Her sister had not moved once during the drive. "Hey, Sis, you need a pit stop? We're approaching another town. I think it's pretty sizable, and I'd rather not stop until we're past it. Okay?"

Still she received no answer. Anne sighed. The road unfurled before her. It shimmered in the rising heat. The sun's rays glinted off lots of metal. How bad would the blockage be? Her pace was a steady forty-miles-per-hour. She dropped even lower. The wrecks became more numerous, at times forcing her to creep around and through the debris.

A large sign informed them they were a half-mile from the Greensboro exit. All the centers of the letters were shot out. Anne couldn't stop the shudder that ran through her. As she passed the sign, she noticed movement ahead. It soon resolved itself into a pack of zombies.

"Oh no, oh no, oh no," the younger woman moaned. There's no way for her to avoid them. She doesn't think they even have guns to defend themselves with against the horde..

Maybe if she kept driving, she could get through them. The first zombie hit off the front driver's side and staggered away. Anne gritted her teeth as more of the pack pushed against the front of the truck. Others came alongside. Their hands reached for the vehicle. The pounding of rotting fists against the glass startled Joan, who screamed.

Anne felt panic well up inside. It seemed like the zombies were preventing the truck from moving forward. Her sister kept screaming, barely leaving off long enough to suck in air. The whole situation rattled her nerves.

"Shut up, shut up, shut up," she screamed at her sister.

Anne pressed down on the gas. With a groan and a lurch, they moved forward. The truck bounced and rocked as zombies hit it, and fell to be crushed beneath the wheels. The sound of shattering glass made Anne press the gas pedal to the floor. They broke free of the horde, only to narrowly miss plowing into the back of a car. She brought the truck to a halt in the middle of the two-lane highway. The sounds of gunfire came to her ears. Out of the shimmering haze appeared a small convoy and an even larger pack of zombies.

Anne could only stare. Her bottom lip trembled, and tears spilled from her eyes. Beside her, Joan's screams had diminished to a wheeze. The tide of undead swarmed around their truck and pounded on the glass. Their moans drowned out the sound of gunfire.

"No no no no nonononononononono," Anne wailed.

Any moment now the glass would shatter, and she and her sister would be dragged out of the vehicle and eaten alive. Frantically, she cast about for a weapon as the truck rocked. Joan's hoarse thread of a voice keened in terror. As the younger twisted about, she spotted a garbage bag that had come undone. Its loot spilled out onto the backseat. Anne saw the sheathed handle of a knife. She unbuckled her seat belt and lunged for it just as a zombie fell headfirst into the back. Pieces of shattered glass crunched beneath the zom.

The next few moments became a blur for Anne as she fought to remain alive. Soon, she could barely see past her gore-soaked hair. Strong hands clamped around her wrist and shoulders. She screamed and fought more wildly as she felt herself dragged from the truck.

The young woman landed with a thud on the hot pavement. The knife skidded away.

"Hey, hey, hey," a male voice yelled. "Calm down, you're safe now. We got you. That's it, Ma'am. Calm on down. Everything's gonna be all right."

Little by little, the soothing tone penetrated the haze. Anne blinked. Tears streamed down her face as she looked up at the person attached to the voice. Combat fatigues, boots, and an automatic rifle greeted her. She gazed around, noticing a mix of civilians with the military.

"Come on, let's get you on your feet," another voice, an older female, spoke nearby.

Anne felt helping arms lift her up, and despite the hot sun shining down, someone wrapped a blanket around her. It felt good. She shivered from shock. She couldn't seem to keep her gaze on one spot for long. Her eyes flitted from each member of the rag-tag group. The female introduced herself as Nancy, and led Anne to the back of the truck. She lowered the tailgate and helped her sit on it, bringing her sister to be with her. She, too, had a blanket wrapped around her.

Voices and conversations floated around her, but she couldn't always understand what they said.

"Both of them are in shock."

"They're not much older than my two daughters. You suppose they're from one of the colleges?"

"There had to be someone else with them. The bed is fairly well stocked. By those bullet holes, I'd say they ran into some trouble. It must have cost them the life of whoever was traveling with them."

The young woman blinked several times and finally focused on the face in front of her. It belonged to the older woman. Her red hair had faded some, and freckles and creases covered her face.

"Hey there, I'm Nancy. Can you tell me you and your friend's name?"

"A, A, Anne. And, and my sister, J, J, Joan."

Patiently, Nancy drew the whole story out of Anne. When the young woman lapsed back into silence, the older introduced the members with her.

"I'm sorry for your loss, Ma'am," the young lieutenant Higgin's said. "Your father did a brave thing back there, making sure you and your sister got away. I know it's not much comfort, seeing the way in which you lost him."

He paused a moment before continuing. "Excuse my bluntness, Ma'am, but it seems to me you two ladies are not adequately equipped to deal with the reality of our new world. We've been escorting refugees from the surrounding areas to safe centers. We've got several set up over in Winston-Salem, and Durham. Now, I don't know where you're headed, but I highly suggest you consider joining the other survivors we're escorting there."

Nancy had been scrutinizing the two women during Higgin's speech. "Where was your dad planning on taking you two?"

"S, S, South Carolina. Charleston. Some island," Anne replied dully. She was starting to feel warm again, but her mind felt wrapped in layers of cotton.

She missed the looks shared between Higgin and Nancy. The woman gently probed further. "Is that where the rest of your family lives?"

"Our, our dad is, was, our family. We, we don't have anyone else, except our uncle. And, and, my father's girlfriend. That's where, where, she lives."

"Have you heard from your uncle since this all started?" Higgin asked.

Silently, Anne shook her head in the negative, taking another sip of water from the bottle that had somehow made its way into her hands.

"He's a Navy man," dully she recited his name, rank, and what little she could remember of his duties.

Once more, she lapsed into silence, leaning against her sister for comfort and resting her head on Joan's shoulder. Anne let her eyes drift close. Her father's warnings echoed dully in the recesses of her mind, but she was so tired. She just wanted things to be the way they had been before everything went to shit. It wasn't long before the young woman slipped into a light doze.

Anne woke with a jolt, heart pounding in a panic,

before she realized where she was.

Higgin's eyes, while weary, also shone with determination. "Ma'am, my squad and I need to be moving soon. I'm sorry to rush you, but there's more of those hordes roaming about. We have to complete our mission. So I'm letting you know your options."

He paused to make sure she was listening and waited for her acknowledgment.

"Option One: You and your sister join my squad, and the civilians we're escorting to the safe centers. Option two: Adler can show you the basics of using the weapons your dad stowed in the truck, and the best route to take to your island. Option Three: You can join those survivors who are planning on making their way to a coastal city and joining up with others forming their own fortified enclaves. Unfortunately, I can only give you a few minutes to discuss it with your sister before I'll need your answer."

He walked off to his men and issued orders to them.

The older woman lingered, "I know you young'uns don't generally think we oldsters understand what you're going through. Or that we're behind the times. Either way, I believe you'd be smart to pick one of the groups to travel with. Besides, how likely is it your dad's girlfriend is expecting you, or might be still alive?"

Anne heard the words, but they formed a jumble in her head. She pictured her dad's girlfriend, Spacey. The woman had basic life-saving knowledge, and worked at a hospital. She and her dad had often held lively discussions on the world around them. Mostly, she remembered the older woman as quiet, a bit distant but with a wealth of practical knowledge, and not tolerant of willful stupidity or ignorance.

"Where, where on the coast are they going?" she asked Nancy.

"Well, there's a Navy and Air Force base in Charleston, which happens to be a coastal city. Last Higgin heard they were holding out against the horde. The problem is getting close. Those that are heading that way may have to eventually find boats. Of course, there's also no guarantee any of them will make it alive."

"What, what are you planning on, if I can ask?"

"Me? Heck, I'm heading to the coast. I always did want to live near the beach, and well, since the world's ending, I might as well try for my dream. There's nothing but my life I have left to lose."

"You, you don't have any. . . . "

"No, dear. My family is dead. I consider myself extremely lucky to have found a group such as this. I'm sure you can appreciate the sentiment, considering all you and your sister have gone through."

Nancy bent to peer intently into the younger woman's eyes before she straightened up. "I've been with this group for three weeks now, and while everyone has their quirks and idiosyncrasies, they're basically trustworthy. It's more than I can say for some of the others we've run across. You want my unvarnished opinion, you could do a lot worse."

She briefly squeezed Anne's shoulder, before walking off to join the civilians who stood a little way off from the military. The young woman squinted in the sun, taking the first good look at her surroundings. The squad consisted of two Humvees with mounted guns, two large transport trucks, an assortment of civilian vehicles, and a few motorcycles.

The military members wore full battle kit and kept a perimeter guard. The civilians also had their own assortment of weapons and homemade armor. They, too, helped patrol and keep watch so nobody could sneak up on them. Anne turned to her sister.

"Joan, Sis, we, we gotta make a decision. What do

you wanna do?"

Her big sister's head hung down, her dirty blonde hair a greasy curtain hiding her face. "How could you leave him there? You killed him. I hate you. Get away from me. I want Uncle Tom."

The venom in her words pierced her sister's heart.

"Please, Joan, please don't. I, I need you. You're the only family left. Please."

The older sister kept her head down, "I don't care. Nothing matters anymore."

Tears spilled down Anne's cheeks. *I don't want this responsibility! It shouldn't be this way. I want to be back in college, studying with my friends, drinking beer.*

The clomp of boots brought her head up. Lieutenant Higgin stood before her. "Ma'am," his address to her kind and firm.

"C, C, could you show us how, how to use the guns? We, we wanna join the group heading to Ch, Charleston."

"Yes, Ma'am," the soldier waved Adler over and briefed him before Anne was left with the hard-faced, older man.

CHAPTER TEN

I was in the woods surrounding the house I had taken over when I heard rustling and whispering. I finished making knots, then stayed crouched in the tree. Zombies don't whisper. They moan. It wasn't long before the two kids appeared. What were the little shits up to now?

"But Colonel Travis said . . ." the girl whined.

"I don't care! He's not the boss of us, and Mom said she's selfish and mean. If we wanna play with the horses, we can."

"What if the mean lady catches us? She has a gun. She threatened Mommy with it."

"She wouldn't dare, The colonel will take it away and lock her up, and then the whole place will be ours."

Oh, it would? I continued watching as they made their way through the trees. A breeze blew, causing an eerie moaning sound. The kids froze. The little girl whimpered in fear.

"Shut up!" her brother fiercely whispered. "Do you wanna bring them to us?"

He crept forward as the moan died down. I slid silently out of the tree and used the shade and concealing vegetation to crawl closer to them. Each time the wind came , so did the eerie moans. They both jumped. I was almost there. I added a moan of my own, reached out a hand, and snatched at the boys' pant legs. They screamed and bolted in panic, not watching where they went. The girl raced to her right. She would eventually come out near the visitor center. The boy slammed into a wire fence, cutting himself on it, as I had added a layer of barbed wire. His screams reached new heights as I moved farther into the woods. It wouldn't be long before he brought someone/thing to him.

# # #

I had just entered the paddock, crossing from around the house, when I saw the military, and civvies crowded around the boy. Ashleigh had her head buried in her mom's enormous gut. I crossed quickly, coming up to the group, acting as if I hadn't been the cause of all the commotion.

"Oh, my God! Bradley! My baby! What did that nasty ho do to you?"

Classy, real classy. No wonder the kid had an attitude problem.

"Ma'am, where were you?" Colonel Downing asked me.

"Out in the woods, bolstering my defenses. Why is he near this place? That's a direct violation of our agreement."

"We need to get back to safety, no telling what'll come." The gunner had his rifle up, constantly scanning.

I could see Downing opening his mouth, and I just shook my head no. He gave orders to retreat to the center. We quickly made our way, the kid still screaming from the bleeding lacerations on his upper torso. I figured any zombies who might come ashore would make their way here. I re-checked my guns, rifle, and mags. All good to go. Lugging so much around while trying to work is a pain, but better safe than sorry. I continued with my 'noise-makers' and other various chores. I itched to explore, to see how much the bikers had left behind. I didn't dare leave this place with idiot guests. No telling what they would get up to while I was gone.

# # #

I was blissfully left alone the rest of the day. In hindsight, I suppose it should have worried me, but I was too overcome by joy at having my solitude back to worry. I had done all I could on my own for defense, both against zombies and unwanted humans. Next on the list was a trip to the farm across from the plantation. I hoped they had seeds, not the genetically modified kind. Those didn't propagate, more had to be brought, planted, grown, etc. each year. Heirloom seeds topped my list, those I could harvest from what I grew, and re-plant year after year.

The injured horse I left behind. Ed used to be a farmer and knew about livestock. He taught me more about caring for the horses, including how to properly tack up. Half a month of putting up with guests, he became just as disgusted with Mrs. Breckson and her undisciplined children as I, for he took every opportunity to help me. I saddled the Appaloosa after setting the house defenses. I didn't want anyone to know I had left. They might decide to snoop around. I took the long way, skirting carefully. I barely ran across any zombies, which unnerved me. Where were they all? The farmer had managed to plant his fields before the world ended. The recent storms had given the plants enough water so they managed to hang on. The major crop seemed to be corn, with some veggies.

I should have brought the truck, I soon realized. A lot of the stuff was ready to be harvested, except the corn. I rode farther, making sure the barn, outbuildings, and house truly were empty. I didn't need to be surprised. I cleared out the trapped zombies, then got down to work. The amount of fresh produce was more than I could eat before it spoiled. I hoped I had grabbed books on canning, dehydrating, and the like. The farm equipment all used diesel. Now if I could figure out how to operate them. It would be too convenient for owners' manuals to just be left lying around.

That was another concern: the diesel tank at the plantation. I'm sure Downing and company had already inspected it. No doubt they would confiscate the contents when they managed to get their vehicles back. I needed to find containers, lots of them, to empty and move the stuff. Food-wise the farm was better, but survival-wise, the plantation was easier to defend. Background noise filtered to me on the breeze. I wasn't paying as much attention to it as I should. If I had, I would've run into trouble. I stuffed my empty backpack as full as I could. I also managed to find empty feed sacks to put more in and tie to the saddle. I made it back with no problems , those issues waited for me.

As I approached the house, I noticed the covering to the tiger traps lying in the now-trampled high grass. A quick look inside showed my zombies dead, amid fresh blood, gnawed bodies, and crumpled metal. WTF? Someone was going to have a lot of explaining to do. I cautiously rode closer, the stable hiding me from the elevated first floor of the house, but not if anyone was posted on the roof, or in nearby trees. I didn't see any movement from curtains or blinds. I stabled the horse, not bothering to un-tack or brush down. I would take care of that later after I examined my place. The house had been breached. I noticed the moment I got close. Large caliber bullet holes riddled the outside, along with more bodies and bikes strewn around. Parts of a person lay at the foot of the back stairs. The rear door had a large puddle of congealing blood along with bits of stuff. The place looked as if a small war had taken place. The duck-walking thing was a pain in my knees. I crept closer to the door when it was abruptly opened, showing a highly irate Downing.

"What the fuck? Why are you in my house?" I demanded, sword at the ready as I stood in a popping of knees.

"No choice. Where have you been?" he replied curtly, gun pointed at me.

"You're not my dad. I don't have to tell you shit."
Real mature. I sounded like a bratty teenager.

"I need to know you didn't play a part in the attack."

My eyes narrowed. "What attack? I didn't hear anything."

"Ma'am, I repeat . . . "

"Oh, for fuck's sake. I was out scavenging with one of the horses. Now, let me in. I need to know what kind of damage those walking idiots have done to the place."

"They weren't zombies," he answered.

"I'm talking about the survivors. They do more harm than the zoms."

He sighed, holstering his weapon. "What did you find?"

"Nothing of import," I replied, stepping past him and the blood. I wasn't about to let on I had fresh food just yet.

The kitchen was a mess, not just from body matter, but from people eating my supplies. My temper went from irritated to I-want-to-kill-someone.

"They were hungry, Ma'am. There's plenty left." Downing answered before I could let loose with more expletives.

I stomped into the living room. Mrs. Breckson sat shell-shocked on the couch, her kids curled beside her.

"Where are the others?" I asked.

"You'll be happy to learn, no doubt, Branson is dead. Tanya, and Rondel, the female soldier, tasked to guard him, kidnapped." The colonel spat bitterly. "I lost two good men. Your traps took out the civvies who weren't taken as hostages, and some hostiles."

"Sweet! I was hoping they'd work, I wasn't too sure when I set them." Uh-oh, that was out loud.

I received a hostile glare. "Um, sorry. I mean,

what exactly happened?"

It didn't look like I was going to receive a reply, then Downing said, "The bikers."

I blinked, words slipping out, "And they didn't use your toys against you? What a bunch of pussies. Guess you should have retaliated sooner."

I watched jaw muscles clench, veins pulse. Probably shouldn't taunt him with the loss of his remaining squad so recent. "Seriously, I am sorry for the loss of your men. They were useful," it was the best I could come up with. "Is there anything else I should know of?"

"It's not safe here any longer. They know we're here. We have to leave."

"Motherfuckers!" I fumed. "I am not letting all this fall into their hands. That is it. Colonel, we're at war."

A sneer was his reply. "There is no way a civvie such as yourself can take on a pack of thugs with military hardware."

"Watch me. I've survived this long, not because I'm some ninja or super soldier, but because I can be a cunning, unforgiving bitch, especially when crossed. Now, if you'll excuse me, I have some rounds to make."

I made sure nothing lurked outside. Stupidity getting me killed after a grand exit tends to ruin it. Then I headed into the tree line, The colonel followed me. Why, I had no idea, and really didn't care. I did my best to look for traps not of my own making. I shouldn't have bothered. There was none. The bikers apparently believed their large numbers, and ruthlessness didn't need supplanting. Smoke rose lazily from the direction of the visitor center I saw when I peeked out from behind a tree. They had set the place afire in retaliation. I was more concerned about the fate of the diesel. I darted across the road and made my way to the back of the building.

I didn't see any puddles of liquid. I circled

cautiously, sniffing the air, no smell of leakage. The traps had all been sprung I saw, impaling at least one biker.

"Nice," fist pump included.

"Has anyone told you that you're insane?" Downing hissed behind me. "Do you realize what could've happened had anything pierced that tank? We shouldn't even be this close to it with the fire."

"I was counting on it."

"What?!"

"Insanity is just un-recognized genius."

A snort of disbelief was his answer. I continued around the building, scouting as I went. The nearest trees had been scorched. The recent rains helped to dampen the spread of flames. I continued toward the entrance, stayed off the road, and moved through the wooded parts.

The colonel held a hand up. Somehow during all this he had gotten ahead of me. Well, if he wanted to sacrifice himself, so be it. Although I was hoping it wouldn't come to that. I needed his expertise to help me get payback. I waited, mentally cursing, then moved up to him when I got the come-ahead signal. We lay side by side in the grass, gazing out at the entrance.

I didn't hear nor see anything. "We gonna lie here, or stand and go closer? This is making my allergies flare." I sneezed several times, having to use my sleeve to wipe my nose. "Gross, now I gotta do laundry."

"Tell me again how you've managed to survive this long?" he snarked back, rising and approaching the mess.

I considered it a rhetorical question. "Oh, this is so cool! They worked!" I was bouncing up and down on my toes like a little kid, including clapping hands in glee. "Hee hee!" I thought I heard more mumbling about my mental state, or lack of, from Downing as I inspected my handiwork.

The caltrops had blown quite a few tires on the

bikes, judging from the discarded Harleys, before they wised up. The monofilament had also helped, but not as much as I had hoped. Oh well, can't have everything.

"So, please tell me you raided the bikes and bodies for anything useful."

I received a scowl. "Sheesh. It's the end of the world, every little bit helps." I started to inspect what saddle bags there were. He stood guard. I guess looting was beneath him.

I barely kept from shouting out in happiness. One of the bikers, perhaps a leader or second-in-command, I hoped. Nah, that would be too easy, had grenades. I left them in the bag, taking the whole thing off. I figured, if the wreck hadn't disturbed them, my moving them around shouldn't either. If I were a nice person, I would have alerted the Colonel, seeing as it was stolen military stuff. Lucky me. I no longer cared about social conventions. The other few bags contained shells, back up guns, knives, and a taser.

"Hope it's charged."

Downing barely glanced at it, instructing me on what to look for. It still had a charge. "Okay, now the bodies," was my way of informing him I was moving on.

"Now I've seen everything," he replied, shaking his head as I took gloves out of a pocket and pulled them on.

"What? Who knows what diseases the nasty bastards have. I'm not risking it."

"Exactly what did you do before all this started? Normal people do not go around with medical gloves." He had to help me turn most of the bodies over. They had been mostly big, fat, or burly guys in life. Only two of the corpses were female.

"Funny you should mention that," I said as I pulled items out of pockets and off the corpses. "I did work in a hospital. I barely escaped. And no, I wasn't a nurse. I was an Imaging Tech. Giving meds wasn't part of my job. I don't know anything about them beyond what was needed to do my job and keep my patients safe."

"Dare I ask how you escaped?"

"It was smelly and nasty. I hid under a dead body for most of it." That was also a partial truth. "When my co-workers and the staff realized what we were actually dealing with, it was everyone for themselves. I used the opportunity to snatch badges off corpses, making my way farther into the place. Crazy, since a door to the outside, and freedom was mere steps away."

"How did you survive without a weapon? And why'd you go farther into the danger zone?" Downing asked.

"One of our patients was bitten, but we didn't know it was from a zombie. She turned on the scanning table. The paramedics who brought her in had placed her wooden cane on the stretcher with her. I took the cane and the oxygen tank, and I vented my frustrations. The pharmacy was about one hundred feet from where I was. I passed up three different exits in my determination to get inside it and retrieve what could be much-needed medications before any looters got to it."

Downing's face remained impassive. "Did you manage to complete your mission?"

"Not in the way I hoped to," I lied. "It turned out I shouldn't have bothered." I realized too late that admitting I had medicine was not smart. *Please let my lying skills work for once.*

He narrowed his eyes at me. I looked like a pack mule. "Look, these things aren't exactly light. Help a lady out here?"

"I would if I saw one."

"Ohhhh, burn, good one. Seriously. Help."

He took a few bags, and we made our way back to the house, a temporary truce between us, to plan mass destruction and chaos.

CHAPTER ELEVEN

Anne woke, confused, not sure why the truck had stopped, and said as much.

"We need to re-fuel the vehicles, and ourselves," Nancy replied.

The young woman peered over at Joan, asleep still, with drool coming out the side of her mouth. She decided to leave her sister be. Anne opened her door and joined Nancy and an older man who had introduced himself as Mitch. All along the line of assorted vehicles, survivors stretched and surveyed the woods around them. The small military convoy, with Higgin, had escorted their band through Greensboro. The leaders, Ruth and Sam, had chosen to stick to backroads. Anne had found them a pleasant, middle-aged childless couple, if a bit eccentric.

"All right, you know what to do," Sam called out. "Group B, your turn to guard."

"Let's get re-filled first, then we can eat," Ruth said, as she opened the trunk of their SUV.

Everyone moved to comply. The couple loved to joke and have fun, but they also insisted that work get done. Their quirky sense of humor reminded Anne a lot of her dad and Spacey. Anne helped Mitch with the gas cans while Nancy stood guard.

"So," Mitch began, "your sister doing any better?"

"Um, she's sleeping."

"Yeah, she does a lot of that," he replied in a carefully neutral tone

Anne bristled. "She's missing our dad, and so am I."

The man kept his eyes on the can, his tone never changing. "It's hard, losing someone. Heck, everyone here has lost a loved one. Only . . ." He fell silent.

"Only, what?"

The man shrugged, switching out the empty can for a full one before resuming his watch on the nozzle.

She had a feeling she could guess what he was thinking. That Joan needed to get over it. Both sisters did. Anne felt a trickle of anger. Who was he to judge? Not everybody could just seal their emotions away. Besides, he could always find a spot with another member of their band. He didn't have to ride with them. They would be just fine with Nancy, thank you. She opened her mouth to voice her thoughts when the guards began to shout.

She turned to see a dozen zombies shamble out from the woods. "Oh, no, why—"

Before she could finish her thought, the guards had re-killed the zoms. Anne tried to control her breathing while her heart pounded furiously, and she shook all over. Mitch had not once stopped in re-filling. He merely kept an eye on the situation. Casually, he re-capped both the tank and the empty can. Her view was momentarily obscured as he walked past her to store the container in the truck bed. *How can he just act like nothing happened? What if the others hadn't been able to kill the zombies? Daddy, I miss you.*

Anne sniffled, and hastily wiped her tears. She wondered for the umpteenth time if she had made the right decision for her and her sister. Maybe they should have stayed at one of the North Carolina refugee centers. What if they died out here before they made it to the coast? She drew a shaky breath in, and swiped once more at the tears, which she couldn't seem to stop. Mitch and Nancy ignored her crying. They offered her food and water from the supplies her dad had packed in the truck bed.

"Do you want to try to wake up your sister?, See if she'll eat and drink something? Or do you want me to?" Nancy asked.

The young woman shook her head. "No, I'll do it." Anne took the portions meant for her sister and climbed into the backseat of the truck.

"Hey, Joan. Sis, wake up," she nudged gently at first, then more insistently when Joan wouldn't awake. "Come on, Joan. Wake up,"

"Everything okay?" Nancy asked from outside.

"Yes," Anne lied, and pinched her sister's upper arm.

After a few moments, Joan sluggishly responded. "Ow. Are we back home? Where's dad? Why are there so many trees?"

"No, Joan, we're not home. Here, you need to eat and drink something. You've been sleeping the entire trip."

Her sister made no move to take the offered food. Joan's brow wrinkled with confusion. She groaned as she shifted position, her eyes flitting about the interior. "How much farther? Did you ask Dad? Go ask him," she whined, rubbing her eyes.

"Joan," Anne tried again, then shoved the food into her sister's lap. "Here, I'll go ask. Just, just, eat something."

Her heart filled with dread while her sister fumbled with the packaging on the protein bar. She didn't get it open before laying her head on the seat, and she slipped into sleep. Anne crammed a fist into her mouth to muffle her sobs. She looked out the window, and straight into Mitch's eyes. She thought she saw pity for a moment, and not his usual neutral expression. She blinked, and he had his head down as he opened the front passenger door.

"Anne, how are you and your sister doing? Did she eat or drink anything?" Nancy's concerned voice came a second later.

The young woman could only stare at Mitch's profile as he kept watch on his side for zombies or other undesirables. *Just say it!* She wanted to scream at him. *Just say what everyone's thinking.* But she didn't. She turned and climbed out of the back.

"No, she, she woke up briefly, long enough to ask for our dad. She's sleeping again."

Nancy lay a hand on Anne's arm in sympathy. "Oh, honey. I'm so, so sorry."

An unreasonable anger rose in the young woman. *No, you're not!* She screamed inside her head.

"Why don't you take a break, and let me try? She needs to drink some water if nothing else. Okay?" Nancy gently steered Anne toward Sam and Ruth.

Sam's eyes showed worry, but his greeting was genial. "Hey there, Anne. Hope the little bit of excitement we had there didn't upset you and Joan. Ya know, I'm kinda glad we're going the back roads. I think that's the most zombies we've seen since Greensboro. And as an added bonus, nary a banjo in sight, heh."

Ruth gave her husband a look, and he widened his eyes at her from under the brim of his black straw hat. "Sorry," he apologized, "Sometimes my attempts at humor don't go right."

"We've met a lot of friendly country folk, very helpful," Ruth stressed. She turned her gaze back to Anne. "We're not that far from Charleston. One more day of travel, and then we'll have to decide how to navigate without increasing our chances of running into hostiles or too many zombies."

"I knew things were going too smoothly," Sam joked besides his wife. His eyes lifted to the person walking up to them.

Anne turned at the sight of Nancy. The older woman gave her a sad smile and patted the young woman's shoulder. "I got your sister to drink a little bit of water. Not enough, but it's a start. So, are we ready to move on?"

Sam craned his neck and surveyed everyone. "Yup. Let's round 'em up and move 'em on out," he raised his right hand and arm and gestured to everyone. "Rawhide," he sang softly to himself as he walked back to his vehicle.

Ruth briefly closed her eyes, nodded at them, and followed after her husband.

# # #

Ruth slowed the SUV, and in the rearview mirror she could see the rest of their group doing the same. They had made surprisingly good time on the back roads. Most of them were free of the massive wrecks and abandoned vehicles which clogged the main highways and arteries.

"I think we may have missed a turnoff somewhere," she said to her husband.

"Duh, someone failed a roll check," he grinned. "Lemme see what the bent-over sign says." He nodded toward the intersection twenty-five feet ahead of them.

"Be careful," Ruth called after him.

He grinned again, and slowly picked his way through the debris. Mrs. Resick propped her rifle on the window edge, scanning through the scope for any sign of movement other than her husband's. Sam took his time, even going farther ahead than she thought wise. He came back quickly, face pale despite the heat, and sweating freely.

"Definitely failed the spot check," he used a bandana to wipe the sweat off his face, head, and neck. "The sign says 'Bee's Ferry Road.'" He scrambled to unfold their map.

Up and down the line, doors opened and shut as the occupants took the short break to get out and stretch. Anne's anxiety rose.

"What's wrong?" she asked.

"Good question," Mitch answered. "I'll go find out." He slipped from the back seat, gently closing the door.

The women watched as he walked up the line to the lead car. They saw Sam get out of the car, map in hand. The two men spread it over the hood, and their hands moved while they frequently looked around. Anne turned around in her seat, to check on Joan. Her sister still slept. The afternoon light illuminated just how much weight she had lost. Her hair hung in lank, greasy strings. Her eyes were sunk in dark pools of flesh, drawn tight over bone. Joan refused food, and it was a struggle to get her to drink enough water to keep her hydrated. Anne bit her lip, debating on whether she should try waking her sister. She decided against it and turned around. Mitch came back, stopping at each vehicle to converse with the occupants.

Come on, hurry up. What's the problem? Anne silently urged.

Mitch stopped beside Nancy's door. The young woman thought his eyes flicked her way briefly before he addressed them.

"Well," he drawled, "it seems we missed a turnoff somewhere. The best we can figure out, we're somewhere in West Ashley."

"How long will this add to our time?" Nancy asked.

"Depends. There are a couple of islands not too far from us. If the map is correct, we can get to Charleston from here. But it means taking the main roads. Sam doesn't feel comfortable with 'em, and frankly, neither do I. We'll be lucky if they're passable."

Nancy and Anne both picked up on the mention of islands, but the older woman spoke first. "So what do Sam and Ruth suggest?"

"We take a vote."

"What? Why? The whole point of this trip is to join up with the survivors' community and the military."

Mitch's eyes definitely flicked over to Anne, before he shifted his gaze back to Nancy. "I think they're spooked." He held a hand up to stop any protests. "I don't know why, but after looking at the map, they're definitely more in favor of checking out the islands."

"That makes no sense," Nancy insisted. She opened her door, forcing Mitch to step back or be hit.

She walked with purpose past the other survivors, who stood in small knots, talking. Anne looked away from the woman, feeling eyes on her. She found herself staring into Mitch's deep brown eyes.

"Looks like you may get your wish to find your dad's girlfriend."

She remained silent. She wasn't sure what she wanted, beyond a safe place to live.

"Come on, you get a vote on the matter, too. Let's get this over with." His rough voice interrupted her thoughts.

Silently, after one last check on Joan, Anne exited the truck. She took a breath in. The heat pressed down on her. Around her, the sounds of a southern spring filled the air. The two joined the group of people milling about.

Ruth clapped her hands to get everyone's attention. "All right, people. We missed the turnoff somewhere. Now, we can use these roads to get where we need to be. However, it's not going to be easy. This is an extremely populated area. The roads might be impassable in spots. So, we have a choice."

"Hold on, I fail to see what the problem is," a strong male voice cut her off.

A few muffled groans were heard, along with some eye rolls.

"We just turn around, and take our time finding

the missed turnoff. Problem solved," his smug features plainly said what he wasn't voicing aloud.

Ruth took it in stride, "Yes, we can. We are also close to a few islands . . ."

Once again she was interrupted, "Oh ho, I'm just gonna stop you right there. I didn't join this party to bow to the whims of a single person."

Anne was about to protest when a hard, masculine hand lightly squeezed her shoulder in warning. She glanced sideways to see it was Mitch. He and the man protesting, Devon, often had arguments about the group's direction.

"No one's asking you too" Ruth retorted. "If I can finish?" her tone biting, as she glared at Devon. "Sam thinks, and I'm a mind to see his reasoning, that one of the islands might be better than a possibly overcrowded survivors' center."

A disbelieving snort came from the quarrelsome man. "It won't be any safer. There won't be any guarantee of food."

"You could say the same of the center," Mitch spoke calmly. "People draw zombies. The more of us there are, the more of them there will be. An island might be easier to defend."

"To get trapped on and killed sooner!" Devon shouted, red-faced.

"That can happen anywhere, including the safe center," the other man retorted. "Look, folks, it's simple. We're splitting up . . ."

"The hell you say! And I suppose you expect to just take half of everything?" Devon demanded.

"I expect to take enough to sustain those who agree to head toward the islands," Mitch growled.

Before either man could say more, Ruth clapped her hands together. "This is wasting time, and you're acting like children. Those who want to continue to the safe center, step over here," she pointed to her right. "Those who wish to check out the islands, step left."

Devon grabbed his wife's arm, as she rounded up their four kids. They stood on the side for the safe center. Anne chewed her lip for a moment, then joined Mitch and Nancy to the left, the island side. The rest of the members argued among themselves.

The debate raged for almost thirty minutes. In the end, most of the members decided to stick with the original plan. Devon's smirk grew broader.

"Well, looks like I'm the new leader," he announced.

"Yup," Ruth replied placidly, "good luck to you all."

"Wait just one minute, we still have to split up the supplies," the other man said.

"Oh? Why? Everyone's got the vehicles they originally had. It's even. Six and Six," Ruth walked back to the SUV.

Behind her, Devon spluttered and raged.

"Let's go," Mitch quietly urged the two women. "Anne, you think you know how to get us onto the islands from here?"

"Um," she cast a nervous glance back at the other group.

They had gathered around the red-faced man, urging him to just let things be.

"It's been a while since Joan and I were down here. I'm not sure."

"Mitch, you sit up front with her. I'll take the back with Joan. Are all the guns fully loaded?"

"Always."

Anne climbed into the driver's seat and started the truck up. Her heart beat fast, and her breathing sped up. *Calm down, you're almost there. It's not home. Dad won't ever be there. But maybe it can become home.*

She pulled out from behind the two SUVs carrying Devon's group and crept toward Ruth and Sam's ride. He was driving, and his wife had a rifle propped on the window frame.

A sudden crackling made her jump, and she had to slam on the brakes or rear-end the couple before her.

"Easy now, nice and smooth," Mitch soothed, as he brought a walkie talkie up to his lips. "Yeah, boss?"

"Hey, Easy Rider, be on the look out for hostiles. I've got a feeling we'll be running into them soon."

"Will do, boss," Mitch put the device in his lap and went back to scanning the area around them as they drove. "Keep close, but don't crash into him. Keep alert, and calm. We may be making a run for it."

Anne nodded mutely, trying to keep her breathing under control. She glanced in the mirror at her sleeping sister. Nancy had belted Joan and herself in. Their pace was a slow five miles per hour as they navigated the many pile-ups. The two trucks turned onto a divided, four-lane highway. In the distance loomed a massive wreck. As they got closer, birds rose from the bodies. The remains seemed oddly placed, almost if someone had deliberately displayed them.

"Be advised, we may have company soon. Keep close, and don't let them cut us off." Sam's voice came through the walkie talkie, and he repeated himself twice more.

"Copy that, boss. Nice and steady, Anne," Mitch kept his tone even, neutral. "You're doing good."

She sucked in a shaky breath and nodded. Ahead of them, Sam turned right, and she followed closely. The sides of their vehicles scrapped the wrecks, jostling them before they got through. More cars and trucks lined the road, in an almost straight line on both sides.

"A little more speed, Anne," Mitch commanded her, as she had let her foot slip a bit, increasing the space between the two trucks.

"There's gotta be a trap somewhere. None of this is natural. Keep sharp, Anne," Nancy added.

They crested the first rise and came over the top. To either side, roads led off into neighborhoods. A loud roar came from behind.

"We've got incoming," Mitch yelled into the radio before dropping it and training his gun as cracks sounded out.

"Full speed ahead," came Sam's voice on the radio.

"Anne," Mitch warned her as Sam and Ruth's SUV suddenly charged forward.

"No, no, no, no,"

"Yes, yes, yes, if you don't speed up. Do it! Now!" Mitch barked.

Anne mashed her foot down on the gas, closing the gap. The truck's powerful engine thrummed. A quick glance in the side mirror revealed three bikers, with a passenger each. They brandished rifles, flashes coming from the muzzles.

"Shoot the riders," Mitch instructed, "and if they get alongside us, ram them off the road."

The young woman could only nod as she tightened her grip on the steering wheel and closed the gap between their vehicle and Sam's. The sound of gunfire echoed in the cab, as Nancy and Mitch returned fire.

"Got one," she yelled, as the rider and passenger went soaring before hitting and skidding along the pavement. Their bike crashed into the barricade of vehicles, and parts went flying.

The sound of shattering glass had reached Anne's ears before Nancy called out, "Back window is gone."

"Shit, more incoming. They're trying to block us from the bridge. Go to ludicrous speed. Prepare to ram them." Sam's shout crackled through the radio.

"Oh no, oh no, I can't, I can't. . ."

"Yes, you can," Mitch yelled at her, "you have to unless you want to find out what they'll do to you, and trust me, you don't."

He fired out the window, toward the four trucks pulling forward. Debris hit Anne's window as a bullet took out her side mirror. She let out a little shriek, startled into jerking the wheel. A thud came immediately, as she unknowingly hit one of the bikes.

"Good girl," Mitch praised her, as Nancy shot at the riders. "Faster, they've almost closed off the bridge access," he yelled.

Two of the four trucks faced each other, and as she watched in horror, Sam plowed between them. Shrieking metal and crumpling plastic reached their ears. They were too close. Anne instinctively lifted her foot off the gas, only to feel the rifle against her leg. The butt ground against her foot as Mitch forced her to mash the gas pedal down.

"Drive it like you stole it," he barely had time to yell, as the front end of their truck smashed into the front sides of the blockade vehicles. More metal and plastic tore. The impact snapped them forward, then back, as the seat belts were engaged.

"Eyes on the road, keep sharp, go, go, go," Mitch yelled as he struggled to yank the rifle back and switch out mags.

The gap between Sam and them had widened by a large margin. She could hear bullets pinging off their truck, or the puffs of concrete as they hit around them. Anne swerved hard left to avoid a wreck. She was barely aware of Mitch hooting beside her, and of Nancy returning fire.

Anne saw Sam make another sharp turn. Then he and Ruth's SUV briefly became airborne as they hit the highest point of the bridge.

"Come on, Anne, they're gaining on us," Nancy yelled.

Tears streamed down the young woman's face as she swerved to miss the same wreck Sam had. The tires chirped and smoked. The truck tilted up. Mitch's steady voice talked her into keeping them upright as he scrambled to belt himself back in. The crest of the bridge was upon them. Anne felt them go airborne, not able to see what lay before her for a moment. Then the front end tilted, crashing down a second before the back end. The seat belt cut into her, she couldn't breathe. A large wreck lay before them. They were going to hit it.

At the last moment, Anne jerked the wheel. Time seemed to slow as the driver's side ricocheted off the edge of the wreck. Distorted screams filled the truck, over the crunch and shriek of tearing metal as they pin-balled back and forth between the concrete bridge side, and the wrecks.

CHAPTER TWELVE

The gunner came back as I was losing my patience. Mom and kids refused to move out to another house, and the colonel had long since given up trying to argue with her. My poor cats spent the greater part of the day hiding from the shits, and I spent mine having to disrupt my war preparations to stop the kids' destruction. My last nerve snapped when the children raided the food supplies yet again. They opened cans carelessly, spoiling what was inside, eating very little, if any of it. After that episode, I gathered all the edibles, and removed every bit of it from the house. I made sure no one followed me, or saw where I hid my supplies. They could all starve if they were too lazy to fend for themselves.

The two soldiers waved me over to join them, more I think, to keep me from strangling the brats than because they wanted my help. "I swear if that bitch doesn't do something about her kids . . . "

"That doesn't matter."

"It is to me. My cats aren't play toys to be tormented. The stress alone is making Pepper sicker."

"Ma'am, do you want to help us take care of those bikers, or what?"

"Fine, but if I come back and discover my cats have been harmed, then I'll find a zombie and feed the little shits to it myself. Where are they?"

"Not at the club. They had been there, I could tell from the mess they left behind. At one point, it seems they took over the distillery you mentioned. That's not the worst of it." He used condiments to show the layout of where everything was, as he spoke. "From what I could tell, they've taken over all the houses lining this road. All our stolen hardware and vehicles are there. There's a cluster of dwellings."

"I know the area. There're docks behind them."

He narrowed his eyes at me. "Sounds travel over water."

"Not if we start early and go slow enough we might as well be paddling. I bet they won't think anyone's dumb enough to try sneaking up on them like that. But, it's just a thought. I'm bowing to your expertise."

"Getting stuck in pluff mud and being used as target practice is not my idea of fun," the gunner reminds me.

"I've heard skis are an excellent solution."

"As in water skis?" Speary squinted his eyes at me.

"Yeah, I haven't had a chance to test the theory out yet. But I will, once I actually find some."

"Please don't stand so close to me. I'm afraid your insanity could be contagious," he retorted.

Downing made a loose plan. He was more concerned with getting back the military stuff. Freeing Rhondal, along with the others who had been kidnapped, was a secondary mission. I figured they'd be lucky to be alive and unharmed.

The men loaded up a boat as I replaced the parts I had taken out, and got it ready. Our tasks became more difficult because we had to stop and kill zombies walking out of the water. It would be noon before long, and the humid day already had us soaked in sweat.

"If only I could be guaranteed no zoms lurked below, I'd so jump in."

"Hoo-ah!" Speary called, dumping a bucket of creek water over my head, then slapping my back hard enough to send me stumbling forward a few steps.

"Gah!" turned out the best response I could

muster as I blinked water out of my eyes and used a pillion to stay upright.

Speary re-filled the bucket, dumped it over himself, then repeated the process and handed it off to Downing. Great, now I was wet yet still not cooled off enough. I lowered my pack into the boat, secured my swords and guns, and climbed down the ladder for the last time.

I fired the engine up. The two men came aboard, which sent us rocking and bumping against the pillions. They cast off the lines, gently pushing us away from the dock. I reversed into the creek, turned, and eased us forward. I navigated out of the creek into the main waterway. We could increase the boat's speed for the first half of our journey. The men had binocs out, constantly scanning the banks to either side. Occasionally, they commented in military speak to each other.

At Wadmalaw Point, I reduced to an idle. Speary tossed out the anchor as I cut the engine. We bobbed peacefully as the men hauled up water in a bucket. They leaned so their upper bodies hung over the gunwale,and poured the liquid over each other to cool off. They did the same for me. We reapplied sunscreen. I fixed my old floppy hat back on my head to their amusement. We sat down to eat and replenish our fluids.

I loved the color black but was re-thinking my choice in the harsh sun, even under the small canopy. Never mind that I would change opinions when night came. I fell into a stupor with the gentle rocking, the heat, the occasional breeze. We all must have, for I awoke startled, confused, heart pounding, and sensing violent rocking.

"Wake up, and get us out of here!" Downing bellowed to me.

Without stopping to think of consequences, I gave Speary a hearty shove and snatched my hands back before his ingrained training tried breaking them at the rude awakening

"Speary!" Downing barked, "They're climbing the anchor rope."

Oh, hell no! The port side dipped as waterlogged, rotting hands gripped the edge. Don't flood the engine, stupid! Pinged in my brain. I probably would have if I hadn't been trying to fight off zoms at the same time. The engine roared to life while the propeller made a high-pitched noise before settling back into its rhythm. Viscera and body parts landed on me. I couldn't help it. I puked right on a zom's head.

"Screw the anchor. Cut it loose!" I screamed, and used a hunting knife to play a modified version of whack-a-mole, water edition.

If they didn't pull the boat down, they'd toss us out. I don't normally get sea-sick, but I made an exception this time.

"Go! Go! Go!" Downing yelled. "Anchor's away!"

I opened full throttle. Screw being heard by roving bikers on land as the water conducted our noise over it. The engine roared with the effort, then we took off with a mighty jerk, flinging us all back against our seats hard. I had to immediately throttle back to half speed, as our unwanted company created enough drag to potentially stress and crack the motor. The men continued working on the remaining zoms, as I plowed down the Wadmalaw River.

This monitoring of the men and the waterway brought on an immediate migraine. Or it was the culmination of too much sun as well. I slowed back to idle when Downing signaled the all clear.

"Aspirin, before my eyes exploded and my brains leak out," slipped in a whimper from my lips. I jammed my curved thumbs into my upper orbital sockets, trying to massage the nerves.

Squinting against the pain, I let Speary haul me out of the seat, and into his. He took over pilot duties. Downing rummaged through my pack, found my careful horde of drugs, some rags, and water. I downed the pills and sipped the water, willing myself not to puke. He dipped the scraps of cloth in the river and laid them, dripping, over the back of my neck.

The only noise was the rustling of paper, clothes, and the gentle swish of water.

"I'm pretty sure we passed the off shoot we needed," Speary eventually said.

"Doesn't matter, there are two half coves beside each other that'll get us there," I replied, eyes closed.

Downing re-wet and replaced the rags. I'm not sure if he heard my whispered thanks.

CHAPTER THIRTEEN

*"Ease up on the gas. Apply pressure on the
brakes."*

The car jerked to a sudden stop.

*"Not that much pressure," her dad shouted as he
braced his hands against the dash. "You trying to give
your old man whiplash?"*

"Sorry, Dad," Anne apologized.

*"Try again, carefully. You don't want to be
causing a wreck," He instructed her.*

*The words echoed, "You don't want to cause a
wreck, a wreck, a wreck. . ."*

*"Daddy?" came out pitiful and little girlish. "I
hurt so bad. What happened to the truck? Did we run out
of gas?"*

*"No, sweetie, the truck decided to take a nap, it
didn't run out of gas, we wrecked. Bad news, you're never
driving again, and the worse news, the bad men are still
coming for us. Coming for us, coming for us. . ."*

Gunshots sounded over the ting of cooling metal.
Anne heard her name called, but not by her father. A
whimper of pain slipped past her lips. She didn't think
there was a spot on her body that didn't ache. For a
moment, Anne didn't remember where she was, or why.
Then it all came rushing back with the next wave of
gunshots.

"Anne! Mitch! Nancy! Anyone?" Sam's voice
called out. "Keep firing, Ruth."

The young woman groaned again, forcing her
eyes open. A spiderweb of cracks filled the windshield
before her. The rest of her view was blocked by the hood,

imitating the Great Pyramid of Giza.

"Joan? Dad?" Anne couldn't help but call out for her father, then abruptly stopped.

"Yo, Adam, Shane. Get over there and see if they're alive. Kill the man and the old woman, we don't need them."

Panic flared through her, and she tried to move, but sharp pains forced her to abruptly stop.

"Joan?" she tried again, fear tinging her word.

Another burst of semi-auto fire came off to her left, and Sam's voice seemed closer.

"Mitch? Nancy? Guys? If you're alive in there, I need you to answer. We gotta get you out and away from here. We've got bad company."

Slowly, Anne turned her head, blinking her eyelids. A sticky film wanted to keep them glued together. She raised a shaky hand, and it came away bloody. The interior of the car reeked of blood and other scents she didn't want to contemplate.

"Joan," she tried, calling her sister's name again to no results.

Anxiety mounting inside, her eyes flicked to the rear-view mirror, hanging crooked. The image of two people were there, but her gaze refused to settle on any one spot. A hand slapped down on the window frame, forcing a cry of fear from her.

"Hey there, little lady. It's me, Sam. We gotta go. Ruth can't hold the gang off too much longer."

He paused to swivel and poked the rifle over the hoods of nearby wrecks. He shot off several bursts, and by the cries that came back knew he had hit a few of the gang members.

"Come on, wakey, wakey," The older man yanked on the driver's side door as a hail of return fire peppered the area around them.

"Pop the buckle, honey." Sam talked her into

releasing the seatbelt.

He caught her as she tumbled out of the high car and gently set her down. Anne cried, the hot concrete burning her skin even through her thick jeans. Sam crawled inside the truck. The trading of gunfire continued.

Joan, she thought, *I have to get her out.* Despite her aching body, Anne hauled herself into a crouch. Backpacks came tumbling out, followed by weapons, and Mitch. A cut along the right side of his face poured blood, and bits of glass from the passenger window twinkled all over him.

"Come on, girl, don't just sit there! Grab what you can and head to Ruth," he barked out.

"Joan," Anne screamed, trying to be heard over the fighting.

She lunged upward, only to be sharply pulled back down by Mitch.

"You trying to be used as target practice?" he demanded angrily. "How's it going, Sam?" The bearded man grabbed a rifle off the pavement and shot in the direction of the enemy. Heavy return fire answered.

"I can't feel my arms or legs," Nancy screamed. "Oh, God, Sam. I can't feel them."

"Shit," Mitch muttered while trading gunfire.

"We gotta go, people. Come on," Ruth yelled as she ran to them, hunched over to present less of a target.

Inside the truck, Nancy continued to wail.

"Mitch, I need you," Sam called.

The middle-aged man let go of Anne and crawled inside the truck. The vehicle appeared smashed between the concrete wall of the bridge on the right, and previous wrecks on the left. The only way in or out was by the driver's side door. A temporary lull in shooting from Ruth and the gang meant Anne could hear the conversation inside the truck.

"Why can't I feel my arms and legs? Why?"

Nancy kept sobbing, over and over.

"Maybe if we . . ." Sam began.

"We need to brace her neck and back. If we move her, we could cause more damage," Mitch replied.

"Help me, please. You have to help me," the older woman pitifully moaned.

The rest of her words were drowned out by the sound of engines. Ruth risked a quick look over the hoods of the cars and trucks she hid behind. The enemy took the chance to drive to them.

"We gotta do something quick," Ruth called out to the men. "The enemy is coming closer."

"Joan," Anne called frantically. She crawled to the running board and used it and the seat to haul herself back to a crouch.

"Shit," Mitch said, the rest of his words lost to the sound of automatic gunfire.

Anne watched as he and Sam tried to cram themselves into the footwells. Her hands flew to her ears to block the noise. "My sister," the young woman shouted. "You can't leave her." She accused the men.

"Move, damn it," Mitch vehemently bellowed.

The uncharacteristic angry tone directed at her gave her pause. Anne flinched, and Mitch took the opportunity to ungracefully flop out of the truck.

"Move, move, move," he yelled, while he scrambled on hands and knees.

A short break came in the gunfire, which Sam took as an opportunity to also scramble out of the front of the truck. Both men crawled the few feet over to Ruth, grabbing rifles.

Anne used the chaos to haul herself inside the truck. Her eyes once more refused to focus on the spot Joan occupied.

"Damn it! Grab her, she doesn't need to see that." Sam shouted.

"JOAN," Anne screamed in despair.

"You assholes think you can get by us without paying the toll?" An enraged voice yelled at the small party. "You think you can just assault our people and kill them? You're gonna pay for it."

"Anne," Nancy cried. "Don't let them leave me here. Tell them I don't care what they. . ."

Her words abruptly cut off as her face blew outwards. Blood, bone, and brain splattered over the interior of the truck. Some of it landed on Anne, who let out a shrill scream of horror. Suddenly, she zipped backward out of the truck. Her hands scrambled for purchase on the front seats, the dash, the wheel, anything within reach.

A sharp ringing assailed her ears as a rifle went off next to her. A hard, male body held her tightly .

"Let me go! I have to get Joan!" Anne struggled even as they dragged her away from her sister.

"Joan. Jooooaaaaannnn!"

Hard faced men, bristling with rifles, swarmed over the top of the massive wreck. Some of them paused long enough to shoot inside the truck. The interior lit up from muzzle flashes.

Tears and snot streamed down Anne's face as Mitch dragged her, at a stumbling run, to Ruth and Sam's SUV. She didn't remember getting in, or what the remaining group shouted at her. The young woman fought the arms and hands trying to keep her inside the moving vehicle.

CHAPTER FOURTEEN

Night would be falling in a few hours, and the men wanted to be in place by then. We had spent a few hours land side, hiding out in a shed, grabbing quick naps. Now headache free, we were back on the water, and close to the shoreline. We slowly motored up the river past the back of houses. The guys wedged themselves as flat as possible in the bottom of the vessel, only letting their eyes show above the gunwales. Speary was the first to spot which dwellings the bikers had appropriated. We continued past.

"At least three houses seem to be in active use, minimal guards river side," he reported. The sounds of barking and baying floated to us, along with wild laughter, cheers, screams, and the occasional gunshot.

We continued our slow putter upstream. I docked half a mile past the target. We had to hurry, in case the bikers decided to do a sweep of the area. Speary would be on his own while Downing and I made our way back downstream to another docking point.

Except for the zoms which had attacked us when anchored, we didn't spot any others. The lack didn't sit well. I took up a hunting rifle with a scope, slowly scanning the area as Downing helped Speary gear up. We waited until he made it off the dock and sprinted toward the abandoned house.

"Alpha Two to team leader, cover achieved."

"Team leader to Alpha Two, acknowledged. Good hunting," Downing replied through the throat mic.

The men had given me an extra com set and shown me how to use it.

Downing and I shoved off, puttering back past our target in the advancing dusk. Our slow speed kept engine noise and wake at a minimum. It gave the gunner time to work his way closer to the biker's base and deal with any perimeter surprises they might have rigged. He also intended to set a diversion. This sucked, it meant my imagination, and nerves had longer to run away with me. I tried to keep them at bay by concentrating on the waterway. Spotting floating debris became harder because we ran without lights. Downing scanned the far bank with his nighttime binocs. The closer we got to our destination point, the more anxiety I felt.

By the time Downing guided me to our drop point, my nerves had overtaken me. The docking could only be described as a disaster.

"Crashing and sinking us is not part of the plan. Calm down. Slow, deep breaths in and out. You're going to get us killed. Or yourself," Downing said.

"Excuse me. I think I'm having a heart attack from fear."

"It's called a panic attack. Want me to slap it out of you?" he casually asked.

It took a moment to answer. "Maybe, I don't know. Lemme get back to you on that." I wasn't sure if I wanted to pass out, throw up, or pee myself. Maybe if I just did all three, I'd feel better. "Are you sure about this? I mean. What if they kill you before we get there? Or Speary?"

"Now you're having doubts?"

"Well yeah, you both know you're worth like, I dunno, ten of me."

Downing clapped me on the shoulder. "Breathe, and don't accidentally shoot me."

"Crap, we're doomed." He ignored my words as he finished gearing up, and helped me when my shaking hands interfered.

"Move out, civvie," Downing ordered me, "follow my lead."

I nodded, struggling to get control of myself. This wasn't a game, but I might have to start deluding myself into thinking it was so I didn't freeze in terror. The colonel turned back to me, hand raised. Before I could formulate a question, he liberally smeared pluff mud on my face. I stood dumbfounded, snapped out of panicking.

"Now, we're ready. Team Leader to Alpha Two, landing completed. Moving toward target now."

"Copy that, Alpha Two, ten minutes out."

"I just. . . not even right." He ignored my outraged splutter as he motioned for us to start moving.

From here, we would walk. I followed the colonel, reminding myself to keep my finger off the trigger. Didn't want to be the movie fuck up, or the chick who got killed by stupidity. I had an uncontrollable urge to chatter. I tried to keep radio silence, but the closer we got, the harder it became.

"Um . . . what if they have night vision goggles and scopes?"

"They do. It's part of our kits."

I nearly shit myself. I stopped dead. "What?! That's supposed to reassure me?"

Downing came back to me. "There's only a handful of nigh vision goggles. If the enemy's smart, they'll give the hardware to whoever is manning the roadblocks. Remember what I told you."

"I need to puke now."

"Buck up, civvie. Puke, and walk. We can't let Ryan down, or we will lose him."

I whimpered, but forced myself to stumble forward. Okay, okay, so it seemed more like Downing dragged me forward while searching for traps. After a few feet, it got old. My body started functioning on its own, mimicking his hunched over posture. The traps we came across appeared simple, and easily avoided. *Too easy*, I thought, as we kneeled in the high grass and weeds. We crawled the last hundred yards or so. I distracted myself with the lovely round hump his ass made. Hey, whatever works, right? We came to the furthest empty house which delineated the bikers' territory. Across the broad expanse of what had once been manicured lawn sat another house. Candles or oil lamps made flickering lights into shadows that danced across the windows. The barking grew much louder, more aggressive sounding.

"Great. I'm allergic to dogs. Please don't be zombie dogs," I whispered.

"Radio silence," I was sternly reminded. "Alpha Two, we're in position."

"Copy Team Lead. Standing by."

"On my signal."

My anxiety reached all new levels that not even my incessant slapping at mosquitoes could overcome. I was in grave danger of passing out. Downing tapped me on the shoulder, I rose to a crouch. Another tap, we ran the last few feet to the empty house, hunched over. The lack of guards seriously un-nerved me. I took out the pop bottles filled with gasoline. I could tell the gas had started eating its way through. The colonel steadied his suppressed rifle, taking aim at the waterside guard fifty yards away. The sounds of cicadas and frogs covered. the slight noise it made. I splashed the liquid against the house. I had a bag full of the things. I forced myself to count out each bottle.

I lite a rag on fire, placed it on the gas trail, and waited for the flames to start. They raced up the house, catching hold of the overgrown grass. Shit, I didn't think it was that dry. I followed the path of the flame to the front of the house, another bottle ready. I could hear yelling. I used the flames to catch another Molotov Cocktail on fire, then tossed it onto the porch before I sprinted to a clump of trees.

I checked briefly, before running toward a darkened bulk. The sound of gunfire followed in my wake. "Fuckfuckfuckfuck."

I nearly bashed myself unconscious on a tree, but managed to avoid it by falling to the side and sliding on the ground. Another handy tree stopped me, adding to my growing collection of bruises. I knelt, panting, watching a group of armed men with hysterical dogs on leashes go by. The group wanted to head to the engulfed house. The dogs desperately lunged in my direction. I couldn't seem to get my fear of the slathering beasts under control, as I slipped from tree to tree. That was bad. I would definitely get killed this way. If it hadn't been for the smell of decay, and the large bulks of horses I nearly stepped in, I might have continued to panic.

"You bastards." There was a small stable facing the first occupied house.

I went in. Thankfully, no nasties waited for me. I bolted the doors as best I could except for one. By this time, half of the men had split up. Some checked on the fire, the others followed the dogs who barreled toward my shelter in a pack.

The growing conflagration helped to outline the threats. I pulled the pin on a grenade and lobbed it. I ducked just in time to miss a face full of bloody bits. I popped up, sighted through the night scope and fired. I kept pumping rounds in a line across the lurching shapes until I was out of ammo and had to lock a new mag in. I crawled out of the stables in a hail of flying splinters, and bullets from return shots delivered by the first half of the group. Some of the shots came uncomfortably close..

"Alpha One, coming out front with hostages. Hold fire."

"Negative, too many hostiles left! You're about to be Bar-B-Que." I quickly dumped some gas filled bottles and used a lighter to set them burning., I zig zagged between trees away from the soon-to-be-flaming stables. More gunfire and splinters followed me.

The small copse loomed before me. I crashed into a tree to stop my forward momentum, and use it as cover.

Wait for it, I sternly told myself. I half-leaned out from behind the tree, and stitched another line of gunfire across the dark, moving shapes. I then did the zig zag thing again, except across open lawn, heading for the side of the house the colonel infiltrated.

A sudden pain bloomed in my side, only briefly replaced with the pain of kissing the ground. I couldn't breathe! Moaning brought me out of unconsciousness. I did a credible imitation of a gasping fish until I wheezed in. My uncooperative limbs flailed about, as I tried to turn over. I managed to sit up, realizing the sounds were me. *Shit! Was this what it feels like to be a zombie?* Nope, I was alive, the tac vest taking the hit.

"I enjoy breathing without cracked ribs," I groaned, as I untangled myself from the rifle's cross-body strap and got it resettled properly.

Were the bright, flashing lights a concussion or gunfire? Downing met me as I hauled myself upright, needing every pain-filled breath for air, and not cussing. He had several women with him, filthy and shell-shocked.

"Move, move, move!" he bellowed to me.

At least I think that's what he said, as a carillon now occupied the spot my eardrums should have been.

I staggered after him. This whole episode was gonna leave marks, and not the good kind. We gained the tree line again, hustling along to the next house.

"What about the women?" I gasped and gestured to them, doubled over in pain when he stopped. Only two still followed us. The rest freaked out and ran.

"Liabilities," with a negative head shake.

I figured he meant they were on their own while

we took care of business. I had been so panic stricken I didn't realize gunfire had been raging for a while. It didn't take long to reach the next house. Downing was a move it or get-left-behind kind of guy.

He provided cover fire while I splashed the remaining bottles of gas liberally over the back porch before setting it alight. I paused to suck heated air into my lungs via my mouth, my ribs a protesting chorus. Great, I'm now a member of mouth breathers R us.

"Fire two burning; moving out." I didn't wait for a reply. I couldn't hear it anyway.

Ever tried to talk underwater? That's what everything sounded like: heavily muffled. I gained the tree line at the back of the house. Downing was gone, headed to the rendezvous point with Speary. I wasn't sure if they'd wait for me or not. Still, I had to slow down, or I'd pass out. As I leaned panting against a trunk, rifle pointed toward my feet, I noticed fast movement. It resolved into the surviving members of the dog pack.

"Why me? More mental trauma. Now I really hate dogs!"

The single shot I could get off took out one of the animals. I was bowled over by the two remaining dogs leaping at me from both sides. Only my old armored biker outfit and tac vest saved me. We tumbled in a nasty mess. Anger replaced fear as my backpack jabbed into my spine. It gave me the impetus I needed to ignore the weight and the pain, and stand. Claws and teeth scrabbled on the body armor, trying to take me back down. An old friend's advice flashed through my thoughts. I grabbed the ears of one dog and slammed it onto the ground. Before it could move, I stomped down on its face, putting most of my weight on the foot while I dealt with the other animal. I ripped my knife out of the thigh sheaf as the remaining dog leaped up at me. I slashed upwards, going from the breast to the throat. Hot blood sprayed over me. The dog beneath my boot struggled, claws digging into the ground as it tried to pull out from underneath me. The rifle swung from its cross-body strap. I snatched it up and finished off the remaining dog.

"Sorry, puppies," I whispered, gulped air, ribs screamed. I could feel a warm wetness running down my legs.

"Damn it. Every fucking time. Oh, spike collars," I took them off, and happily strapped them around my exposed neck.

Yes, I have issues . . . In fact, my issues have subscriptions to their own issues

A quick gun and pack check, then I moved on. I was pissed off now. "Be Alice, be Selene, be Violet." I chanted as I maneuvered toward the meeting spot.

"Be Aeon Flux, wait, scratch that, wrong choice," I whispered to myself.

My hearing was coming back by degrees. I heard bikes growling, guns chattering, and an explosion shook the air. I hoped this meant the enemy was engaged, and wouldn't notice me or where I was headed.

I shot out the back picture windows of my next target, the third house. I stepped from the cover of marsh and trees and hurried to the edge of the deck. I paused only long enough to pull two grenades out of the backpack. I armed and lobbed them through the windows I had just shot out. I saw shapes shuffling toward me, moaning.

"Unfuckingbelievable! An entire gang of bikers, and the damn zombies head for me. I swear I've got an invisible magnet attached to me that calls out to them. I really need to get it removed."

The nasty biters get closer while I dropped flat on the ground as the side of the house blew out. I barely had time to shield my head with my arms as shrapnel flew. I felt stuff land on me, and I made no effort to hide my grunts of pain. I peeked an eye open. Smoke roiled out over the area. The zombies no longer shuffled. Most had been shredded by flying debris. A few still managed to drag themselves close. They reached hands out to grab my boots as I turned my rifle on them and blasted heads until the mag ran out.

The carillon was back full force. I wouldn't be able to hear who, or what was sneaking up on me. I concentrated on breathing as I locked a new mag in place with shaking hands. I got another grenade out.

"You can do this, superstar," I babbled, forcing myself to rise. The condition of my ribs held me to a fast walk. A bunch of the enemy still needed annihilation. I headed to the primary fight. "Yup, I'm now officially, certifiably insane."

Angry wasps zipped past my head. Shit! I ducked behind another tree, letting the rifle swing on its strap. I armed the grenade still in my left hand. My plan didn't include blowing myself up from stupidity. I turned sideways, stepped out, and lobbed death.

I ducked back behind the tree as white-hot pain scored my arm, "Shit, the bastard hit me. Oh fuck, it hurts."

Tears streamed down my face as I sank to my knees, clutching my wounded arm. I wasn't aware of the shrapnel flying past me, embedded in the surrounding trees. A fireball rose into the air, as something flammable must've been nearby. A wash of super-heated air followed. I dug in a pants pocket for a rag, pulled it out, and clumsily tied it around the wound.

"Please don't let zombie gore get it in," I whimpered, as I was covered in nasty stuff.

Before me was a whole wide-open yard to cross. I wasn't looking forward to it. Hell, I wish I had hearing instead of the constant ringing.

"Mawp, mawp, mawp." Nope, still mostly deaf.

I peered around the tree I sat behind, light from the flames providing medium visibility. A truck sat on the far side of the clearing, near another line of trees. My left arm and hand didn't want to obey my brain's commands to shut up about being hurt. I got the rifle ready. I was about to do a lot of bucking up, buttercup, when I would have to shoot. I forced myself to stand, and jog to the vehicle.

The driver's door opened, but nothing dangled from the ignition. "Of course there'd be no keys. Can't a gal catch a break?"

I prepared to move into the trees that lined the long driveway when I spotted headlights and ducked down as bikers roared past. They skidded to a stop.

My hearing was coming back by degrees, but not enough for me to make out what they said. If their faces and gestures were any indications, they were pissed. Next, I saw twin headlights approach., A Humvee passed while I peeked over the hood. The occupant shot at the enemy. Silently, I cheered. At least one of the military men retrieved some of their stuff.

He was gonna need help, as bikers chased behind, and the ones in front returned fire. This was really, really going to hurt. I propped the rifle on the truck's hood, lined up body shots through the night scope, and began shooting. I had to occasionally duck as return fire came my way. I was soon going to be shit out of luck. Those remaining riders who had avoided the spilled bikers in the lead came up fast. Of course, that was when the mag clicked empty.

"I've got to learn to keep count while being shot at," I grumbled, as I dropped on the ground to position my back against the tire. It took me a few fumbling tries to drop the spent mag out and lock in a new one. I stood up again, and helped whoever drove the Humvee finish off the few surviving bikers.

# # #

Ryan helped me disinfect and stitch up my gunshot wound. Okay, it would be more accurate to say he threatened to really cause me pain if I didn't hold still and quit squirming around. Hey, that shit hurts when you don't have numbing medicine. The gunner was also able to determine I had severely cracked ribs.

Downing came up to us—not even a hi or a thanks. "We haven't found all the prisoners. We need to search for them. How much longer will you be?"

"Thanks for helping. Why, you're welcome." The sarcasm slipped out. "I'm tired and hurt. I'm going home to see what those brats have done to the place. You have Ryan, what do you need me for?"

I got The Glare. "One of my own is still out there. We don't know how many zombies continue to roam around, and some of the enemy escaped. I will not let them have the chance to re-group, and return to their base. Not with all the military hardware and vehicles they still have access to . . ."

"Um, injured here."

"This is not a request, nor an option. If you want to act like some hot-shot military wanna-be, then you better be prepared to nut up when the time comes."

I was unable to form words. I don't think I've ever thought that. I'm more the sneak around and sabotage type. Or the run while you still can. The whole go in guns blazing we just did was my last resort effort. Besides, did he just forget all the help I gave them to flush the enemy out?

Ryan acted as if he couldn't hear as he took care of his own minor wounds. Before I could protest, Downing kept talking.

"The mission isn't completed. You will return to help," he emphasized, "or I will confiscate all military hardware you have. Including those grenades you somehow illegally obtained."

Since being a bitch got me nowhere, I decided to turn asshole.

"Did I not just help you at great, personal expense to myself? Did I not follow your orders? Did I not help you? What. The. Fuck."

Downing looked ready to rip heads off and shit down them. Pissing contests, great fun, another thing I try to avoid.

"You do not want to tangle with me, civvie, or the only hell to pay will be the shit storm that's about to come down on your head. You do NOT fuck with the U.S. Military," he spat. "We move out in fifteen minutes. Do you understand?"

"Yes, sir," came out of my mouth, heavy with sarcasm, along with a one fingered salute. Monkeys flying out of his ass would happen before he chilled out.

"Fifteen minutes," Downing reiterated before he stalked back to the Humvee, presumably to reload, or do whatever it was he had too.

"I just want to curl up with the cats, and sleep forever," I grumbled to myself. "I'm completely unneeded."

"Forever sounds a lot like dead in your context," Speary commented, causing me to jump.

"As long as I don't come back a zombie, I'll count it as a win."

The gunner shook his head as his colonel turned to us.

# # #

We drove back to the site without any further complications. The houses still burned, fully engulfed in flames. To me it seemed the battle had been longer, but time's funny that way I guess. The abandoned house which had been used for the main club of the gang yielded a treasure trove: everything from guns to ammo, and food to drink. We also found survivors—women who had been

147

kidnapped, and forced to be the night's entertainment. There were even a few children, held hostage to make their parents compliant with their captors' wishes. It was from the adults we learned the house I had tossed grenades inside was the main prison for the hostages. Uh-oh. Trouble apparently decided to piss on me a little more.

I watched Downing hustle toward the ruins, anxious to see if anyone had escaped, even though he knew better. Ryan guarded his flank. I tried to get comfortable in the Humvee and take a nap.

Ryan woke me briefly when the men got back to the truck. No survivors made it in the bombed house, but a shed out back yielded the female military member, and a few other women. Rhondel was in a far worse shape compared to the others. The male members of her unit decided to stay and guard the remaining house with its valuable supplies.

I didn't remember much of the ride home. Only of Ryan heaving me in a truck looted from the former bikers so we could get everyone back. I think I recall mentioning the plans we needed to do, and him telling me to shut my brain off already. I barely made it back to my home before I passed out from exhaustion. It seemed a fortuitous state considering the mischief that awaited me from the brats when I awoke the next morning.

The house was a smelly mess, making me believe a pack of zombies had torn through the place. But, no, it was just two grade school kids. They had tracked mud and shit inside, broken trinkets, scribbled on walls. That was all fixable. What angered me the most, was what they did outside the master bedroom door. The little shits had tried getting inside. When my traps worked, one or both had decided to defecate outside the door. The excruciating pain of my wounds took a backseat to my wrath. Those same pains had been the only thing that kept ing me from chasing the brats down and strangling them. I spent most of the next day comforting my traumatized cats.

CHAPTER FIFTEEN

The refugee camp stunk, of unwashed bodies, garbage, and over-flowing latrines. The Resicks, along with Mitch and Anne, had only been there for half-a-day, and already they wondered where else they could go that would be safe.

"This isn't what I was expecting. I thought there'd be a bit more room." Sam gazed around glumly.

"We can't stay here. Too many people. It's only a matter of time before sickness breaks out," Ruth stated.

"They took our supplies, the ones Mitch didn't help us conceal—even the gas. Where is he? Or Anne?"

"I think he went to find out if there are plans for more permanent housing, and when," Ruth answered her husband's question. She glanced about the crowded parking lot as she continued repacking their backpack. "She's lost in a fog of grief, and depression. I wish I knew how to help her."

"So do I." He idly picked up crumpled clothes, smoothing them out and folding them smaller.

After they had almost finished their chore, Mitch showed up. He appeared agitated.

"We need to talk." He kept his head down, but his eyes shifted constantly from side to side. "Now, please."

"Sure," Ruth replied.

"What's so important?" Sam asked.

Before he could say more, a military woman with a bullhorn called for everyone's attention. Survivors slowly stopped what they were doing to listen.

"Attention. May I please have your attention. Will all survivors make their way to either the gymnasium, or the auditorium, please. We have an important announcement to make."

She paused a moment, then repeated herself. Many people approached, but she only shook her head and gestured toward the building behind her.

"We should probably . . ." Sam began.

"No," Mitch replied, "I don't fancy being stuck inside with a group of nervous people."

"I'll go," Ruth stated, handing the bags over to Sam.

Before either man could protest, she briskly walked through the front doors. Mrs. Resick let the crowd carry her along. She slipped to one side of the gym doors, so as not to be trapped inside with the sweltering mass of humanity. For one brief moment, she thought she spotted Anne, before her view became blocked.

# # #

Anne shifted her weight from one foot to the other. She was crammed against the side of the bleachers. The mood inside was anxious. She had tried looking around for the Resicks, or even Mitch, but gave up as more and more people crowded inside. Voices rose in a deafening babble, the heat rose, causing sweat to pour off everyone. She was beginning to think she had made a mistake in following the crowd when the squeal of a bullhorn cut through the noise. Slowly, the gym fell silent.

"Folks, I'm going to make this quick, because it's hot in here, and we don't want anyone passing out from the heat. The United States Government has issued a nationwide mandate asking for all survival centers to be moved closer to the interior of the country. This is to consolidate food distribution, and security."

Voices rose at the announcement, and it took several moments before the man speaking could resume.

"All military, police, and medical personnel are being re-called. Those who choose to stay do so of their own accord, and at their own risk. I repeat, re-location is not mandatory, but those who stay behind will be responsible for their own well-being . . ."

A loud roar of voices drowned out the rest of his words, and even with the bullhorn he couldn't be heard. Suddenly, an airhorn went off several times. Most of the people clapped hands over their ears until the shouting died down.

"If I may have your attention again?" the military man called out.

Slowly, order returned. Anne bit her lip, shaken out of her haze. She felt light-headed, and a queer sensation fluttered in her chest.

"We will begin evacuations in two hours. Each person is allowed only one carry on and one backpack or purse. They must be able to fit either under an airplane seat, or in the overhead bin. Buses will be waiting outside to ferry you to the main airport. Thank you. That is all."

Shouting broke out, the mood quickly turned sour. Anne felt as if she couldn't breathe.

"I can't breathe!" she yelled, pushing at people in an effort to get through the crowd.

"Hey! Watch it!"

"Quit shoving and wait your turn!"

Several people angrily yelled at her. A few in the crowd noticed the look of distress on her face. They reached hands and arms out to help her. She was half-unconscious from the heat and anxiety before the kindness of strangers managed to get her outside.

Anne slowly came around to find herself lying on the ground. Two teenagers crouched nearby, and she could see a few younger kids near her feet. They helped her sit up, and the girl passed her a dented water bottle. Gratefully, Anne took the bottle and sipped. The water inside was warm, but she didn't care.

"Did you get separated from your parents?" one

of the kids, a girl who looked to be six, asked.

The question caused a fresh spurt of pain. "I came with a group. I don't know where they are," she answered instead.

"I hope y'all have a spot to meet at. It won't be easy finding them in the crowds," the teenage boy replied.

"Yes, we do," she simply replied. "Thank you, for helping me out of the gym, and for the water." She held the bottle out to the girl, not wanting to drink all of their water.

"You talk funny," the little girl noted. "Did you come on vacation and get stuck?"

"Emily!" the little girl was scolded. "Be polite. Sorry. I'm Dawn. This is my brother Jeff, my little sister Amy, and my other little brother, Taylor. We're the Willetts."

"Nice to meet you, I'm Anne."

The two girls tentatively smiled at each other.

"Don't mind Emily," Jeff said. "We lost our parents, too. We came over from Georgia to visit relatives and got stuck here."

"My father died trying to rescue my sister and me. She didn't make it."

"Your mom alive around here?" Jeff inquired.

Anne shook her head negatively. "No, my dad lived down here with his girlfriend. My mom and he have been divorced for a long time. I don't know what happened to her."

"Wow, so, you're what," Jeff persisted, "planning on finding your dad's girlfriend?"

"Jeff!" Dawn hissed at him, with a sharp poke to his side.

"I, I guess so. I don't . . . I thought the refugee centers would be better than this."

"So did we," Dawn rolled her eyes. "We don't know if any of our aunts, uncles, and cousins are left alive back home, or we would've tried going back."

Anne carefully stood, and they stared at each other for a moment. She didn't know why, but the words just popped out. "If you're not planning on trying to go home, or joining the other survivors, you can come and meet my group. They're nice. It's just an older couple and a guy. We, we lost a few people recently."

Brother and sister seemed to have some sort of silent communication with each other.

"I take it you're planning on staying behind then?" Jeff probed.

It hadn't originally been her intention. She wasn't even sure how she felt about trying to find her dad's girlfriend. Plus, her feelings about the announcement were mixed.

"I haven't made my mind up yet," was what she did say.

"Oh. Well, let's go find your group then."

Anne and her new friends wended their way outside. It took a few moments before she found the Resicks, and Mitch. As she came up to them, a small family stopped beside her traveling companions. Anne and her new acquaintances stood off to one side, silently observing, and listening in. The family called out greetings, which were returned. Mitch made introductions.

"Sam and Ruth Resick. Gary and Susan Heartsman, and their children: Chris, Brian, and Jennifer." Mitch continued. "The Heartsman's live one island over, called Wadamalaw?"

Amused grins came from the family, as Gary spoke. "No middle A, folks. Wad-ma-law," he carefully pronounced.

He noticed Ruth glancing behind them, at the crowd of people frantically milling about. The noise of people talking and shouting became momentarily overshadowed by the sound of a fleet of school buses pulling up in a line.

"I wouldn't worry about all that. Besides, y'all don't wanna be caught up in that mess. My eldest son, he's inside with the rest of the troops. Word came from the higher ups to evacuate the islands. They're gonna tell folks to get on the buses. The plan is to fly everyone out of the main airport toward permanent camps in the heartlands."

"Why? I thought there was enough of a military presence here to fight off the zombies." Sam pondered.

Gary grunted, casting his own gaze over the parking lot before replying. "They say it's because of food stores. That there isn't enough. I call bullshit. We've got some good farming land around here, and there's the bounty of the sea and rivers. Of course, we are at the start of the tourist season, so there're more people here than normal."

"But surely the government can make food drops? Or organize search parties to go out and forage." Sam persisted.

Gary snorted. "Look folks, you believe what you want. I wouldn't bother with any of you outsiders during this crisis, except Mitch here vouches for y'all. And, well, he's a former fellow brother-in-arms. And y'all seem like decent folk."

"Thank you," Ruth replied. "What can we do to help put your minds at ease?"

"Well," he drawled, "I was told there's a young lady with you who's looking for her step-mother, or her dad's girlfriend, or something?"

"Yes.It's Anne," Ruth replied. She spotted the young woman and the group of teens and youngsters with her.

At a gesture, Anne stepped forward and explained her situation, and the code word her dad had spoken before he died. She also introduced her new friends.

"Well," Gary replied, "I know exactly where she's at. It's well known down here. I just hope she's still alive. When we left, there was a large group of bikers intent on messing up the peace. They're kinda the reason we haven't been too hasty on getting back."

Sam fidgeted. "If it's that dangerous, where else could we go?"

"Could be the danger's passed. Them military boys sent a small squad out to search the island for folks in need. They were to check out the rumors of any gangs and break 'em up if they were a threat." He paused to adjust his cap. "Either way, folks, we're heading back. Y'all are welcome to join us."

"Thank you," Sam replied. "I think we'd like to discuss your offer first. If that's okay?"

"Sure," Gary smiled. "We're gonna leave at dusk. If you're coming, just meet up." He and his family said their goodbyes, and went off to finish their errands.

CHAPTER SIXTEEN

Anne clutched the 'oh shit bar' as Mitch slammed on the brakes. In the back of the van, Emily and Taylor clutched each other and howled in fear.

"Hurry, please," Dawn whimpered, white faced and wide eyed.

"Stay calm," Mitch's rough voice soothed. "No need to panic. There're too many people left back at the center. Unfortunately, they'll keep the zombies busy for a while."

Jeff remained quiet, but anxiously gripped his rifle as he peered out the window. Greg and his family led the survivors in a bewildering series of turns, taking them further away from the carnage at the survivor center. The taillights in front of them winked off as Sam accelerated. Mitch twirled the wheel, and the van made a sharp left turn before heading straight again. After a few minutes, silence descended inside the van.

Somewhere farther toward the center of Wadmalaw, thick smoke rose.

"Are we sure we made the right decision?" Dawn whispered to her brother.

He gave a curt nod, head and body twisting as he kept watch for zombies. His sister had doubts again. A surprisingly clear, two-lane bridge lay before them. Water gleamed on either side, and a thick line of trees hid the shoreline. They passed over mud flats, dotted with trapped zombies. The disturbing view receded behind them.

Mitch followed Greg and Sam. They spotted abandoned vehicles, and flocks of carrion birds rose from corpses as they drove past. Their speed reduced to a crawl as more and more wrecks loomed before them. To either side was the dark mass of tress. They gave Anne the feeling they were crowding the road, and that at any moment they would come alive and squash the intruders.

The group's headlights washed over a Y in the road. Greg took the left turn, still driving slowly. The smell of burning organic and non-organic matter leaked through the air vents. After a few more minutes of driving, the three vehicles came to a halt twenty feet from the biggest wreck they had seen since crossing onto the island. Anne watched as Ruth and Greg exited their respective vehicles, and cautiously approached the mess. After what seemed like a long time, they finally walked back to their cars. Taillights flashed briefly as Sam and Greg put the trucks in park.

Mitch did the same, and opened his door as Ruth approached.

"Well, we're here," she said. "But it sure looks like no one wants company. Assuming anyone is alive."

"Are you sure, this is the place?" Anne hesitantly spoke up.

Ruth gave a sharp nod. "Yup. Mitch, you and the other men wanna go check the place out? Make sure it's safe?"

"Yes, Ma'am, I can," he placed the van in park. His eyes met Jeff's in the rearview. "You stand guard for me, son. Keep everyone safe."

"Yes sir, I will."

Mitch got out, then walked to the cargo area and opened it up. He took a few minutes to arm himself, before walking past the van to join Sam and Greg. The three men held a hushed conversation, then began to thread their way through the wrecks. They hadn't gone far before the darkness swallowed them up. The rest of the group did the best they could to get comfortable and wait.

# # #

Anne must have dozed off, for she started awake when Dawn shook her shoulder. The girl silently pointed out the windshield at moving shapes. A flickering, bobbing light was at the forefront. They watched as the shapes resolved into the men from their group, led by a fourth, much older man. He carried what looked like an old lantern with a flickering flame. At Ruth's call, the young people slipped out of the van and walked over to the men. Introductions were made all around.

"I don't suppose you know anything about that mess a smoke?" Greg asked. "Or a group of bikers?"

"Might be, might be," the old man replied. "Now, I do know the young lady what took over this place left with a few of them military boys to take care of the problem. They haven't returned yet. If' n she survived, I gotta warn ya, she ain't the most friendly of types."

"Uh, what are you saying?" Sam asked.

"Well, depending on how you conduct yourself, will determine if she likes you or not, and if she'll let you stay," Ed replied.

Sam, Ruth, and Mitch exchanged glances.

Ruth spoke first. "We really don't have anywhere else to go. Besides, we told this young lady we'd get her to her dad's girlfriend."

"Oh?" Ed inquired. "You have a name, honey?"

"Anne, and his girlfriend is Spacey. My dad and sister didn't make it."

"Huh, so you're the 'family' she spoke of," he made a come-along gesture. "I hope you folks don't mind sleeping on the floor for a night. We're a might short on beds."

"Frankly, sir, that's a lot better than the seat of a van," Mitch replied.

"Mmm, I imagine it is. Well, you'll have to leave your cars here for now. I advise getting any personal stuff out. Come on in, and I'll find you spots. It shouldn't be too long before we hear back from Spacey and the military boys," Ed smiled.

Sam turned toward Gary. "Thank you for your help, sir. Ah, if you plan on heading back to your place, I can come along if you think you'll need an extra set of hands."

"Not a problem, and don't mention it. We'll be fine. If not, you might see us back here. Y'all take care now." Gary tipped his cap at the group, then walked back to his truck and got inside.

The survivors watched as he headed further down the road, until the darkness swallowed his taillights before following Ed to safety.

CHAPTER SEVENTEEN

"Downing, don't make me have to start insulting your manhood. You and Ryan are so exhausted even I could get the drop on you both." Must keep my temper and not take my bad mood out on those with the knowledge and firepower to help keep us safe, even if they were being dick heads.

Greasy waves of pain from my ribs and arm wound rolled through me. When it all got to be too much, I just puked, passed out, woke up, and was fine until it got to be too much; then I would do it all over again. Stubborn was my middle name, or stupid, depending on who you listened to.

"Those remaining men,"

"Are still out there. Yeah, I know. I have a plan for them. Relax, it'll work. After all, trouble finds me, and I know how to deal with it."

"You are dead on your feet, and refuse to stay down."

"Ouch, that hurts pot, kettle, black. We're going to check out the distillery first, then the surrounding houses. I have a theory. . . "

"Save me from your half-baked ideas," Downing barked, coming out much less formidable than he wanted.

"Those bikers probably rounded up every zombie on this island they could find, and didn't have to kill, to use for their twisted plans. I believe we won't find many left, not unless they've managed to walk under the water from the other land masses, and struggle through the pluff mud. A highly unlikely scenario. I mean, have you ever gotten stuck in that stuff? I have, and trust me, without someone else helping out, well, let's just say it's got a lot in common with quicksand. Except, not as quick, death-wise. We'll check back with you around noon."

"Sir, Colonel Sir, for once I agree with the civvies."

"Will wonders never cease?" slipped out my mouth as Downing glared at his man before transferring it to me.

"Dude, I despise the ass-crack of dawn, yet here I am, doing the hated to keep this little piece of land safe and infection free. The least you can do is get some sleep so when I need you, you can come charging in to save me, and say 'I told you so'."

Ryan did the fake cough thing. "Technically, it's noon."

I ignored him. Downing snorted, but after a few minutes gave a reluctant nod. I gave him the rundown of my plan, so any shots or explosions wouldn't overly alarm them. I collected Anne and an older, brown-haired and bearded man called Mitch. We left ten minutes later.

I sat in the driver's seat, idling by the side of the road a few yards down from the distillery. My opinion of Mitch and the group he arrived with was still unformed. He, along with Sam and Ruth Resick, seemed like nice people. I only hoped I wasn't being fooled. The couple immediately earned good will points from me by staying behind to supervise the children. including Breckson's hellions, while I tried to figure out how to help Anne.

We drove to the distillery in silence. Mitch—a man of few words. The sun already blazed, and it wasn't even noon, It would be a hot and humid day for killing things. The woods were unnaturally quiet, something nobody wants to happen. I know silence means something or someone is scaring the wildlife.

"From here on out, we stay as quiet as possible."
"Why?" Anne asked.

Mitch responded, "Zombies."

I drove in at a creep, tires crunching over gravel. As we got closer I could start to hear the telltale signs of deadheads, moaning.

"We're going to have to do this quick and quiet. We shoot from a distance first, and move in to clean up," I whispered.

I stopped the truck at the edge of the parking lot before the distillery. There were about thirty or so deadheads in sight. Mitch and I started shooting. Anne did her best to help out, but the most she ended up doing was removing legs or arms. It took us fifteen minutes, alternately shooting and knifing the zombies to re-kill them all. Mitch and I locked in new mags. I laid the rifle on my legs, ignoring Anne's snuffling, which grew to loud sobs. I put the truck in drive, and pulled through the parking lot. I stopped at the edge of a patio dividing the distillery and the winery. Anne's sobs slowly gained in volume. Mitch looked to her, then at me. I was not about to touch whatever mental trauma she was experiencing. We left Anne in the truck as we walked around, clearing the buildings. After a few more minutes the place was secure.

The bikers left a mess, trashing both of the buildings. At least they didn't find all of the booze, mainly the stuff they didn't like. Now the part I hate the most: clearing out the dead for burning. Good thing I wore old clothes. They would be useless after this, if they didn't just disintegrate off me first.

Using some of the diesel we brought with us, Mitch and I set the pile of bodies ablaze. We retreated to the truck to re-load after our second round of shooting, and to see if anyone alive or undead would come out of the woods. While we stood around and waited, Anne's sobs turned into sniffles.

Crap, looks like I'd have to ask. "What's wrong,

Anne? What's got you upset?"

"I . . . I thought, once my Dad found us, we . . . we'd be safe from zombies. That, that we wouldn't have to constantly worry about if they'd just show up and try to eat us. I didn't expect him and Joan to die. I'm all alone. We barely know each other. I just want this nightmare to end."

"I'm sorry for whatever you suffered, but holy fuck! Grow up!" I flung my arms wide. "This is our new reality. You either learn how to be hard when it's needed, or you fucking die! The unknown can, and often will, kill you. . Did I expect all three of you to die? Yeah, I did. I told your dad not to go. I knew his chances, and yours, of surviving unharmed were slim to none." Not the best way to go about comforting a bereaved soul. I suck at this.

"What?! Fuck you. We would've died if he listened to you," Anne screamed back.

"And if he died before he got to you, the outcome would've been the same. Death, and becoming a zombie. Guess what? This nightmare? It's not going to end anytime soon. You want a secure place to live? Well then buckle up, cupcake, and deal with what's happened. You will either learn how to become self-reliant, or you can get the fuck off my island, and take your chances with the really evil assholes of this world." My smile didn't reach my eyes.

Mitch remained quiet, and didn't once comment or speak up during the conversation. I ignored Anne's epithets, and got inside the truck before I cranked the engine over. Mitch jumped in the passenger side. Before Anne had a chance to join us, I pulled out and left her behind.

# # #

I fumed. It was official: mentally, emotionally, I no longer cared who lived or died. I'd continue. The place was devoid of zombies, and had been raided.

It was still no excuse not to double check. Mitch and I searched the place as thoroughly as possible. We found a few useful items, and some which could be used to jerry-rig stuff. The most important items I placed in the truck bed, and stacked the remainder in a pile under the trees. Mitch covered the pile up, and we moved on. It was past noon by the time we checked out every place leading up to the National Fishery, a big area with lots of forest around it.

As I sat in the cab, motor idling, windows rolled down, enjoying the small breeze, I noticed movement in the rearview. I watched the heat shimmer on the road, and finally made out a human figure stumbling along the verge, one which resolved itself into Anne.

I sat, continuing to scan the area, angled the side mirrors a bit to minimize the blind spots on the side of the truck. I sipped water. My rifle lay across my lap. The other weapons sat on the back foot space. I powered up the passenger windows enough to prevent her from reaching in to unlock the door. Mitch just gave me a sideways look, but maintained his silence.

"Predictable, so predictable." I spoke, as Anne tried just that.

She leaned a sweaty brow against the window, red-faced, panting. "Let me in," she croaked out.

Three-sixty degree check, including the upper reaches of the trees, and the far sight lines. "Nope.

"I hate this state. It's too hot. Water, I need water."

I gestured around us. "Take your pick: creek, swamp, river."

She glared at me, yanked again at the handle. "Bitch!"

"We're past the point of flattery getting you anywhere."

She sniffled, tears leaking in a slow trickle down her sweaty face. The locked entrance to the fish hatchery was a mere forty feet away.

"One: Crying is only going to dehydrate you even more. Two: Tears annoy the fuck out of me much faster."

"Your family,"

"Is dead along with the rest of the world. And even if by some small chance they did make it, I'm not fool enough to chase after infinitesimal unknowns. My memories will have to comfort me for however long I have left."

"My father and sister . . . "

I brutally cut off her whining. "You know what? I. Don't. Care. At least you got to say goodbye to your family before they died. You got to be with them, even if it was only for a moment. My family? I didn't get that. I left voice and text messages. None of them were returned. I don't know how, or when, my sister or my parents died. I don't know if they ever got to hear or read my last words to them. For all I know, they're zombies. At least you have the comfort of knowing your family is truly, and thankfully, dead. Fuck you, and your expectations."

She gasped in outrage, her reply garbled with tears and anger. I turned the engine off and got out of the truck. I had to get away from her, and give my temper time to cool down, before I did or said something more vile.

"You see the physical trouble you're in now? How close you're creeping to death from heat stroke, and lack of water? It's not pretty. If you wanted someone to come along and save you, you should have stayed at the survivor centers."

Her face crumpled. "You don't have to be such a hateful bitch."

"Sweet pea, if I really want to be an evil, hateful bitch, I'll just say a zombie ate you, and I couldn't save you in time. Look, I'm not in the mood for anymore bullshit. Just go away so I can get back to my life, such as it is."

"Please, I . . . I'm not gonna ambush you. I was, I am, angry about all this. I want, I need help. Please, just, just give me a second chance, a chance to prove myself. You, you don't have to give me a weapon, even."

I weighed her words, not sure I could, or wanted to, trust her. I turned the vehicle off, slid out, and walked to the tailgate while simultaneously hitting the button to lock the doors.

"Fine. Take these bolt cutters, and snap the hasp on the lock. Un-ravel the chain, but don't get rid of it. I expect you to pull your own weight and follow orders from here on out."

CHAPTER EIGHTEEN

The three of us cleared the outbuildings just inside the gate. Anne did her best to keep up with Mitch and me. We then slowly drove farther down the road toward the main buildings in silence, keeping an eye out for deadheads and gators. As we got closer the wind shifted, and I could smell decay. It was more potent than just being a zombie. Fish left to rot is worse.

"We've got a lot of ground to cover, and a shit ton of woods hiding who knows how many rotters," I whispered.

"I don't know if I can take the smell."

"Puke out the window, or you're riding back with your own vomit until you clean it out."

I moved ahead, the stench getting worse. I tasted bile in the back of my throat. A horde of deadheads, perhaps twenty, milled between us and the first of the many structures. They hadn't spotted us yet. This many in one place means there might be living people in the buildings somewhere.

"Can we leave now? We can't survive them all," Anne tried to keep her voice low. She fidgeted with her seatbelt, casting her gaze about.

An irritated sigh escaped me. "Anne, the point I was trying to make back at the distillery? This, before us, is. If any of that offends you, please take your pack, some water, an extra rifle and ammo, and head back to Downing and the others."

Her wide, fear-filled eyes darted around our surroundings, drawn back again and again to the horde, which had still not smelled, nor noticed, our presence.

"They wouldn't be grouped together for no reason. Living people must be inside. Great. Starving refugees. More mouths to feed. If only we knew if they were going to be useful or not."

"We can leave. They don't know we're here, and you certainly have shown you don't care," Anne hissed.

"Tempting, so incredibly tempting. But, we leave and who knows how long it takes for those inside to die. We don't know if they were inoculated with the shot, or how many potential zombies will be added."

"You can't be serious! You call trying to take on a group that big smart?"

"So, I'm a hypocrite. Here's what we're gonna do." I gave Anne and Mitch a quick rundown of the plan.

Naturally, she didn't like it, but when I once again pointed out she was free to leave, she just shook her head and geared up. I drove the truck to a building on our right, putting us slightly out of view of the horde. We discovered the back door was closed and locked.

Anne followed me, pulling rear guard, as we made a cautious circle around the building and toward the front. By the time we verified the inside held only dead fish, and my ribs screamed in agony from all the heaving I did, a stiff breeze was blowing.

"Okay, action time," I told the young woman, and waved her to get going as I stood guard near the open front door to the building.

Anne walked up the road a pace, almost at the limit of my sight. Then she began yelling and waving her arms. I waited, and waited, and waited. Seriously? Were these zoms not hungry? I heard two gunshots, then saw Anne jogging backward. The horde slowly following her.

As she got closer to me, the breeze blew, wafting my scent their way, along with hers. The group shuffled faster, moans beginning. Anne turned and ran. I admit, my bowels wanted to crawl out of my body at the sight, too.

She reached me, panting heavily with fear.

"Steady. We can't lose their interest." I tried to calm us both

When they were about twenty feet away, Anne broke, and ran inside the building. I followed, not wanting to give her the chance to change her mind and lock me inside with the damn things. The sounds of the horde filled the building, and I was still three-quarters away from the far door when it began to swing shut.

Without thinking, I squeezed off a burst, and forced my much abused lungs to work harder. I hit the metal door with my right side hard enough to send it slamming open and nearly dumping me on the ground. I stumbled a few steps, noting Anne was gone.

"Double-crossing bitch," I wheezed out, disappointed my expectations in this matter had come true.

I heard Mitch holler, and looked around to see him sitting in a golf cart. I stepped out of the way as a rifle went off near the front of the building. The man used the cart to block the back door, before jumping out and jogging over to me.

"Come on. I've got you," He supported my weight as we headed to the truck.

We hoisted ourselves inside. It seemed apropos to imitate a fish out of water as I started the motor. The cart would not keep the rotters contained for long. I drove around the building, screeching to a halt at the front door. Anne battled the stragglers.

"Spacey!" She screamed my name as I tumbled out, hanging onto the door, willing myself to not pass out as she finished off the last one.

"Oh, shit! I'm sorry! I'm sorry!" The look of terror which filled her face when she met my glare would've been comical if I had air to laugh.

"Grenade!" Mitch yelled at me, coming around to

the front of the truck. "You two get behind the passenger-side wheels.

I handed over two death-dealers, before taking his advice. The front door to the building remained propped open. I admired Mitch's aim as he lobbed the grenades through the door. I didn't have time for much else, as he yanked me down.

They went off, leaving our ears ringing. We shielded our heads with our arms. The wheels helped block the worst of the explosion and flying debris as we crouched behind them. I kept trying to take deep breaths, but it didn't seem worth the pain-laced effort. Over the ringing in my ears, I barely made out Anne's voice.

"It worked. I can't believe it worked. Shit. You make my mother look sane."

I gave up with my efforts to get air, and lay down on the ground, tears streaming down the sides of my face. Hell isn't other people. It's broken ribs, and other people. I stared up into the sky.

Crunching sounds met my ears as I contemplated how much moving to shoot myself, and put me out of my misery, would be worth.

"Um, shit!" Anne's voice floated to me. "The truck is, um, shredded? I guess you could say."

I think I may have managed to lift my arm and give a thumbs down. How did turtles turn themselves right side up?

"So, would self-reliance include you managing to, oh, I don't know, haul your ass off the ground?"

I may not have been able to breathe very well, but my middle fingers worked great. Slowly, I stood, hating life, and everyone left in it. Mitch, silent as always, helped. As I slumped against the remains of the truck, Anne managed to get my tac vest off. She and Mitch probed my ribs, checking to see if the breaks had gotten worse. I hung onto the side and did my best to gulp down what was left of the wine.

Ten minutes, and my entire gamut of swear words later, Mitch declared no new breaks. He helped me put the tac vest back on, and tightened it enough so I could still breathe. My head swam from a combination of pain and inebriation. Anne did a quick scout, and found a working truck with keys in the ignition. Mitch transferred what was left of the gas from our ruined ride into the new one, while she salvaged what she could of the stuff in the bed. They helped me into the cab, and Mitch seated himself behind the wheel.

The older man eased the truck farther down the road and parked so we could see the main group of buildings.

"Remember, conserve ammo if you can," I reminded them.

"Just tell me what to do. You stay in the truck. You can barely breathe," Anne replied.

"Stepping up. Good choice."

She glared at me as she got out of the cab, and slammed the door. Mitch gestured to her, and while I kept look-out, they cleared the buildings.

It took Mitch and Anne a while to clear a building. As they headed off to check another, the breeze temporarily cleared the air of fish decomp, but added human.

"Shit, please don't let the incoming be too unmanageable."

Cranking the truck on, I eased closer to where Mitch and Anne had gone. I got a glimpse between the buildings of the forest. A line of zombies staggered forth. Briefly I wondered how many crawlers hid in the tall grass and weeds.

I put the truck in park, steadied the rifle on the window frame, and took my time to make head shots. Anne and Mitch finally came bursting out of the other building. She only froze a moment, before she ran for our vehicle. Mitch was already by the passenger door, reloading his rifle. At this point, the zombies managed to reach the back of the farthest building.

"More are coming from the woods," Anne screamed.

"Numbers?"

"A dozen. We need to leave!" She clambered inside, shaking.

Mitch calmly lined up shots, and started dropping rotters.

"Chill. Take out those closest. We've got this."

When the smelly biters tried reaching inside the truck, I just powered up the windows a bit, then used my dagger. I was struggling for breath by the time we finished, and Anne rocked herself in shock. Once my heart rate settled, and my breathing became less of problem, I handed Anne and Mitch a protein bar and some water.

We munched in silence, eating our lunch. Once done, I drove forward enough to clear the pile of bodies, so we could step down and not twist an ankle. Refreshed, and out in the open, Anne rounded on me.

"Do I need a white jacket, or a bullet to your head? Are you in your right mind? Who the fuck died and left you in charge of deciding what's smart and what isn't? That was some grade A crazy-ass shit. Where the fuck do you get off on telling me what to do when you don't even follow your own advice?"

"Hey, I already admitted I'm a hypocrite. Besides, I'm not some princess in need of saving. I'm a queen. I got this shit handled." A wave of dizziness hit me, and I'm sure my eyes wheeled in my head from pain. I leaned against the truck shutting eyelids, breathing in and out for a while before straightening out. "I'm okay. Don't mind me puking my guts out."

Anne sent me a disgusted look. "When your ribs stab your lungs, and they collapse, and you die from it, you're gonna turn. I should just do you a favor and shoot you before it happens so you won't endanger me yet again."

"The only person I'm a danger to is myself, and I'm pretty sure we've already established the only danger to you is you."

Rage flashed through the younger woman's eyes and she muttered a string of obscenities.

I paid no heed to the epithets, Anne watched in hostile silence, arms tightly crossed before her chest, as I cleaned my knife and sword before re-sheathing them. I changed mags on the rifle, then hauled out my backpack. Mitch had taken over look-out.

"Rule number two: Always keep a watch out. Thank you, Mitch." With my chores done, I gingerly got my pack and swords settled. I added a lumpy bag to my belt, and extra ammo to the pouches on my sweat and gore soaked tac vest.

"Seriously? You expect me to believe you can handle shit when you can barely breathe?"

"Watch me."

"I'm what, zombie bait yet again?"

"There is merit in your suggestion. However, I'm actually going to give you a vest like mine, along with a hand gun, and mags for it and for your rifle. I will be extremely pissed if you shit all over this display of trust and shoot me."

"Kind of hard to do if I do decide to kill you."

"You better hope there's no afterlife, 'cause if there is, your ass is mine when you die, and I promise you, you'll wish you had gone to hell," I matter of factly stated.

A niggle of fear shone in Anne's eyes. I could almost hear her thoughts: This woman has a bullet wound, a bunch of cracked ribs, and yet she keeps going. Wade's daughter swallowed, hard, and nodded once, letting herself be kitted out. Not once did Mitch say a word as Anne and I verbally sparred.

Finally, we started toward another building. My stride remained purposeful even with my breathing problems, and despite the late spring's heat and humidity.

# # #

We made a full circle of the building, testing doors. My partners in crime silent and sweating beside me, before I breached the front. There were a few deadheads inside. We made short work of them, before we lost the battle with our stomach, and hurled up the protein bars.

"Please tell me these buildings are not all full of rotting fish and zombies."

Gagging and hacking, feeling as if I was suffocating, I finally managed to clear my nose and sinuses of puke. "Gross," was my reply as she repeated her question. "Um, yeah, it's all rainbows, puppies, and cotton candy from here on out."

"I really, truly hate you." Anne hacked once more before we moved on.

The second and third buildings were empty, of people and zombies. Just lots of rotting fish. This was going to ruin my desire to fish in the future. Maybe I should save a bullet for myself for when I started to starve to death.

At the fourth building, I heard movement inside as I tested the door. I raised the gun as I backed up, fully intending to shoot through the locked door.

"Wait," Mitch frantically hissed.

He reached out and knocked, hard. After a moment, we heard a muffled voice from behind the door. "'Don't shoot. We're alive.'"

"How many, and are any of you bit?"

The response was a quick no.

It wasn't convincing even to me. Anyone replying that fast has something to hide. I couldn't call them liars to their face, not without knowing how many there were. Even if half-starved, they would be desperate, and could potentially overpower me. If they thought to try to hide bitten members, they'd soon find out I'm a shoot first, question later kind of person when it comes to potential survivors. I tried to distract those inside.

"Back to the original question: How many are there?"

A pause met me. "About a dozen."

"When's the last time you had food, or water?"

"Well, there's fish in here, and the tanks have fresh water. Not that it was good to begin with. Are you with the army? We were told you would be coming to save us. What took you so long?"

Great, people who couldn't be arsed to help themselves. Of course, there was no need for them to know the truth. It might make things easier.

"The world as we know it has ended." Cheesy but apt. REM started playing in my head. "My colleagues and I will do our best to help you, but you have to work with us."

"I can check them out medically. I know what to look for," Mitch whispered to me.

"Why are there still stupid people left? Why haven't they been Darwinized by now?" I grumped.

Desperation is a sad emotion, especially when everything else has been lost. Most people were not as strong as I have always been, or had the stamina to try to be.

"Here's how this is gonna work," I said. "Everyone comes out slowly, in a line, hands in the air. You can hold your weapons up if you like, but if they point toward us, then you will be terminated. We are under strict orders to question and inspect all survivors for signs of infection."

A babble of voices rose and fell inside the building as a short, furious discussion took place. They tried bargaining with us. I remained firm. Life sucked all around, but it only took one infected person to ruin everyone's happily ever after. They would thank me later, or curse me, depending on what their relationship to each other was. I had seen enough horror/zombie movies to know how it worked. Compassion for others would only get you so far, then it got you killed—usually in slow, horrific ways.

"I don't think they're gonna comply," Anne said, gaze nervously switching between me and the door.

"I am too hurt for this bullshit. If they don't shit or get off the pot soon, I'm gonna take the decision outta their hands, and light the place up."

"Holy shit, psycho, chill. They've been trapped for a while I bet."

"Dumb shits who can't be bothered to save themselves have no business being picky when rescuers show up."

"Just, be patient. It's like I'm talking to my dad, in female form," Anne muttered.

"None of us are bit," came a voice from inside.

"Which just guarantees one or more are," I remarked as they continued,

"So there's no need for inspections."

"I'm sorry, folks, but if you want our help, you submit to inspections, or you're on your own." Mitch firmly replied before I could open my mouth, or gun.

More arguing came from inside, a few voices rising in anger, one almost hysterically before being cut off and shushed as they debated again.

"Look, this is no time for a debate. I know it might be loved ones, but I WILL BE damned if I'm

177

bringing the infection back with us. So what's it going to be?"

The whispering started up again.

"They had to know they would be asked to prove they're infection free if rescue came. I know people can be stupid, but this is a whole new level. How did they think they'd get 'em past the government? Tug on their non-existent heart strings?"

Wisely, Anne and Mitch decided to take my questions as rhetorical.

I banged on the door once. "Don't make us have to come and pry you out. Anne, go around back, would you? I have a bad feeling any infected members are going to go out another door and hide until the group finds out where they'll be relocated. Then they return to fetch them, sneaking them and the infection inside to kill us all, because reality is too hard for them to face even now."

"Shit, can you be any more paranoid?" Anne shook her head, swiftly making her way around the building, looking for another entrance, and zombies.

"Time's up." I heard shouting from the other side. Anne.

"I'll keep watch here," Mitch said as he grabbed a pouch off my belt. "Go see to Anne."

"Let's see how they like your caltrops," he muttered to himself as I double-timed it toward the rear of the building.

"Down, down on the ground. Stop right there!" Anne shouted, rifle at the ready, shaking a bit.

I rested against the side of the building, peering around with rifle at the ready. I did my best to silently suck air in. Through the rifle's scope I saw one person holding an improvised weapon, and another with a pistol.

"Drop your weapons! Drop them now, or I drop you!" I yelled at them, or attempted to.

They didn't seem to want to comply. Really?

What was it with people pushing their luck with me today? I pulled the trigger, hitting the pistol wielder center mass, he dropped like a marionette whose strings had been cut . . . Good thing I dressed Anne in the tac vest I had 'borrowed' from Downing. The second shooter's gun went off. I heard more than saw Anne gasp, and stagger back before she collapsed.

"Wrong move mofo! Wrong move!" I was already shooting the second weapon holder when hell broke loose yet again.

I heard agonized screaming from the front as ungrateful escapees found my surprise with their feet. I could barely make out Mitch's voice barking commands. The backdoor into the place flew open as I gimped over to Anne, breathing harsh in my ears. A woman came screaming at a run toward me. She had something metal in her hand, and looked crazed. Oh, hell no! Sorry lady, I love me a lot. Her blood sprayed those who charged out behind her, giving a few pause. One person tripped and fell over her body. Voices screaming in terror, alarm, and rage echoed all around. When this brought more zombies out of the woods around us, I was so feeding them to the rotters.

"Do you all want to die? Drop it now! On the ground! Do it!" I yelled out as a small figure detached itself from the center of the group in an attempt to sneak off.

Great, the fuck up fairy wasn't done shitting all over me. A small girl raced to the fallen woman, screaming and crying. "Mommy! Mommy! You shot my Mommy! Mooommmmmeeeeeee!" She fell on the still body, tugging its arm, trying to get a response.

I saw what was in her hand. It was a nail file of all things, and not the cheap ass one. It was the metal one about four inches long. I'm pretty sure my thoughts should've been remorseful instead of, *Hey, cool, I can really use one of those.*

"Anne?" I called out. No response. Great, the bullet hitting the armor had temporarily knocked both wind, and consciousness, from her. Through all this the fucktards still hadn't stopped screaming, from either the front or back of the building.

"Last warning, assholes! Face down on the ground!" I commanded.

We were all close enough I could see the hesitation. Movement from my peripheral vision showed other survivors coming to their comrades' aid. Mitch brought up the rear. One survivor had a fire ax held in a double-handed grip as he ran at me. Try to help people out and be nice, and what do you get? Another squeeze of the trigger sent Ax-man to the afterlife. Some of the remaining members did an abrupt turnabout, taking off at a stumbling run away from me. There was no way of knowing if they were infected, or terrified beyond reason. I swung the rifle back around toward the door, as a woman hefting the fire extinguisher aimed the nozzle at me. I fired before she could spray me with the contents. My shot knocked her down. The canister thudded to the ground.

"Don't shoot! Don't shoot!" A female voice frantically shouted to me. "Everyone stay still. We don't need more deaths!" the person hollered.

Slowly, the screaming subsided to whimpers and crying. I should say most of the screaming. I motioned with the rifle barrel for them to walk left, where there would be sufficient space.

"Put your hands on top of your heads, kneel real slow, then lie on the ground," I instructed. It's hard to sound intimidating when you can barely breathe. Here's hoping my willingness to shoot first counts for something.

Coughing from the vicinity of Anne let me know she's awake. "Oh, fuck it hurts! Even with the vest."

"As a consolation prize, you've won an awesome set of bruises, and the matching broken ribs," I sang out in cheerful game announcer style, before dropping the tone. "I need you to stand and help me out here, number two. The train has derailed again."

"Huh? Oh. Right," she said as she heard the weeping and wailing. Anne stood shakily. If she could keep her fortitude up, she might just survive.

The little girl continued to scream and cry at our feet.

"Lady, please," came a muffled voice, "the little girl."

"Anne, try and get the kid away from her mom."

"Sure." She approached the girl, but the air-raid siren sound of the kid's screams increased.

"Or not. Never mind, Leave her. Pat them down, take anything off them that looks like it could be used as a weapon."

Yup, it was only a matter of how many zombies would be coming from the woods, drawn by the noise and my gunshots.

I just hoped the rest would cooperate so one of them could comfort the child and quiet her. Mitch and Anne began searching the survivors for weapons. There were a few people left in the building who never had a chance to flee. They filed out one by one, and lay face down on the ground in two rows. We received a mixture of nasty, frightened, or defiant looks.

"Let's try this again, shall we?" I asked.

"Murderer! Cowards!" Spat a female voice from the ground.

"Shut it. You were given an option, you refused to comply. Not only did you refuse, but you tried sneaking infected out, didn't you? Now they're on the loose and will have to be hunted down. Don't blame us for your poor decisions." I ranted at them.

"This is why you're in the mess you are. The world's changed. A bite or a scratch from one of them is a death sentence. You still fool yourselves into thinking it's just a bad dream. Wake. The. Fuck. Up. You lost people you didn't have to. Now, we can't trust any of you. We certainly can't let you into our haven."

This made some of them angry, and they started to lift heads, or in a few cases upper bodies, to yell back at us. I fired a round into the ground at their feet, and they shut up, and backed up, real quick.

"Everybody lost loved ones. But harboring infected only insures you die much quicker. You want to kill yourselves because you don't have the balls to do what's right, what's needed for the safety and survival of your group. Fine. But don't you dare put me, or those under my protection, at risk for your selfishness and stupidity."

This is all we need, more dumb-ass people thinking their loved ones will pull through. A scream came from where the child was crying over her mother.

"Watch them. They do anything funny. Shoot 'em," I told Anne.

I turned around in time to see the re-animated mother ripping into the girl's neck. "Seriously?" I shot the mother, then the little girl.

I was already Public Enemy Number One to these people, and no doubt a monster as the cherry on top. I walked over to those I had shot earlier, putting a bullet through their brains.

Resting bitch face firmly in place, I addressed the group, "I hope you're all happy with yourselves."

"You monster!" A shrill female voice accused me.

"None of you had the balls to do what needed to be done, so that makes you all the evil ones. This is how we're gonna do this. Each one of you is gonna strip down, and be inspected for bites or scratches. Those who pass, you get a ticket out of here."

"Whoa, whoa, whoa! You can't be tearing apart families. We've got rights." A once fat, middle-aged male protested.

"News flash: The only right anybody has now is the right to die, and not come back. Those who want out of here, put your hands up. Dick head, didn't you hear before, a bite or scratch is a death sentence?"

At first, no one moved. Well, shit. It wasn't in the plan to waste bullets on these idiots. Anne chose to speak up.

"We'll do the best we can to protect everyone's modesty. Mothers can choose to stay with their children. It's hot out, and only going to get worse."

Hesitantly a hand went up, a younger male. I really didn't wanna see a man's junk. If he tried some dumb pick up line, or thought he was gonna try and charm me or some other bullshit, I was gonna geld him just on principle.

I motioned for him to get up, and kept him covered with my rifle. I directed him to the corner of the building while Anne and Mitch kept guard. We would be within hearing range of everyone else.

"Face the wall first, if you want. Everything comes off. Arms held out at shoulder height, legs apart." I used my professional member of the medical community tone.

The guy did as requested, thankfully, without any lame attempts at conversation. His back appeared free of zombie marks. I had him move his hair out of the way of his neck. Then he slowly turned around so I could see his front and both sides. He was filthy, and half-starved. His ribs stuck out, skin pulled tight over bones. His eyes sank in sockets, from lack of proper nutrition.

"Clean. Get dressed," I commanded him, trusting Anne and Mitch to come up with a method to keep order.

"So, who's next?" I asked as we came back, indicating a spot away from the group where the male was to sit.

In answer to my question, a young woman raised her hand.

Several hours later, we had two groups of people. I put the throat mike on, and powered it up, speaking softly as we kept watch.

"Downing, this is pain in the ass. Over."

"Can the shit. What do you want?" he asked.

"We have survivors at the fish hatchery."

"You're shitting me."

"Why does no one believe me? No, I'm not. But we have a situation. Some of the survivors want to be saved. The others don't. Either way, I need more transport Some food and water, too."

"You're just full of good news. Any infected?" Downing asked.

"Not anymore."

"Anything else I should know about?"

"Oh, my ribs have been upgraded from merely bruised to cracked."

"I'll be there shortly. Over and out," the line went dead.

It didn't take long for the colonel and Ryan to arrive with the troop transport. The sight of actual military seemed to hearten some of the survivors. The compliant group got water and energy bars. Downing went to talk with the rebels. Ryan came up to me.

"Go sit, before you fall down. I've got this."

I nodded, and made my way to the truck's back bumper. I sat and leaned against the side; unabashedly eavesdropping.

"That woman is a monster! Bitch shot those people in cold blood!"

Another said, "What they're asking is a violation

of my rights! They should be locked up. I'm gonna sue."

"Everyone just calm down, and we'll straighten this mess out. Firstly, we do need to check for infection. The United States Government has decreed those who contracted the virus, and are in the first stages of infection, are to be shipped to medical facilities. If you refuse to submit to checks, you will be considered enemies of the nation and treated accordingly. Now, are we going to continue having problems or not?"

CHAPTER NINETEEN

I didn't think it possible the colonel could lie. I also didn't think there was an antidote. My over-active imagination kicked in to overdrive with visions of secrete government labs where they experimented on the infected. Or cramped holding cells where 'enemies' rotted if they couldn't be rehabilitated.

The complaints continued. Downing patiently listened to their side of events before coming over to the waiting survivors, and us.

"Medical Facilities? Really? Is that what your superiors told you to say? Who believes that bullshit anymore?"

I got a glare. "I don't care what you think. It is the truth. We need to get going with evacuations."

"To where?" I asked.

"The navy base is the first staging ground. All survivors will eventually be air lifted to the new capitol."

"Uh huh." I didn't believe a word of it. Okay, maybe there was some truth to it; however, I was more inclined to think the worst. "What about the ones who don't wanna be checked for bites?"

"We leave them. We have seventy-two hours to get to the base."

"Hold on, what happens after that time frame? Is the government planning on nuking the rest of the country outside of their arbitrary safe zone? You never mentioned any of this when you crashed my pad. And, I don't want those people staying and wrecking my plans."

"Ma'am, all non-coms are on a need-to-know basis. I'm only telling you because we need some help.

While I do not condone your methods, you have proven to be up to the task of helping rebuild our great nation."

Holy time warp, Batman. He was all military speak and stick-up-the ass rigid protocol again. I smelled a rat, or maybe the stench was just me. It is hard to keep clean during end times. I didn't like that he just assumed I would be happy to learn all of a sudden I rated a spot on the salvation train. There was no chance to argue as Downing and Ryan got the first group loaded up. I sat, eyeballing the 'rebels'.

"Isn't it great? We get to go to the new capitol. We'll be safe, and we won't have to constantly fight for survival," Anne happily chirped.

I just grunted. The colonel went back to speak with the holdouts, trying to convince them it was better to submit than be left behind. Only a few more people decided to join, and after being cleared of infection, returned to the survivors.

Downing left some jugs of water and MREs for the others, but essentially from here on out, they were on their own. I pulled out behind the troop transport, following Downing and Ryan back to the bikers' hideout.

# # #

I called a meeting once home, and laid out the facts for gramps, in-pig, her kids, and Tanya. I refused to speak of my fears. Only gramps seemed to be able to read between the lines. He harrumphed before walking off to think.

It didn't take us long to get back to the hideout with the people from my place who wanted to join the survivors going to the new capitol. I sat on the running board, my wounds bothering me more than I wanted to admit. Mitch talked with Downing. The more I mulled over my conversation with the colonel, the more concerns I had. I heaved myself up, and sauntered over to the men with my questions.

"Look, right now I need to know how big the hoard is, and where it's heading. And don't hand me the 'I'm not at liberty to say line,'" I told Downing.

"As far as we can tell, a large group is heading for the safe zone."

"How large is it?" I asked again.

He hesitated, which gave me all the answer I needed, but I wanted confirmation. "Estimates put it at several hundred million."

"Are you fucking shitting me! This paradise is where?"

Downing grudgingly told me.

"There is no way you can outlast that many. The zombies will overrun anything and kill everyone. There aren't enough bullets in the world."

"The military is not without a plan," the colonel began.

"To have everyone fucked," I muttered, and received a glare.

"You should make your choices soon. We need to leave so we make the rendezvous point. We don't know how many zombies are still left, or what other problems may crop up."

He gave me a nod and walked over to the others. A scowl grew on my face. I stomped up to Anne. The brain to mouth filter busted. Words spewed forth.

"News flash, you can't do any good in the 'new capitol.' Downing won't tell you, but over a hundred million zombies are making their way toward the ringing dinner bell the military and government fucktards have set up. I hope you enjoy your one-way trip to hell." I gave a chilling smile, whirled around, and stormed off to be by myself.

Well, the bruised ribs made it hard, since I sounded asthmatic, so it was more of a fast limp. I passed Ryan, who had raised brows from my outburst, and a strange look on his face I failed to interpret.

CHAPTER TWENTY

I know Anne is thinking I'm moving too slow, but I don't know if the gang will try to ambush us right away, or let us get inside their territory

I coast down the other side of the bridge, noting nothing is moving on the banks or among the wrecks. My anxiety level ratchets up.

"PIA 1 checking in, still clear," I say into the mike.

We get about ten miles when the first heads on poles and hacked-up bodies start to appear.

"Anne, you see anything moving through the scope yet?" I ask.

"Not yet," she says. "Wait. Five miles up the road a couple dead people are lying around by the side, and the clear left lane. There's also a kid holding a teddy bear beside a sideways van with a flat tire. It looks like his mom is sitting on the rear floorboard. The dad is crouched, trying to change the flat. Three living and two deceased."

"All units, we have contact," I briefly give a run-down.

"Are we gonna stop?" Wade's daughter asks me.

"Hell no," Is my reply. "It's a trap."

"That's pretty shitty to use a kid and his mom."

"That's what shitty people do. If they don't bring up weapons, don't shoot 'em."

I sit up taller in my seat, trying to see a way around the van. It's there, if I run over the bodies lying in the road. I bet the family is counting on most people stopping to help, not wanting the guilt that comes with killing innocents. I don't want it, either. The situation reeks of being a set-up. I don't believe the corpses in the middle of the road are truly dead, but living beings playing decoy.

"Hold on, it's gonna get messy." I tell her, while keying the mike. "All units, Operation Kick-ass is green."

I keep my steady pace, and when we get a little closer, I act like I'm slowing down as the mother leans over briefly to speak to the man. Then she pops out, and frantically starts semaphoring her arms at us. The man fiddling with the tire still hasn't looked up, and that just cements it for me.

"Wait! You're not gonna just . . . " Anne bursts out as I floor the peddle.

The truck smoothly picks up speed, big horsepower engine throbbing. Dumb fucks wanna play chicken? They picked the wrong person. I just hope what I'm about to do doesn't wreak the undercarriage so bad we can't drive. Now, that would really suck.

Downing is squawking in my ear as we surge forward. I risk a quick look back to see if he's sped up.

"Come on fucker, move it," I shout, bumping the mike on accidentally as I brace myself for impact. "Being around us civvies musta made him soft."

The woman and child realize last minute that I'm not stopping. She starts screaming, and bumps the kid out of the way as she runs forward. I'm not sure if she means to warn the 'dead' decoys, or thinks I'll stop for her. Sorry, toots. You picked the wrong side.

I catch her on the right front bumper of the truck. Anne screams along with the woman as she gets flung forward, then tumbles backward over the front of the van. My front tires hit the man who started to get up, realizing I called his bluff. The truck shudders. The top of his head was level with the top of the grill.

I feel physically sick, and faint at the same time. I

don't like the choices I have to make. A moment later, my emotions turn to rage when I hear gunfire.

Anne continues screaming in horror beside me. I can't let go of the wheel at this speed and miss roadblocks to slap her out of it.

"Shoot. Goddamn it. We're gonna be swiss cheese. Fucking shoot 'em," I scream, but doubt she hears me.

We're past the two remaining men by this time, fast coming up on mile twenty of our trip. I'm trying to divide my attention between the road and the enemies. It's a shit load harder at the speed we're going. I wrench the wheel almost too late, ramming into a pair of bikers who suddenly appear out of nowhere.

The jolt is much bigger, flinging us back and then forward. The truck skids out of control. I hear the shriek of tearing metal, a whistling, and a wasp sting past the right side of my face as the windshield explodes outwards. The roadway is doing donuts. Wait, that's so not right. I smell burning stuff, metal, rubber. Thick smoke has obscured the view behind us.

I get the truck straightened out, mainly by slowing down. Anne cries and sobs next to me.

"PIA 2, Package 1 and 2, you still behind us?" I shriek into the mike.

"Yes, we are," comes the calm reply, "It looks like you got company coming."

"How many?" I ask, and Mitch answers me.

"Oh, about fifty, give or take. Is Anne still hysterical?" he asks. I can hear him popping off rounds at the enemy.

"Yes, but it's not as bad as it was," I tell him.

"Good. Anne, I know you can hear me. They're closing the gap. We need you."

Anne clicked the mike and said halfheartedly, "Okay."

I look in the side mirror as one of the enemy trucks flip as it goes off the road. It spills the five in the back out of the bed like rag dolls.

My adrenaline is flowing now, breath harsh in my ears. We need to lure them away from both packages. I push the gas pedal, picking up enough speed to look like we intend to flee from them as we pass the needed turn-off.

"Keep sharp, Anne. Package 1 and 2, safe traveling. Yippee ki yay, motherfuckers," I shout, and do a one eighty, the truck groaning with the effort. I have to be careful with the shitty center of gravity the things got not to rollover.

"Wait. What? You're crazy. Lemme out," Anne shrieked as tires spun. Smoke came off them before they catch on the pavement. We lurch forward as Downing appears out of the smoke.

"Shoot, Anne. Do it," I scream at her as we race toward the gang.

She's freaked out beside me again because any sane person would have turned tail and driven away, not toward them. I'm mad enough to play the biggest game of chicken ever. I just hope we don't end up tangled in the truck remains.

A couple more rifles pop up, all training on us. Uh oh, not sure I can miss them all. I hear thunder all around, almost see the bullet trails coming toward us.

"Anne, if you don't wanna be Swiss cheese, start fucking firing."

I dodge and weave amid the wrecks, clipping vehicles, tires chirping and screeching. Rotted body parts splatter and blow everywhere as I mow on over them. Yuck! The stench of trapped gasses exploding from the corpses is enough to make me pass out. That, and the side windows, which are fast becoming coated in gore and ichor. I really wish the windshield was still there, as some of the noxious mess flings up high enough to splatter in on our faces and bodies. Boy, those men sure seem excited, if the waving guns and arms means anything.

Anne is now actively vomiting out the side of the truck, the wind helping plaster it to the side and back. The enemy is not moving over, but coming straight toward us in a staggered line. Clearly, they hope I'll lose nerve first as the available free space narrows rapidly, and alarmingly.

Over the sound of screaming comes the big booms of the .50cal as Speary tried to take out the oncoming vehicles before I crashed into them. Shrapnel, blood, body parts, made a nasty mess, especially without a windshield. I gunned the truck, side mirrors smashing off with how close we come to the enemy. Anne barely got her head and body back inside. The near miss seemed to wake her up a bit. She grabbed up the rifle she had dropped in her lap, firing rapidly into the maelstrom as we passed through,

We roared out the hole made for us. I couldn't hear a damn thing over the ringing in my ears. I would have to trust in my eyes. I took the turn on two wheels. We were behind the gang now. Up ahead on the new road we had taken, I could see the remnants of government sandbags piled halfway across both lanes with gun emplacements. And more enemy numbers inside, bristling with rifles. Oh, shit!

I had a split second to make a decision before we: A) slammed into the forefront of the abandoned vehicles, or B) got trapped in the one-vehicle wide lane they made.

I wrenched the wheel left, Anne's shot ruined as her arms flung up, her seatbelt straining. She slammed into me briefly and then flew toward her door as my body acted like a flipper in a pin-ball machine, and she was the ball. The bed of the truck slammed off a random, abandoned vehicle.

We get tossed about like rag dolls, my head briefly making contact with the door frame, stars sparking behind my eyes. The truck engine shrieked, the body shuddered, and groaned. I didn't have time to return fire,

"Fuck you, motherfuckers!" I jam the gas pedal down. This would be the last run for this heap. I could tell by the way the motor responded.

Speary never let up on the .50 cal, and the return fire dwindled. With the enemy briefly suppressed, I raced the truck down the single lane. Anne and I barreled toward two cars parked nose-to- nose, cutting off access to the rest of the road. We slammed through in a crash of ripping metal, safety glass, and pops. Air bags punched into our faces. My face felt on fire. I contemplated passing out from the pain as my foot left the gas, and we drifted to a stop.

After a brief loss of consciousness, I forced my battered, unwilling body to move. I released the seatbelt, shoved the door open, and grabbed my rifle. I pretty much tumbled out of the high truck cab and landed on sun-heated pavement before passing out.

I smelled a sharp scent as I swam back into consciousness. The tanks had ruptured.

"Anne, get your ass out of there. The gas tanks are leaking!" I tried to scream as I flopped on my belly.

I felt my ribs move in ways they shouldn't. This is how I die, from a punctured lung. Please let someone be kind enough to put a bullet in my brainpan so I don't come back as a zom.

I'm sucking in air, my wounded arm deciding a good option is to go numb right now, to my disgust.

"Jesus Christ! We could have died if we weren't strapped in, and I think my left arm broke," Anne states as she throws out what is left of our supplies.

I blinked as I struggled up—blood, powder, and sand gluing my right eye shut. I cursed as my ribs throbbed, lungs spasmed in pain. Fine! I used my hands and legs to scoot my body backward over the hot asphalt as fast as I could. I didn't care how much my arm protested. I had no clue what was behind me, or where I was headed. Of course I slammed my shoulders, neck, and head into a solid object in my haste to get out of shooting range. That did not help the head wound I had received earlier. The world swam. I blacked out briefly. I woke to the faint sounds of screaming and gunshots as my hearing came slowly back.

I looked over at the offending object which had helped knock me out. Well, what have we here? Military camouflage, fat tires. Could it be? Cha Ching! I got on hands and knees, and left bloody lip prints on the door as I kissed my good fortune. A hot wind smashed me against the metal. My face protested this new abuse by making my brain shut itself down.

I woke to Anne slamming a mostly empty sand bag all over my poor, battered body.

"I hope you like the bald look," she told me.

"Well, that'll save time washing," I joked. "Maybe I can change my name to Riddick."

She rolled her eyes, muttering something I didn't think was meant to be complimentary. I painfully forced myself to roll over, using the running board, jutting door hinges, handle, etc., to pull me mostly upright.

"Please tell me the smell of overdone meat isn't me," I whimpered as sharp pains stabbed me from my movements.

"Pretty much," came her response.

"That's gonna leave a mark." I got the door open, and more or less crawled into the passenger seat.

CHAPTER TWENTY-ONE

Mitch watched impotently as Spacey and Anne made their suicide run. The older woman's no-nonsense approach to life appealed to him.

"Damn," Sam spoke. "I hope they make it."

"Let's make sure they do," Ruth answered, shooting at gang members.

Mitch joined in the firefight. "Sam, get close to those gun emplacements. We've gotta take them out." His AK clicked empty. Quickly, he locked in a new mag. "Keep her steady for a minute."

Sam did the best he could to not weave. Mitch fired three bursts apiece into any remaining enemy stupid enough to pop up from the emplacements. The .50 cal fell silent while Sam came to a stop before the two wrecked cars. Mitch and Ruth hop out of the vehicle. Mrs. Resick kept watch, while the older man jogged over to the two women.

"Are you crazy? Wait, never mind, you've already answered the question with your antics. How bad is it?" Mitch asked Spacey.

"Well, firstly: Call me Riddick. Secondly: I prefer my meat medium rare. I got cooked a little too much. And thirdly: Hello, military Humvee." She leaned forward and smooched the dash. "Ow."

"She broke my arm," Anne cried, as her late father's girlfriend drooled all over their new transport.

Spacey worked her way into the driver's seat. She was ass up, leaking blood and clear fluids from her burns. Her jeans had been scraped and burned almost to hot pants, showing she went commando. She hit the button to warm the glow plugs up, and get the Humvee started.

"Trifles. Suck it up, buttercup. We've got ass to kick, and I don't give a shit about names," Spacey wheezed.

She kept talking to herself, attempting to get comfy in the seat.

"Anne, grab what you can from the other truck. We'll get your arm set in a moment."

Mitch can see how much pain she's in, but the young woman does what he asked. Mitch is proud of her, as they shuttle gear into the Humvee. Spacey helps them load it up.

"Heads up, P.I.A. More incoming," Downing warned over the throat mikes.

"Thanks for the warning," Mitch spoke for Spacey.

"P.I.A., we are coming up behind you," came over the mike.

"Anne, keep a sharp eye out. I'm going to see if there's any usable ammo left behind the barricades." Mitch holstered his rifle, and double-timed it over to the sandbag emplacements.

Over the mike, he heard Spacey ask, "Can we loot the bodies now?"

Downing answered with a stream of harsh words that made Mitch recall an old drill sergeant he once had.

"Kidding, kidding," she answered. "Not," before falling silent.

To his satisfaction, Mitch discovered a stockpile of ammunition. He began ferrying cans of ammo over to the Humvee. As he worked, he half listened to the conversation between Anne and Spacey.

"I quit," Anne announced. "Shove over. I'm driving. You can still fire with the arm wound. Plus, you probably need your ribs re-set. I hope you're happy with the mess you've gotten into. How are the lungs?" she asked sarcastically.

"Guess again, pumpkin. I'm the only other one who will plow a path through the debris, and not think twice. Besides, do you really wanna sit in body fluids? My blood and leaking burns are now on the seat. My lungs will be just fine, I hope."

"Ewwww. Why must you be so uncouth and nasty?"

"It's all just part of my innate charm. Yo, Mitch, you need help?"

"No, Ma'am. I've got it," he replied, and continued to work.

# # #

Downing is genuinely shocked at how much trauma I willingly took on a second time for him and the group. He pulled out one of their first aid kits, which was way better stocked than my civilian one.

"You may attract trouble, but damn if you don't dish it back." He was trying to rinse my head off, and see how bad the burns really were to put ointment on. I was trying to hold still and not swat his hands away.

Ryan helped Mitch take care of setting Anne's broken arm. She screamed shrilly before passing out from the pain. Then the two men turned their attentions to my ribs. I was rethinking the whole being alive deal by the time they got done. Downing took out a small packet, and passed it over to us wounded women. It contained Oxycontin.

"Shit, dude, I take that now, I'm useless the rest of the trip. I'd be happy to kill for some regular ibuprofen, or acetaminophen. The pain is kicking in."

"I think you've proven you can hang with the big dogs Just take the damn stuff." He shoved it into my hands.

"No, seriously. I rarely take meds, and it will knock my ass out."

"Keep it. You'll need it later."

I shoved it into a pocket of my backpack, rooting around for a pair of pants that didn't resemble a thong. I began the laborious process of unlacing my shit-kicker boots and changing inside the Humvee as the men conferred.

CHAPTER TWENTY-TWO

Once Spacey had changed, the group continued to the secondary landing zone. Mitch took over driving duties to let the injured women rest a bit. Their pace held at a steady twenty miles per hour, owing to the need to avoid pileups, barricades, and assorted small groups of zoms. Downing cautioned everyone not to shoot unless absolutely necessary. He wanted to keep as low a profile as possible once away from the gang zone. Mitch utilized every open bit of road and berm just to keep moving.

Anne lay passed out from pain in the back. Spacey dozed on and off next to her. Ed kept an intent look out from the front passenger seat. All the jouncing and jarring around was taking its toll on everyone's wounds. So far, they had yet to see any living souls, just re-animated ones. Many buildings had spray painted messages on them, begging for help.

The convoy stopped two miles away from the airport. A long line of abandoned vehicles, some holding zombies, spoke of failed evacuation attempts

Doors slammed as everyone exited their vehicles, and walked up to Downing. Someone let out a low whistle. The road was chock full of mostly high-end vehicles.

"Sir, Colonel, Sir. What would you like us to do? I don't think we'll be able to take the vehicles farther. The thick trees make going off road out of the equation," Rhondel spoke. Her eyes hid behind shades, dark hair in a neat bun. If she was in pain from her ordeal with the bikers, she didn't let it show.

"Fuck that noise," I growled, causing Anne to

whimper a bit in fear at my words. "We're at the back of the airport. We just need to cut through the wire fencing, and we're in."

The colonel brought his binocs up, and surveyed the highway before lowering them. "I concur. Good thinking, civvie." Downing raised his voice, and motioned to everyone with a weapon. "Gather 'round," he addressed everyone. "Here's what we're gonna do. I need a couple volunteers to cut through the wire fence so we can get the vehicles through. The rest of us will stand guard. We don't know how many zombies are lurking nearby. Once we've gained access, Rhondel, you'll follow directly behind Ryan and me, then Sam's group, and Spacey and her crew can bring up the rear."

The colonel walked with his troops over to the transport and spoke to the emaciated refugees from the fish hatchery who carried makeshift weapons and a few firearms. His words clearly floated to us on the still air.

"You lot will guard those inside if we are attacked by zombies. It is imperative to keep you survivors safe. Let's do this, people!"

Gramps and Ryan got to work on the fencing, choosing to cut a side closest to a ground pole. The two men had been at it for a while before someone spotted the first zom. One of the survivors, nerves frayed, immediately shot it.

"Let's hope the sound goes unnoticed," I muttered. My mouth tightened in displeasure.

"Um," Anne tentatively began, "I don't think trees are supposed to move."

I risked a quick glance, noting she was right. I raised the rifle's scope to my eye, and used it to scan the woods surrounding us. Movement immediately caught my attention.

"Rear guard to Downing, a herd is coming at us from both sides." I spoke into the throat mike.

"Heads up, we have contact."

People in the troop transport starting shouting. Hysteria seemingly broke out at the sight of the oncoming horde.

"Can't anyone panic quietly?" I groused. "They draw the bulk of the zoms straight to them."

"Hel-lo!" Anne snipped. "And to us, fuck you very much."

"Hey, is that the Wahmbulance I hear?" I replied.

Mitch snorted with laughter.

"Stick close to the Humvee, knives at the ready, conserve ammo," I snapped to the group with me.

Our world reduced to screams, growls, gunplay, and close combat. Eventually, the survivors ran out of bullets. We watched in horror as a few were pulled from the transport when they leaned too far over the side.

Throughout it all, Speary and Gramps worked feverishly to cut the last of the fencing and roll it back enough for the vehicles to get through. The screams from the survivors never let up until we finished off the last lingering biter.

Rhondel took care of making sure the victims wouldn't rise again. Then we all slowly drove through the opening, and onto the tarmac.

We passed the Coast Guard station, heading toward the corporate airport. The runways were littered with crashed planes, and a few helicopters. We also thought we could see the hazy outline of a small crashed jetliner off in the distance. We pulled up behind the offices/waiting area. The place appeared to be mostly intact, but we still took the time to make sure it was clear of any lurking zoms. Anne and I checked out the parking lot as shell casings crunched under our feet.

"Looks like we missed a hell of a party," I said to her.

"Good," she replied.

Geez, no one wanted to banter. Once we all reconvened inside the airport lounge, Downing set up shift watches. He used all the survivors, more to keep them busy, and hopefully out of trouble, as we counted down the hours until pick up.

CHAPTER TWENTY-THREE

We were woken up by the sounds of shrill screaming.

"Some body better be getting munched on," I grumbled.

I struggled up from the floor to find, and kill whoever made the noise. Mrs. Breckson was alternately yelling for her kids, and at Rhondel.

"You need to wake your superior up so you can go find those kids," Tanya told the female military member.

A few of the survivors had spread out to search, calling out the children's names.

"We need to stay quiet and keep together." Rhondel tried to maintain control of an already quickly deteriorating situation.

"Damn people, why don't you just announce to every zombie in the area where we're at. You're all acting like a bunch of idiots."

"It's your fault we're in this situation," Mrs. Breckson scolded me.

"Alive? You're welcome," I sarcastically replied.

"You need to find my babies," the mother screeched at me. "You should know kids can't wait without something to do for this long!"

"Look bitch, you're their mother, you should be keeping better tabs on YOUR children," I snapped back.

"Who you calling a bitch? The only one I see here is the one before me."

I let it slide. "Look around, everyone. They can't have gone far. Did anybody check the other buildings? Or were you all too busy screaming your heads off?"

"What is going on?" Downing joined us.

"Dumb-ass lost her kids," I replied.

The mother started in with complaints and demands to find the missing hellions.

He made a patting motion. "Calm down. There's a lot of ground to cover. How long has it been since they've been gone?"

"It wasn't more than two minutes. I had to pee."

"I call bullshit, multiply that by an hour," slipped out my mouth, earning me a glare.

"Not helpful," Downing spoke low-voiced to me. He cupped his hands to his mouth, and called back the searchers, waving them to come over.

"We're going to split up into search parties," the colonel told us when everyone had gathered around. He quickly sorted us into groups. We had five hours in which to find the missing kids before pick up.

"What about weapons? You have all those guns and stuff. We need to arm ourselves," a survivor spoke up.

He burst the dam, and they all started to complain to some degree.

"Yeah, we can't be looking around unarmed."

"We lost people back there 'cause y'all wouldn't let us have guns. What we gonna do if we run into zombies?"

"It ain't right you hog all the firearms and bullets."

"Why do they get to keep theirs if we can't have any?"

"People, we're wasting time, and daylight. We don't have enough guns or ammo to arm everyone. Those of us who are armed, will be accompanying each group. As to why they can keep their stuff, they have proven themselves in combat."

"The crazy bitch gets to keep her weapons! She

don't follow orders at all. I'm not trusting her to look after me. She doesn't like us anyways."

"It's nothing personal. I hate everyone equally," I replied.

"We need weapons if we're gonna stand watch."

"Newsflash, it's a little more involved than just point and shoot. It's not a camera, it's a gun," I replied.

"Stop it! All of you. We have a mission to complete. Group one will be led by Ryan, group two by Mitch, group three by Sam, group four by Spacey, and group five by myself." Downing divided up the survivors, and gave them search areas.

#

Mitch moved off toward the Coast Guard buildings. They hadn't been searched when the group first arrived. The others slowly followed their team leaders with much grumbling. He saw the first target had a few windows, and one door. All of which were still intact.

He motioned for a young man by the name of George to try the handle.

"You're the one with the gun. Shouldn't you be doing this?" he complained resentfully.

"Tell me, boy, you have any military or police training? No? I'm ex-army. When I tell you to do something, you do it. There's a right and a wrong way to go about breaching a building. I'm going to teach you the correct procedure. You stand to the side, and open the door, using it to shield yourself. I stand here, gun at the ready to shoot any zombie that comes through."

He opened his mouth for some remark, but the older man didn't give him a chance to voice it. "Everybody else, keep your eyes on our surroundings. We have to move almost as one."

"Ready?" Mitch asked the kid. He nodded. "Now."

The door wouldn't budge.

"It's locked. Now what? Smart ass," George said.

"If it's locked, I don't think the kids are in there," Dan announced.

"Unless it was open before, and they locked the door behind them. I was hoping for a quiet entry." Mitch inspected the window, before turning to Dan.

"Dan, use your bat to break the window for me. I'll go inside and open the door."

Once inside, Mitch flipped on the flashlight and looked in to make sure no zombies lurked.

The office was small, and luckily didn't smell of rot. No thanks to the noise of shattering glass, faint sounds of moaning came from the other side of a second door. Carefully, Mitch crept over, turned the handle slowly, and opened the door. He scanned the hallway for signs of un-life, but saw none.

He back-tracked to the locked front door and let the other team members in.

"Took you long enough," George said.

"Son, I suggest you ease up on the sarcasm if you want to keep breathing. There are zoms in here. I heard the moaning. Stay behind me."

They entered the other rooms in silence. The whole time the moaning grew louder. George opened the next door. He was greeted by the decaying face of a zombie. Mitch didn't hesitate, and shot it in the head.

"Holy shit, dude. You didn't wait to see if they were alive, or nothing," Dan said.

"If they were alive, they would have said something. You can't hesitate. If you do, you're dead."

George demanded, "Give me a gun. NOW."

"You ever use one before?" the man asked.

"Just give me one."

After a few minutes of scrutinization, Mitch pulled out his back up and an extra mag. He handed it to George. "Flip off the safety before you shoot, and you're good to go. I want it back when we're done. Aim for the head."

"I know what to do, asshole."

Now that I highly doubt, but you can't fix stupid. "Dan, what about you?"

"I'm good. You're better than I'll ever be with a gun. I trust in my bat."

They moved to the last room. Mitch pointed at Dan to get the door. The older man heard Spacey over the radio, then Sam, as they reported in. Behind the door was the source of the moans. An equipment room held four deadheads. George pushed ahead of everyone, determined to prove what a bad-ass he was. He was greeted with a click, having forgotten to release the safety. He started to fumble with the gun as the zombie reached out, and grabbed hold of him. The other three deadheads crowded close. Mitch had no choice but to let George fend for himself. He shifted to one side, and quickly shot at zombies. A scream reverberated, followed by the sound of the 9mm.

It went off again, and Mitch felt a hit on the front of his tac vest. He staggered back, breath knocked out of him.

"You motherfucker, you got me bit," George ranted, while lining up another shot. Blood ran from between his neck and shoulder on his left side.

His shot whizzed past Mitch's head. The older man raised his gun and fired, hitting the kid square in the chest.

"I told you the safety was on," Mitch rasped out. He walked over to the young man, who coughed up blood on the floor.

"Fuck you," he spat with his last breath.

"Son, I told you, you should've checked your attitude." Mitch shook his head in sorrow. There was no help for the kid. The older man placed a bullet in George's head, to prevent him from turning into a zombie.

Blowback splattered him. He turned to see Dan still standing in the hallway, a wide-eyed look of horror on his face.

"Come on, son. Let's finish our job."

CHAPTER TWENTY-FOUR

I moved off with my group of malcontents, wondering when one of them would try to wrestle my weapons away from me—not something you wanted to have on your mind while on a search mission. I could tell already that keeping control of the group would end in disaster. The insistent, itching pain of my burns and other assorted wounds left me feeling less than inclined to try to play nice.

"Yo, dip shit. If you don't have ranged weapons, get behind me; otherwise, I'm going to assume you want to be used as bait, and I will treat you accordingly."

The two young punks glared at me, baseball bats on their shoulders. "Bitch, you ain't nothing. You less than nothing without your weapons."

"Maybe so, but I'm the bitch with the gun who helped rescue you. So lets' play who has the bigger balls later. Otherwise, by all means, keep going ahead and get bit. I'll happily shoot you later."

They muttered a few choice insults, just loud enough for me to hear, but waited until I, Ed, and a woman about thirty joined them. I took point, gun at the ready, as we crossed the debris strewn concrete. The overgrown grass beyond the runways barely waved when the wind blew. It came up to mid-chest. I paused a moment, looking for signs of trampling. Unfortunately, I couldn't tell what was normal, and what wasn't. Great, we'd have to form lines and search the area methodically.

"You two," I motioned to the punks, "Fifty yards to the left, an arm's length between you, make sure the kids aren't hiding or injured in the grass from the edge of the concrete to the fence."

"Why? So we can get killed?"

"Hey, you wanted to be all macho, here's your chance," I replied, and instructed the other two to spread out on my right.

The young men sneered and muttered some stuff I'm sure wasn't complimentary, and sauntered off, cracking jokes between them.

"Idiots," I said under my breath. "Keep looking back and out." I showed them what I meant as we slowly pushed into the vegetation, and walked forward. I paused at the fence line, sweat pouring off me, futilely slapping at mosquitoes. I waved to Gramps and the young woman to come my way, while cursing the bugs.

"You," I said to the woman when they came within hearing range.

"Mary," she replied.

"Mary, Ed, we need to keep in sight of each other. I think there's an old fort here-about, and I don't know how much is left or what shape it's in. I'd rather not fall over or into it. Besides, we're getting close to the marsh, and the river."

"Let's hope them kids didn't come this way. A river is a mighty big temptation for two kids, especially on a hot day like this," Ed replied.

"Oh, those poor children," Mary moaned.

Rolling my eyes, I took out a pair of wire cutters, and made a hole in the far side of the fence, which kept unwanted people away from the runways. I held the chain link away, as Ed and Mary slipped through, before I followed them. We started moving off, deeper into the trees. I grimaced as my hurts protested, and held my gun at the ready. I was constantly scanning around me as the other two followed. It was eerily quiet, and the two punks had yet to come back. Just as we smelled water, I heard moans. Mary whimpered. I shushed her.

I brought the sights up to eye level, and cautiously inched forward. My injured ribs protested the abuse. Damn my need to breathe. Zombies in torn, dirty clothes shambled toward me. I lined up on the heads, breathed in and out, in again, and squeezed the trigger on the exhale. One head exploded, gore splashing. I immediately lined up on the next, and fired. The last of the group came so close I didn't need to do more than point and shoot. My ears rang from the shots, so I was only dimly aware of Mary having hysterics behind me.

"Suck it up, buttercup. You were never in any danger. Move on," I stated. Her tears only made me grouchy.

For once, Ed didn't chastise me, only comforted her, and got her following after me. We cleared the tree line to find ourselves on a wide, overgrown swarth. So, this was the old fort site. Water gleamed ahead of us. I really didn't want to tramp about on the river bank. The old man seemed to sense my reluctance.

"Give me the shotgun. I know how to use it, and with your ribs, you're better off keeping watch."

I debated all of several seconds, sighed, unslung the weapon from around me, and handed it over with extra shells. He started toward the edge of the marsh, still spry at seventy. I watched for a few minutes, making sure he was going to be fine, before turning and scanning the area. Just because I had cleared it didn't mean the sounds wouldn't attract lurkers.

"Mary, keep an eye on him. Let me know if zombies appear, or he looks like he needs help."

"Oh . . . okay." she said in between hiccups and sobs.

Fifteen minutes later, Ed verified the bank was clear. He made to hand the shotgun back, so I let him keep hold of it for now.

"I saw a mess of them deadheads stuck in the

mud, struggling toward firm ground."

"Crap on toast. Let's hope they don't come apart at the waist and claw their way to us. Otherwise, we'll have to clear those fuckers out. Let's move."

We fast walked toward the chain link fence, and the two young men somewhere in the high grass. We followed the broken trail they had made, and smelled a sweet scent, not of rot, but of weed.

I keyed the throat mike. "All units, Team Four checking in, be advised there are several dozen zoms trapped in the marsh mud. No sign of the kids."

"Roger, Team Four," Downing acknowledged.

We continued searching and clearing our assigned area, coming across the two punks. They sprawled in the grass, passing a joint between them.

"Gee assholes, glad there isn't two lost kids to be found."

"Like you care, bitch."

"Point taken," I replied mildly. "However, we have a job to do, which means we do it without fucking off."

They just laughed, "Bitch, you do what you want. We's hungry and sick of this shit."

"Yeah," his buddy replied. "Tuck this shit. We're done."

They bumped fists and laughed, toking up again.

I just looked at them and shrugged. "Fine. Don't come crying when the zoms find you. Oh, and if you're not back by pick-up time? Forget it. You can stay behind and rot."

I walked off, back to Rhondel and Anne, with Ed and Mary trailing after me.

CHAPTER TWENTY-FIVE

Downing heard the voices of his team reporting in, scowling at the report from Mitch. It was taking longer than he liked to clear his section. He also didn't care for the ominous silence of his gunner. As point man, he quickly yet efficiently cleared the remaining aircraft, out buildings, and all its potential hiding spots. The others behind him gripped their various homemade weapons, trying hard, yet failing to remain quiet. One person would forget, and shuffle his feet, or another would try to stifle a sneeze or cough. He turned to the others in a clump behind him.

"Clear, let's move on." he commanded.

"Uh, um, Colonel," came a timid response.

"Yes?"

"Uh, what, what are we gonna do if we don't find 'em in time?"

"I have every confidence we will, and so should you. Fall in line." He turned back around and led the way outside, and to the next area.

A few deadheads lurked, which he put down. The silence unnerved him. He knew children were not normally quiet for such an extended period of time. His son never had been when little. A feeling of wrongness crept up his spine. There was no telling how the mother would take the news if he couldn't find and bring her children back. She looked so close to birthing, the strain might cause her baby to arrive early. Downing kept the group moving at a brisk pace, gun and upper body swiveling as they crossed open ground toward another hangar. The large door was closed, so he continued onto the smaller side door.

He placed his back against the hot metal wall, already sweating from the heat, and peeked into the small window placed in the door's top half. It was dark near the middle. Light only streamed in from half-windows placed around the perimeter near the top. The colonel motioned for a man named Wayne to try the knob. It turned easily in his hand. He looked at the soldier, a question in his eyes. Downing gave a nod, and the man thrust the door open and stepped back. Leading with the gun, he made sure nothing lurked nearby.

He walked inside, swiveling and scanning the big space. When no zombies immediately came at him, he reached up and flicked on the gun's light and waited for his eyes to adjust while still keeping watch. In a moment, he signaled his group to follow. They piled in a bit reluctantly. He pointed at Wayne and two others to go right, then at the rest to follow him left.

The young man nodded firmly, griping the tire iron on his shoulder more tightly, and slowly moved off down the inside wall, passing from one pool of sunlight to another.

Downing did the same on his side. Big, silent shapes loomed on the edges of the light. As his flashlight played over and around them, he saw they were massive rolling tool boxes, and other stuff mechanics needed to work on the jets. As his group turned the inside corner, passing by the closed hangar door, a rhythmic thumping suddenly came from further in the gloom to his right.

Someone let out a yip. Others shushed the person quickly. Their breathing sounded too loud and too fast behind him.

He motioned for them to hold, and slowly inched forward a step at a time. The noise grew more frantic. The light played over a cab on wheels, and a zombie inside trying to get at him. The shut door prevented that.

Downing fired, the bullet easily piercing the glass and re-killing the zom.

He went back to his group far enough to say, "Move up."

They shuffled quickly, shoes making far too much noise on the concrete. The cab had a long tow bar extending toward a Cessna. Another zombie came moaning and growling out of the darkness. Gasps went off behind him as he lined up and took his shot. A shout from the darkness on the far side let him know the second group had encountered more of the things.

"Keep moving," Downing exhorted his group low-voiced, and picked up the pace.

He constantly swiveled as he fast-walked, light bouncing over equipment, stairs, up the sides of parked jets, and underneath them. Running and screams greeted his ears, along with growls and grunts. A figure hurtled out of the gloom, and he nearly shot a member of Wayne's group.

"Damn it," he swore.

The woman held her hands out, palms up. "Don't shoot! Don't shoot! Hurry. There's a bunch of them back there."

"Move! Move! Move!" he yelled, and advanced toward the fight, the ragged sounds of steps behind him letting him know they followed, albeit reluctantly.

The colonel got to the scene just as a zombie in filthy, tattered mechanic's overalls took a bite out of a second young man. He gave a shrill scream, collapsing under the weight of the corpse as it chewed and shook its head like a rabid dog. Wayne turned around from finishing off another deadhead, tire iron coated in gore. Downing took aim and fired. The young man's eyes went wide in fear, but he had the presence of mind to step back out of range. Once more a shot rang out, and the screams of the second man cut off.

The stench of fresh and stale blood hung in the air.

"Report," the colonel barked out.

"Damn man! Them fuckers came outta nowhere!" Wayne replied, chest heaving as he sucked in air.

"Yeah," another chimed in. "We had just cleared the space before the second wall and was turning the corner when all of a sudden, there they were."

Downing knelt to inspect the rotters. All wore work coveralls. He looked up toward the tail of the jet looming near them. The door stood open against the side. Wheeled stairs gave access to the interior. He narrowed his eyes. They must have fallen in their eagerness to get fresh meat.

He walked closer, and saw clots of congealed blood, flesh, and a few chunks of bone from the impact sites.

"Anyone else bit?" he asked, as he kept scanning.

"Naw, man. He the only one. We cool now. Damn, you think there are more up there?" Wayne asked softly.

Downing voiced a negative. "We're done here. Let's go check out that downed jet outside."

"I can't. I can't. I just can't anymore." The woman he had nearly shot moaned, crying.

"Hey, Colonel, Sir, I can stay with her here." One of the men in his group offered.

"No, no, no, no, no. I have . . . I have to get out. I can't, no," the woman nearly shrieked. She suddenly bolted, screaming, at a clatter, and the darkness swallowed her up.

"Angie, no! Wait!"

"Go after her, see she stays safe." Downing barked out to the man who had volunteered to babysit her.

He rabbited off, flashlight and a metal length of pipe swinging wildly.

"The rest of you, we have a job to finish."

Grumblings came from the group.

"That ain't right. You're the one with the gun."

"Yeah, shouldn't you be going after her?"

"I thought we all needed to stick together?"

"People," Downing barked louder, as the milling group lost all semblance of order. "We've cleared the building. Now we have to clear the jet site."

It was a tiny white lie, but he felt if any more zombies lurked on the floor, they would have come out of hiding at the sounds of the fight.

A few more mutterings meet his ears, but he swept them all with a steely-eyed stare, wishing Ryan was with him or even, he shuddered to himself, that pain-in-the-ass woman, Spacey.

"Good, now keep close." He started outside and down the runway.

The crashed jet looked to be one of the smaller, domestic types. It was still a tad too large for this particular airport. Whatever happened to the plane, it must have been bad to make the pilot attempt such a desperate landing. Long, black skid marks showed where the jet touched down. The colonel and his group passed by the remains of landing gear, ripped or snapped off. The plane had continued off the concrete, judging by the sheets of metal and strewn luggage. A deep gouge in the earth, containing more debris, led up to the plane. A glint far off in the field was probably one of the missing wings, and pieces of the turbines.

"Holy shit!"

"Oh man, do you think anyone survived?" came in whispers as they walked alongside the trench.

The jet had smashed through the far fencing, and as they got closer, the faint stench of fuel and flesh could be smelled. The slides had been deployed. They lay, deflated.

"Fan out, search the area, make sure no zombies are lurking in the grass. Be careful!" Downing instructed them as he walked along the length of the downed beast.

The engines under the remaining wing were missing, and the plane itself had come to rest at a tilt on the stub of the missing wing. The nose lay buried up to the cockpit windows in the marsh. Mud had splashed up and dried over the windshield, so he didn't know if the pilots had survived and made it off. Heart sinking, the colonel knew he'd have to check inside. Mrs. Breckson's children had so far shown a shocking lack of common sense and discipline.

Downing came back to the remaining wing. He could climb on it, and from there, to the open hatch. Before he did so, he made sure all his gear was secure, tightened the chin strap on his helmet, and pulled on gloves. The metal would be hot from the sun. During all this, a few of his group came back, including Wayne and another man.

"Sir, you aren't thinking of going inside are you? I mean, you really think those kids would be careless or even stupid enough to come this far?"

"I'm not sure of anything when it comes to those children. I'm hoping I'm wrong, but the jet's here, and anyone can get inside. I've got to make sure. You stay here, in case I need back up, and keep an eye on the others."

"Yes, sir," Wayne replied, worry in his dark brown eyes.

Downing tested the wing, then heaved himself on top. He lay splayed out as the metal groaned, trying to ignore the intense heat coming off it. When he was sure it would hold his weight, he slowly kneeled, then crawled up to the opening, pausing every so often to check that the wing would still hold. The higher he got, the more he became convinced a slight sway was taking over.

Downing kept his eyes on the open doorway.

The Colonel ignored the faint voices of his group which floated to him. He had just reached a point where he could see inside. The stench of stale blood and rotting flesh overwhelmed him. He swallowed convulsively before getting his gag impulse under control. The overhead bins had burst open in the rough landing. Suitcases and bags littered the area, or hung from above. He could hear scratching and pounding against a door, and a small chorus of moans.

He crawled back fully onto the wing, lay down to help spread his weight, and motioned for the two men below to join him. The moaning continued to gain in volume. The wing shook and shuddered under the additional weight.

"Sir," Wayne panted, out of breath from the climb. "Oh my . . . " he tried to muffle his coughing and retching.

"I'm hoping the majority are still belted in. But I'm gonna need help. Who knows if any got wedged beneath the seats?"

"No, sir. Yes, sir, I will. Ain't nothing' gonna get you or us while we help clear the rest of this bitch. Hey Adam, get on up here. The soldier needs help."

Downing had to stand once off the wing, and inside the plane, where the sight— not a pretty one. He snapped left, took out the rotter pounding on the cockpit door. The body dropped in a heap. The colonel snapped right, registering movement. A second zombie shuffled up from the back.

Wayne, still gagging, slipped behind the soldier. Due to the slight tilt, standing and moving was difficult. He slowly headed toward the front, killing the few passengers still belted as they reached for the fresh food. He placed his broad, muscular back against the closed cockpit door.

Adam stepped inside, spewing at the pervading stench, and looked toward Downing for his instructions.

"Don't crowd me, son," he said, while he adjusted his stance.

He nodded, one arm up trying to block the smell. He maneuvered toward the aisle. Somehow, he got caught on the seat. He reached the aisle and fell, arms windmilling as he let out a shout. The colonel had to step forward to avoid being knocked down. His boot hit the lower half of a body. The pressure from gas inside caused it to explode. The colonel lost his footing, falling backward across nearby seats.

Wayne's inarticulate shout reached him just as a small hand grabbed his pants leg. A zombie baby pulled itself into view, growling and gnashing its two teeth.

Oh shit, oh shit, oh shit! Downing brought the stock of his gun down repeatedly. Gore splashed upwards, and when the head was a ruined mess, the fingers finally let go.

"Adam, get up and help," Wayne screamed.

What a nightmare! the colonel thought as he heaved himself up, ramming directly into another zombie. His angry curses spewed forth as the thing grabbed at his upper body. Time seemed to slow as they fell in a tangle toward the floor.

"Holy shit," Adam screamed, high pitched.

The gun caught between them, his face all but mashed against a bloated mid-section as hands scrabbled over his helmet, trying to yank it off.

"What should I do, man? What should I do?" Adam babbled.

From what seemed far off, the colonel barely heard Wayne shouting, "Get it off him, ya dumb fuck!"

The colonel used his legs and shoulders to push up and forward, but it didn't do much to move the bulk of the rotter away from him.

If his life hadn't been in danger, the sight they no doubt made would have been comical. Travis got his hands and arm free, just as the zombie's teeth mashed down hard on his raised left forearm. Downing screamed in pain and fury as he struggled to keep the straining zombie away from his face. He groped at the handgun strapped to his right thigh.

"Adam, do something, man," Wayne yelled.

"Fuck! Fuck! Fuck!" the man yelled over and over.

Downing decided his knife was easier than the gun to get out in a hurry. He pulled it out of the sheath, and plunged it into the zom's temple. Pushing the zombie off him, he looked at the two men and said, "Thanks for saving my ass."

The colonel shoved up his sleeve to check the bite area. He noted teeth marks, but thanks to the material of the jacket, no broken skin, but the beginnings of a bruise. Downing let out a sigh of relief.

"Pull yourselves together. We still have a job to finish," Downing told the other two men.

"Sorry, sir. I'm so, so sorry," Adam babbled.

The soldier nodded curtly, cleaning his knife off before re-sheathing it. He took hold of his rifle and with a grunt, stood up. His heart raced, adrenaline pounded, and his stomach heaved with how close to death he had come. He did a quick weapons check, the familiar movements helped to steady himself.

"Stay behind me, let's go," Downing commanded Adam.

The back half of the plane still needed to be cleared. The colonel cautiously inched down the hallway. He steadily moved his upper body left, right, down, and up at the bins. Every muscle tensed, he expected a zom to reach up from the floor between, or underneath the seats, and snag his boots. Or to suddenly come tumbling out of an overhead compartment, and on his head.

He strained all his senses. Sweat ran freely down the sides of his face and body from underneath the helmet covering his soaked hair. He still got scared, despite all his years of service. Only a fool wouldn't be. The colonel reached the last set of seats. Only the bathroom remained. He thought he heard whimpering or crying but couldn't be sure.

"Adam," he whispered.

"Sir?"

"Step there," Downing indicated with a tilt of his head at the right sided last row of seats against the plastic dividing wall as he stood to the left.

The young man did as he was told, eyes wide at the sounds, but trying to hold it together. The colonel appreciated the effort.

Because of how the hinges sat, the toilet door opened outward. The fact it wasn't rattling was the only good sign. The cramped quarters were not meant for rifle use. He let it swing on its cross-body strap and got out his handgun, while placing his back against the plane's wall.

The bathroom door had deep indentations from undead fists pounding on it. The force had dented it inwards, and whoever was inside had enough presence of mind to lock it.

Gently Downing knocked. "Hello? Anyone alive inside? It's Colonel Downing. I've come to help."

No reply. He tried again, "Ashleigh?" Still no answer.

"What we gonna do now?" Adam whispered.

The colonel inspected the door. They needed tools to break the lock and force it open. "Let's let whoever's inside calm down first." He raised his voice, knocking gently once more. "We're going to move to the front of the plane now. I've killed all the zombies inside. It's safe to come out now. I'll be waiting when you decide."

He motioned for Adam to go first. The man did, with a last lingering look back before hurrying up the aisle. Downing followed.

"Let's see who's behind door number one, shall we? Wayne, stand to the side there and on three, open it." The colonel brought his rifle up and sighted down the barrel.

"Yes, sir."

"One . . . Two . . . " The door didn't budge.

Wayne pulled harder "It must be locked," he gritted out.

Downing stepped forward and knocked, calling out as he had to the person trapped inside the bathroom. It took a few repetitions, but finally, the door cracked open. A scared eye peeked out.

"It's all right. I'm here to take you back to your mom. The zombies are dead."

The door opened farther, and the little boy stepped out. His blue eyes wide with fear, he breathed hard. "My sister. We got separated."

"You were exploring inside?"

A wordless nod his answer.

"She's in back, hiding in the bathroom, but doesn't want to come out. She must be as scared as you are. Why don't we go back and see if she won't come out for us? Huh?"

He could have sworn the kid's eyes grew even bigger, and he frantically shook his head no. Downing started to get irritated, but swallowed it. "Come on, buddy. I'll go first, to show it's safe. Your mother is frantic with worry."

Once more the kid refused, and huddled against the cockpit wall, trying to make himself smaller.

He tried again. "I don't want to have to break the door open. That'll scare your sister even more. She's been through a lot, just like you have. I bet it would really help her to hear your voice."

A third time the boy refused. Downing gritted his teeth and stood back up from where he had kneeled down to the kid's level.

"What we gonna do now?" Wayne asked. "We gonna try and break the door down?"

"No, I've got one more idea." He keyed his throat mike. "Downing to base, copy, over."

"Base to Downing, go ahead, over."

"Base, we have the package. Repeat we have the package, do you copy? Over."

"Base to Downing, roger that. Over."

"Base, inform the mother we need her at my location. I am sending an escort for her, copy. Over."

"Downing, you need the mother at your location, and will send an escort, confirm. Over"

"Base, that is correct. Sending escort now. Copy. Over."

"Roger that, standing by. Over."

Downing turned to Wayne and Adam. "Either of you volunteer, or know who would?"

"Sir, I can do it." Adam responded, eager to make up for his earlier mistake.

The colonel nodded and the man clambered down, and took off for their camp.

CHAPTER TWENTY-SIX

Mrs. Breckson stood at the base of the wing, holding her enormous belly with both hands. "You get down here. I can't climb. I'm pregnant,"

At hearing his mother's voice, the boy bolted past the men and slid down the wing. "Mom!"

"Are you okay? Are you hurt?" Frantically, she inspected her boy, and after satisfying herself he was fine, yelled up to the colonel, "Where's Ashleigh? Where's my little princess?"

"She's locked herself into the back bathroom. We can't get her to come out. We're hoping the sound of your voice will help draw her out." Downing called down to her.

He gestured for her to walk toward the back, and call from there. She grabbed her son's hand, and yanked him after her as she waddled.

"Princess, Ashleigh, Mommy's here. You come on out now, and we'll get you a snack."

The men stood and watched the back of the plane. Nothing happened, not even a response.

"Try again, Ma'am, please."

Once more the woman pleaded with her daughter to come out. Adam noticed as she did so, her son kept tugging on her hand, trying to get her attention.

"Stop it. I'm trying to get your sister," she snapped at him.

The boy promptly threw a tantrum, screaming at the top of his lungs. His mother ignored him, trying to coax her daughter out, but her voice was drowned out by her son.

Adam tried to calm the kid. "Hey now, son. Come on." It only made him scream louder. He looked toward the colonel and shrugged.

Downing scowled as he checked his watch. It had taken far too long to search, and the continued silence from his gunner had his anxiety level rising. They needed to get the kid out and back, but he didn't want to further stress an already fragile situation.

"Wayne, let's see if we can't take the door off its hinges. It opens outward, shouldn't be too hard."

"Yes, sir. Lemme just take a look at them. Luckily there're all those tools in the hangar. They should help." He inspected the one nearest them, then clambered out and jogged back toward the toolboxes.

"Mrs. Breckson!" Downing called out, but soon realized he couldn't be heard over the kid's shrieks. He also noticed the people with him had started to grumble and shoot un-friendly looks toward the mother and son. Once on the ground, he turned to the mother. "Mrs. Breckson, it doesn't seem this is working. Wayne and I have another plan. I'm gonna have Adam escort you and your boy over there, so you can both have a seat and rest."

Adam held out a hand to help her, anxious to get them away from the plane. The mother leaned heavily on his arm, snapping out. "Quit your screaming, let's go sit a bit. Mommy's gotta get off her swollen feet."

She didn't look to see if her boy followed, beelining straight for an abandoned golf cart, and lowering herself onto it with a groan. The kid continued to scream. Downing had to work hard to keep the disgust from showing on his face. He had never been more relieved than when Wayne came back with an assortment of tools.

The two men worked their way back up the wing, dragging the tools with them. Downing knocked one last time on the door.

"Ashleigh. It's Colonel Downing, and Wayne. We're gonna try and get the hinges off the door, so we can get you out. Your mom's outside the plane, waiting for you."

There was no response, and when he tried the handle, it still showed locked and wouldn't budge. The men got to work. It was a bit harder than they thought, and eventually, Wayne had to fire up the acetylene torch he had found and try to burn the hinges off. It took a combination of that, a crowbar, and muscle before the plastic cracked and they could pry the entire door off.

Ashleigh lay curled in a tight ball on the floor. She didn't appear to be breathing.

"Oh, shit," Wayne softly cursed.

Downing dropped to his knees, and gently touched the girl on her shoulder. "Ashleigh? Honey?" She didn't move.

Her head was tucked in such a way he couldn't see her face, even when he moved her hair out of the way. He had to remove a glove to check for a pulse. It was barely there, and her skin felt fever hot.

"She's alive," he told the other man. "We're gonna have to carry her out of here. Go and tell her mom we got her," Downing said, as he worked on cradling the girl in his arms.

"Yes, sir." Wayne hurried to the front of the plane, and down the wing just as the colonel stood with his burden.

He was so intent on the unconscious kid he nearly missed seeing the bright crimson puddle her body hid. "Shit," he swore comprehensively under his breath, more sweat suddenly breaking out.

"Please let it be from a wound during play, and not a zombie bite." He sprinted to the front, heart pounding in fear, feeling he carried a defective bomb, and not an injured little girl.

The kid moaned as he sat on the wing, then lay down and tried to control his descent, and he nearly sent them tumbling down in his haste to make it onto the ground. Wayne and Adam waited for him, and despite his efforts, something must have shown on his face.

"Oh, shit, man. No. Not that innocent little kid," Adam said, a tad too loud.

Wayne hushed him. "Shut up, man. It might not be what we think."

Downing lay the girl on a debris free spot of grass, and the men dropped down beside him. Under his guidance, they carefully tried to uncurl her. Wayne swore softly, alerting the others. He looked up at them, fear and horror written all over his face as he held the girl's arm out from her side. A large area of flesh and muscle was missing. The blood had started to congeal, and a rotted scent greeted their noses. Black lines radiated out from the wound, traveling the length of her arm and making their way to the girl's heart.

"Goddammit," Downing cursed.

The men looked at him worriedly. "What, what we gonna do, sir? Her momma ain't gonna like this. Maybe, maybe the army has a vaccine? Maybe she can still be saved? Right? We ain't gonna have to shoot her, are we? Not a little kid. Not with her momma nearby."

The colonel took a deep breath in He dreaded the next few minutes. "No, the army, to date, has no viable vaccination, or cure."

"Maybe, maybe we can just tell her mom she had a-a fatal accident, and you know. Bury the body," Adam suggested.

Wayne glared at him. "You gonna shoot her first, dumb-ass? In front of her mom? 'Cause burying ain't gonna keep the kid from turning, and digging her way out."

"Well, yeah, but, by then we won't be here. We'll

be on the plane heading to safety, see, so her momma won't have to know she was ever bit." he replied. "Right?" Adam turned pleading eyes on the soldier.

"Christ," Downing blew out air. "She's going to want to see her girl. See if there's a tarp around here, or anything we can use to wrap the kid up in. I don't want her to re-animate on her mom. I'll go talk to the mother."

He got up, dreading having to inform a parent her child was dead. Worse than dead. Mother and son sat side by side, eating protein bars and drinking bottled water.

"Where's my Ashleigh? Where's my princess?" she demanded.

The boy had stopped eating, and was fiddling with the remains of his bar and the wrapper. There was something about his body movements, and the way he wouldn't meet anyone's eyes that set Downing's radar off.

You little shit! He thought, *You knew your sister had been bitten!* "Ma'am. We have your daughter." He paused, hating the next part.

She didn't pick up on the hesitation, too busy eating and rubbing her belly. The others, however, suddenly stilled one by one.

"Ma'am. I regret to inform you, your daughter appears to have fallen victim to a fatal accident while playing. I'm sorry for your loss."

Slowly, the woman stopped eating, the silence clueing her in more than what the soldier spoke. "What?"

Christ on a cracker! "Ma'am, your daughter had a fatal accident while playing."

"What? No," she shook her head vigorously in denial. "You're lying! Ashleigh! Princess! Ashleigh! Mommy's coming!" She heaved her bulk up and shoved past Downing, only moving marginally faster than a walk.

The Colonel followed, trying to hold an arm out to stop her, but she swatted it away and cursed at him. He could only hope the two men had found something to wrap the kid up in.

"Ashleigh! Ashleigh! My baby!" she shrilled, and collapsed beside her daughter.

The men had come through. The girl lay wrapped in a dirty tarp, only her head and feet free. Her mother clawed at the plastic.

"Ma'am, you really don't wanna be doing that."

"Don't you tell me what I can, and can't do with my baby! It's your fault she's dead! You're supposed to be guarding us! You're supposed to keep us safe!" She continued to yank, trying to uncover her girl.

"Ma'am, please don't do that," Downing tried again. Wayne and Adam adding their pleas to his.

"You're lying! She doesn't look hurt! I wanna see my baby!"

Downing knelt down and tried to restrain her hands, but her grief and anger lent her strength. She slapped at his hands, trying to claw his face. He grabbed her wrists. She spit at him, and tried yanking free. Their tussling bumped the body, causing the tarp to slip.

"A little help," the colonel gritted out. He didn't want to use more force than necessary on a heavily pregnant, and obviously stricken mother. But he was having trouble. "Grab her upper arms."

The two men hustled over and each took hold under her arms and the three of them started to drag her backward. In all her thrashing, one of her feet kicked her daughter's body. A low, eerie moan emanated, unnoticed by the screaming woman but not by the other survivors.

"Oh, shit!"

"Did she just make a noise?"

"Are we sure she's dead?"

"Hey, something ain't right with her face."

The mother's cries of sorrow turned to screams of pain. "Oh God! Oh God! My water! My baby's coming!"

"Ah, hell no!" Adam exclaimed as a wave of

amniotic fluid suddenly soaked the woman's shorts, cascading down her legs to be soaked into the ground.

Mrs. Breckson lay on her back, holding her belly with both hands, knees bent up and screaming.

Everyone looked toward Downing. He stood, taking a few steps away, and keyed his mike. "Downing to base, copy, out."

"Base to Downing, copy, go ahead, out."

"Base, we need anyone with medical knowledge, and midwifery, to come to my location. Copy, out."

They repeated his request, and everyone milled about anxiously while waiting for the answer. Finally, it came.

The Colonel turned to his group. "Adam and Wayne, I want you two to take the little girl and bury her in whatever spot of ground you can find. The rest of you . . . " he broke off as his mike chattered.

"Base to Downing, be advised a large group of hostiles is on the move a quarter mile from your location, copy, out."

"Downing to base, copy, out."

"It huuuurrrrtttssss! Oh God, it huuurrrrtttsss! I need something for the pain! You gotta give me something!" the laboring woman howled.

"Colonel!"

"Listen up, people!" Downing barked out, over the screams. He fired out orders, crushing any complaints.

The members scurried to do what they had been told. In the rush, those with medical knowledge arrived, and barely made it ahead of the horde. The biggest trouble was trying to load Mrs. Breckson on a piece of large, torn metal in case they became overrun, and had to move. She howled and fought.

The few female members tried to keep the laboring woman calm. She screamed, begged for pain medicine, and cursed when none was forthcoming.

The rest of the group formed a circle around the mother. The hot sun beat down as they fought off the zoms. Downing realized they were in far greater danger of succumbing to exhaustion.

"Downing to base, we need back up. We're out in the open here. Copy, out."

"Base to Downing, received. Help is on the way, copy, out."

CHAPTER TWENTY-SEVEN

Ryan got back before the circus his superior led.

"Where the hell have you been? I mean, seriously! WTF?! I don't report in, and I get my ass chewed off."

Anne watched in amusement, glad for something to break up the monotony of waiting for the other party members.

"Fuck off, bitch. Since it seems you can't see, I lost all my team members to an incoming horde." He shot back with middle finger extended, walking over to grab a water bottle from the dwindling supply.

"Eh," I shrugged it off. "Since it seems you're deaf, Downing found the kids."

"Yeah? Then where the hell are they?"

"Trapped out in the open, probably by the horde you disturbed. And moo cow is actively birthing."

He cursed, tossed the empty bottle in back, and punched the side of the troop transport. He grabbed his rifle back up and ran off to help.

"Um, so why didn't you tell him he could ride with us?" Anne asked as we got in the Humvee

"Because he didn't give me the chance." *I don't want to be anywhere near that woman and the screaming brat she's trying to shit out.*

We followed Rhondel toward the gunshots. Each jolt and jounce of the vehicle caused an agony of pain from my ribs. Anne jumped out, and started attacking the zombies from behind. I stomped on the gas, aiming for a group of rotters, and mowed them down. Eventually, we managed to kill all the zoms, unfortunately losing a few more survivors. Rhondel and Downing got Breckson and her new baby inside their Humvee. We all started back to the concourse.

"All right everyone, rest and refuel. We only have five hours before pick up. Also, welcome to our newest member, baby . . . " Downing began.

"Lexi Wylie," the mom mumbled sleepily.

There was a scattering of congratulations from the people who had stayed behind. But most everyone chugged down water, or nutrition bars, or tried to rinse off blood and guts. Mitch and Sam and both their crews walked in, finally done with their task. Downing and Ryan walked off to have some sort of talk. The boy started to rummage through the supplies, tossing stuff he didn't want aside, not caring where they landed. I walked over and put a stop to it. The kid ran off after trying to kick me. I was left cleaning up his mess.

"I will be so glad when they're gone," I said to no one in particular. "Where's the she brat?"

"Bit, someone told me. That's what set the mom off, brought on labor," Anne answered me.

"Huh, I didn't think he had the balls to cap a kid in front of its mom," I replied.

"Um," a peculiar look crossed her face. "Crap. I don't know if he or someone else did. I do know a couple of the guys ran off to bury the kid right before the horde trapped the others."

"Great. I hope it was shot, or that's gonna give a whole new meaning to the term 'come back to bite you on the ass.'"

Mitch snorted, "Yeah, I know."

"You two are sick. Just completely sick and wrong," Anne said.

# # #

After a few fruitless hours of trying to rest, Downing barked out orders for us to load up and move out. Slowly, our convoy started across the field to the coast guard's runway, which had less debris on it. We teamed up, clearing the runway. Downing got a warning over his radio that another horde had been spotted. No one really knew how large it was, and we didn't want to find out. Everyone sat in the vehicles, waiting for the pickup.

As the sun sank, the sound of explosions and gun fire floated to us on the anemic breeze. The newborn started crying.

"I wish she'd shut the squaller up with a tit in its mouth," I snarked, glaring toward the vehicle containing mother and newborn. "Thing's worse than an air raid siren."

"Now, now," Mitch tried to placate me. "It's not that bad."

I shot him an ice-pick glare. "Let's see how long it takes for you to change your assessment when it brings more biters to us."

He opened his mouth for a retort when Anne piped up. "Shut up! Both of you! I'm fucking sick of both your shit."

Mitch and I blinked at each other in surprise. I didn't know what crawled up her butt and died, but I wasn't in the mood to find out. I turned my head, ignoring her outburst, and futilely scanned the pressing darkness.

Mitch and Anne had a quick snipping contest of their own. For a moment, I thought a fight was about to break out. It settled down when Downing came over the com mikes asking what was going on.

"Have you been in contact with base again, Colonel Downing?" I asked. "I'd really like to know when I'll have some peace and quiet back."

He ignored my jab. "Twenty minutes out. We should hear them before we see them."

Not long after he replied, we all heard the throb of large engines. A large, dark blob approached. Swirling wind and high-intensity beams pierced the night. The huge plane settled down. A ramp extended, and military men and women jumped off before it was fully down. They ran, rifles at the ready, to form a perimeter. One of the figures came toward us.

He wore a marine uniform and stopped by Downing's window, but whatever they said was lost in the sound of the cargo plane.

Over the mikes, Downing gave the order to start the vehicles up. For no reason, my skin crawled, and I found myself taking lots of short, shallow breaths.

"Why are you hyperventilating?" Anne asked .

"We gotta get the fuck out of here. We did our job. We gotta go, now."

"Uh oh, she's losing it again," Anne quietly replied from the back.

"No," Mitch said after a moment of scanning the brightly lit space. "She's right. Any zombies left will be making their way here. Those explosions won't hold their attention for long. We'll be lucky if we can get back to our island."

"Um, Mitch," Anne said.

"What?" he snapped back.

"Yeah, the horde is here."

"Fuck!" he yelled, grabbing up his rifle and lowering the window to shoot.

"We have incoming. All units be advised, we have made enemy contact." An unknown male voice came over the coms.

"No shit, dumb-asses," Mitch grumbled.

I noticed the troop transport finally driving up the ramp. Ryan's vehicle followed close behind as I felt a thump on top of our Humvee. It rocked from the force of something, or someone, landing on it. Downing's vehicle barely made the ramp before it started to rise. What's left of the defenders, fight off zombies who crawled onto the rising platform. I don't notice the figures outside my window until Anne screamed.

I nearly lost it myself, just barely holding on. Gramps and a young woman stand outside, banging and tugging on the door handle.

"What?"

"Lemme in. You're gonna need help getting back. Besides, I don't care to be cooped up in the new capitol. If I'm gonna die, I'll die fighting, not as food for those things."

Great, just great. Anne opened her door before I could reply, and they jumped inside.

"Get on them guns," Gramps barked at us.

"What, or who, is on the roof?" I asked as I hit the gas.

A pair of camo covered legs, followed by a body, wedged itself into the gun turret the wrong way. The sound of the .50 cal spewing death became my answer.

"Move out. Now," Ryan shouted over the mike.

"Kinda trapped here," I replied, as the Humvee pushed against zombies. "And who the hell was driving your rig? You're in the wrong vehicle to go home."

He didn't reply, only kept sweeping the gun to clear a path for us. I pressed harder on the gas, smashing into bodies, trying to turn around to leave. We rocked from side to side.

"Oh, shit," I gasped out at the sight of the horde. "Everybody hang on, and conserve ammo."

How we would get outta this mess, I didn't know. We were all tossed about inside as I gunned the engine and mowed over zombies.

"Come on, baby. Hang on. Don't quit working on us now," I spoke to the Humvee.

Ahead of us, I dimly heard a WHUMP! over the moans of the undead. We all felt the force rock us forward. I had trouble keeping the vehicle from flipping end over end.

"What the hell, Ryan," I yelled out. Shredded limbs and bodies exploded outward in a foul mess ten feet in front of us.

Ichor slapped onto the hood and windshield, I flicked the wipers on. Headlights bounced off the zombies and obstacles in our way. Ryan yelled out which way to drive in an attempt to help me while he lobbed grenades ahead of us to clear a path.

"How can he even see? Anne asked. "I can't see in the dark, and there's no streetlights anymore."

"Night vision goggles. Wish I had a pair on right now." I spotted a small hole in the horde of undead, and aimed for it.

Everyone inside with me cursed as I drove over fields, heading for the fence we breached earlier. If we can reach it in time, we can outrun the horde.

Epilogue

It's been several weeks since we helped Downing and the survivors catch their plane. The journey back to our new home on the island still gives me nightmares. We don't know where the horde is, or if the virus has mutated. Ryan thinks they're still roaming, following the scent of humans trying to eke out a living around us. I think they've moved on, inexorably shuffling closer to the new capitol. Either way, not all have gone. We still discover zoms as we go about our daily business. Occasionally, when the wind is right, we hear gunshots. The sound lets us know the other islands, and the mainland have pockets of survivors.

Some of us think it's eerie, without the sounds of humans and machines. I find it fascinating. The books I risked my life for are providing us with knowledge we need to survive in a world gone back to pre-industrial times. Along with Ed's lifetime of farming, and through trial and error, we will re-learn what our ancestors once knew for daily life.

I know Anne thinks the zombies will be defeated eventually, but I'm more cynical. I believe the time of humans has come to an end. I believe despite all our efforts, all our meddling, nature and evolution have had their way. We will not know who or what comes after us, or what they may think of the artifacts we have left behind. I just hope whatever it is will take better care of the planet than we have done.

Author's Notes

Charleston, Wadmalaw Island, and its environs of South Carolina, are all real, with some embellishments added to fictionalize it. I've lived here since 2008, and I still come across areas I have yet to explore. The beauty and history is just a small part of what makes Charleston a great place to live or visit, or defend from hordes of undead.

When my long time friend, T. Golgan, and I first conceived of trying our hand at a zombie novel, we had a vision. Like everyone else who enjoys the genre, there are things we both hate and love about it.

We finished the rough draft, and had begun refining the story, when creative differences arose. Even with the many compromises made, it soon became clear my writing partner had to be jettisoned from the project after several rounds of Beta Readers feedback. I have salvaged what I could of Golgan's contributions, although they have been heavily edited and re-written numerous times. Most of what is left of his parts bear scant resemblance to the originals. Despite that, I hope you have enjoyed this story.

If you are so moved, whether by love, hate, or

indifference, please consider leaving a review.

I have also written more in the dystopian genre, combing paranormal and fantasy elements. You can explore my Immortalibus Bella Series, set in a future Earth experiencing a second Dark Ages, at my website: www.slfiguhr.com. Please also find me on Twitter @SLFiguhr, on Facebook.com/ SLFiguhr.Author, and on Goodreads.com/SLFiguhr.

Thank you for reading!

SL Figuhr